College Leadership Crisis:
The Philip Dolly Affair

by

Jann M. Contento and Jeffrey Ross

Published by Rogue Phoenix Press
Copyright © 2011

ISBN: 978-0-936403-47-9

Credits
Cover Artist: 'Designs by Ms. G'
Editor: Christine Young

Printed in the United States of America

Dedication

For my father, Michael, whose guidance has helped me recognize the whispered truths
Jann M. Contento

For my son, Quinten Blake Ross, who is teaching me Stewardship
Jeffrey Ross

Section One

Wheat Germ: A Cultural Harvest of Middle Class Dreams

"Every day, somebody gets fired, or quits, or goes crazy.
But not me, not Guitar Bob. And that's because I still got my band together. We can play
both kinds of music—country and western."
—Guitar Bob Zontarg, Custodian Specialist V
Copperfield Community College, Hamilton City, North New Mexico
April 15, 2011

Note from the authors:

This book is fiction—but it is written as fact. Call it a fictional case study if you will. Our characters do not exist in real life, but the reader will recognize each of them.

The places, the names, and the controversies are purely our invention, but they have a basis in the rarified, reified, artificial, and highly entertaining culture known as the American Community College.

[Explanations for acronyms and "specialty" terms can be found in the Appendix.]

Stereotypes have been used purposefully to illustrate both appropriate and inappropriate behaviors at the community college. We are most emphatically concerned with the culture which has developed at community colleges—not with individuals who work on their campuses or students who take their classes.

We are ardent supporters of the community college movement. We wish to see the primary purpose of the community college experience refocused on its historical intent: improving the quality of life.

We sincerely hope this text will stimulate healthy debate about American Higher Education. Let us hope our Leaders function as Stewards first.

Further Comments on Organization of the Text

1. The novel is in three parts. In the first section, we develop, through a series of character and event sketches, the primary players and representative thematic activities in our story—snapshots of life at a twenty-first century community college.

2. In the middle section, we provide a bit of Argentine political intrigue—set in the early 1960's—and explain the mysterious—and yet serious—backdrop for the emergence and behaviors of our main character, Dr. Philip Dolly, Copperfield Community College president. The intellectual, philosophical, and political discussions contained in this section—set in the context of the 1960's social renaissance—provide a "foil" for the "mundane-speak" heard daily at community colleges as described in sections one and three.

3. In the third section, we show the rather rapid professional and personal decline of Dr. Dolly. At the novel's conclusion, the reader is left to determine if 1) Dolly has gone mad; 2) The entire sequence of events was only a dream; 3) The development of an alternative personal explanation exists for the series of events, turns, and counter turns.

(The first Chapter, Call Me Phil, was originally published [in slightly different form] as a Views article in Insidehighered.com on September 12, 2008)

Preface

Ross and Contento's work is a subtle probing of a reality that is, and will continue to be, an enigmatic part of contemporary America culture—the community college. I use the term enigma because this "ersatz" university has come to be representative of many, if not all, institutions in our society.

Yes, the folks who populate the two-year institution have come to symbolize Everyman.

The two authors, in a truly artful, skillful, and delightfully whimsical manner, satirically deconstruct the whispered truths of this American edifice. In doing so, their novel articulates and makes visual what everyone knows but doesn't dare talk about—the phenomena of "The Emperor's New Clothes" which occurs in all varieties of American cultural and economic institutions.

I have thoroughly enjoyed the work and invite not only educators but everyone—Everyman—to participate in this sharply humorous, satisfyingly refreshing novel.

John Paddison, Fools Hollow Lake, Groundhog's Day, 2011

Call Me Phil

I'm Phil Dolly, EdD, recently resigned, or deposed, community college president.

Yesterday I was the CEO at North East Central Community College here in Folsom County, West Dakota. Today, I'm contemplating my own crisis in leadership. Following a faculty vote of no confidence and caving in to growing board pressure, I packed it in this morning. No one was surprised, really, including me. But more about that later...

This evening I am sitting here at the bar nursing a weak gin and tonic, assessing the landscape of my shattered career. This place is nothing fancy, that's for sure. I don't know when it saw fresh air last. Located in Payson, West Dakota, this bar and grill has been owned by the same guy, I.M. Tyred, for nearly a decade. I'm a little bit out of my element— but I'm comforted by the visual relics of my own blue collar past—seed company calendars, jars of pickled pig's feet, softball trophies, and the effervescent aroma of bacon, beer, and cheese. Many of the locals know me and enjoy seeing me stop in for an occasional drink. I probably get in here once a month. Maybe more.

I'm not sure what happened. Enrollments didn't increase, but they didn't decline much, either. We opened up more centers. I had bandwidth upgraded. I was in Rotary Club. I brought in some of my former graduate school colleagues from University of Toledo at Arlington to help invigorate the executive staff and to help bring this district into the 21st century in terms of management. I wanted diversity on the management team.

Hmm, I made all of the directors deans and all of the deans became associate VPs. Only one of the new VPs had emotional problems, but no damage was done. He checked into rehab. Our quality initiatives must have moved the college forward. We redid offices, put in new floors and windows, and really spruced the place up too. We won several national awards.

I remember there was some grousing when I had the president's salary increased to 475K, but the board agreed we needed to be competitive in future presidential searches.

I guess the future arrived more quickly than I anticipated.

The hazy blue smoke in this bar settles at about stool seat level. I wish I.M. Tyred would do something. Why doesn't he install some fans or air purifiers or something? I should say something before I have another asthma attack. The country music just drones on and on. All those sad songs about lying, drinking, and needing to be somewhere else are driving me crazy. How do these people stand it?

The lights around the mirrors seem so harsh. I barely recognize my own face in the mirror—the burdens of leadership, I guess. All those retreats, keynote speeches, conferences, dinners, trips to Europe—just so much, so much over the years.

The governing board said I spent too much time out of state. They said I belonged to too many national organizations and attended too many conferences. They just don't understand the difficult and complicated nature of being a community college president. Networking means survival and prosperity for the institution and for me. They don't understand the community is much bigger now. We can serve China! GIs! Nebraska! Technology has empowered us to do so much more than teach welding, massage therapy, and fertilizer applications.

We ought to do more than just serve the needs of our county taxpayers! We can have the reputation of being a global higher education leader! Oh, I guess it's no longer we.

I remember hearing Tyred worked at a community college out west somewhere before he moved here and bought this place. I heard he was a dean or a director or something.

Somebody said he has a doctorate. I did hear him, once, muttering something about the "illusion" community colleges project. Who knows what that is supposed to mean?

He must be out of touch with community colleges. Maybe he was a custodian or a purchasing agent or an athletic director.

I wonder if anybody ever talked to him about teaching for us as an adjunct.

I guess it's not us anymore.

Well, the faculty senate sent me a letter asking why my own kids didn't attend our college. I tried to explain, directly and honestly, my wife and I had always dreamed of sending them to Nebraska State. We wanted them to have a university experience, you know. Nothing wrong with that. Our kids really didn't need the community college, you know.

I wonder how many of the patrons here at the "Nose Guard Pub" take classes at NECCC? This second drink is really watered down. I wonder if we—oops, they—should work up a transfer curriculum in Bartending? Could we articulate that with NEWDU? Is that part of the guaranteed transfer curriculum? Would bartending fit into the MYJAK or the LOWJAK pathway? Or should it be in an AAS program? I know some of the NECCCT [er, that's NECCC now] faculty thinks we should focus on AAS degrees. Hah. What do they know? We're higher education leaders. We ought to be offering BA degrees. We? I mean they, of course. I'm done. But my future is wide open.

There must be a hundred openings nationwide for community college presidents right now. How can this be? We have millions of professionals trained in leadership skills. Maybe this county is just too rough cut to understand what I was trying to do here.

Based on what I learned at several conferences, I recommended we take "Technical" out of our name and emphasize transfer education. I remember several of the local machine shops, meat cutters, massage therapists, hospitals, carpenters, clinics, and local businesses questioned that move—both the name change and the focus shift. But I was convinced we could become higher education leaders. Just convinced. Six out of our fifty-three full-time faculty have doctorates. One even has a PhD. They are all actively involved in committee work and have been through total quality training. Heck, I sent twenty-two of them to BISON last year. That is Excellence!

The nearest university, North Eastern West Dakota University, is over fifty miles away. They are snooty and elitist. We are the only post-secondary—I mean higher education—institution serving the county. And we serve the entire county pretty darn well when the ITV system is working!

I must have been mumbling out loud. Tyred wandered over and jumped in. "That's the problem, Dr. Dolly"—"Call me Phil," I interjected—"OK, uh, Phil, you have tried to make a post-secondary institution into a higher education institution. The town wants jobs, not philosophy. They send their kids off to NEWDU for an education. And another thing—why do you recruit athletes from Uganda to run track? You've got South Korean tennis players! Why are the football players from Texas? Why is the woman's basketball team from Window Rock Arizona? This is Western Dakota, for God's sake. Let these kids who grew up here, whose folks live here, let these kids play."

He really is out of touch. Some of those NECCC athletes just competed in the Olympics for their own nations! And one of 'em medaled!

"You know, Dr. Phil [nomenclature he seemed comfortable with], I think many of the faculty at Payson High right here in town have better teaching credentials than your full-time faculty. Stop all those leadership speeches! Who is it you think you are leading? Everybody at your college is a leader! Doesn't anybody work? Have you ever asked yourself what the town thinks of NECCC? Really asked?

"And whenever I dial a phone number at NECCC, I get an answering machine. No one ever returns my calls. What kind of Customer Service is that? Are your people in meetings all day?"

Thank goodness, he's wandered off to flirt with that curvy redhead at the end of the bar.

He evidently hadn't heard I resigned—he still seems to think I'm the president. No matter. Tyred is obviously out of touch with best practices of community college management, too.

Oh. The accreditation people were concerned fifty percent of our total enrollment comes from dual enrollment with high school kids [and the classes are taught at the high schools by high school teachers]. How can that be considered double dipping? I am very comfortable with those partnerships. I told the board and the faculty such outreach was important to stakeholder satisfaction.

Uh oh. He is coming back. No—he sat down with a bottle of Scoresby's. Good. Looks like he's eating one of those bar pizzas—the kind that is always half burnt.

I understand Southern Canada Community College and Arctic Region Community College may soon have openings for CEO's, but it is so tiresome dealing with those consulting firms...

I read in the *Chronicle of Post-Secondary Ed* about some school in North New Mexico that just fired their new president for drinking on the job or something.

The smoke in here is really getting bad. This third drink seems to be stronger, anyway. Now I'm eating some two day old popcorn. Is there anybody in here who isn't smoking or wearing a tattoo? All those piercings! Puh-lease! And that music!

It's a darn good thing I negotiated the parachute package back in '06 when they gave me a renegotiated five year contract. But I'm not sure how Molly and I will live on two hundred grand this next year.

I guess I'll email those head hunters at findaprez.com tomorrow. Maybe I'll try www.ccpresidentsrus.com. There must be a community college out there needing my leadership skills, my knowledge of management styles, my commitment to the learn-ed college philosophy, my knowledge of branding and sustainability, my zest for policy governance, and my networking abilities. I really can bring a unique skills set to an institution.

I just hope they don't ask me if I have any publications.

Ach, one more drink won't hurt. I wonder whatzup in North New Mexico?

A Few Months Pass...

Prequel
Mid 2000's

[Horses whinny in the loamy North New Mexico light. Large Thunderheads and Giant Dust Clouds loom in the distance...The CCC orchestra was playing a mixed key version of "Also Spake Zarathustra." The new Copperfield Community College President, Dr. Philip Dolly, stood at the podium with his wife, Molly Dolly, just outside the Staten Information Commons Building. He began his remarks.]

"Yass, my wife Molly and I are happy to be part of the Copperfield Community College family. I have kept my eye on Copperfield for years—your sound tradition of excellent teaching and learning is well-known to me—and to other followers of the community college movement.

Yass, the good work you have done is respected globally..."

[Dust storm begins arriving, splattering crowd with particles—but they sit transfixed by the pulse pounding, fiery oratory of their new president. He seems to be from a different time, a different place, and his influence on them is spellbinding.]

"We know that CCC has an important and significant place in the hearts and minds of county residents, other stakeholders, and state legislators." [Light tinkles of corporate

laughter from the shirt and tie constituency in crowd—a group of ladies wearing Blue Hats was not amused.] A scruffy guy wearing a backpack and brogans sits down, dejectedly, in the front row.

"*We want to continue the good work here at CCC and transition into becoming a Learn-ed College as defined by [Kaff] [Kaff] the well-known and respected community college theorist, Sister Mary Union-O'Leary.*"

"*My hope is that CCC will become the foremost Higher Education Leader in the Great State of North New Mexico—possibly in the South East Southwest itself. My goal is to help CCC undergo a metamorphosis [Kaff], a transition, into a Bachelor's degree granting institution, yass, even a Master's Degree granting two-year institution, during my tenure at CCC. [Kaff Kaff]. Our staff, and faculty, and maintenance crew, are capable of this change as we become fully infused with the Learn-ed College Philosophy. [Kaff Kaff] We can become international leaders in Higher Education, using the very best in technology to deliver our courses to China and even Nebraska! [Kaff Kaff].*"

[Full Fury of dust storm arrives, sending speaker and listeners scurrying into a nearby barn, where they find shelter from the maddening cyclonic blast outside. Rain begins to fall, washing clean the campus and the words...Damp Horses make their way into the barn and compete with Deans and Directors for space.]

Dr. Dolly awoke [or came to consciousness] from this exciting and reflective dream on a lovely, sun-splashed Sunday afternoon. His worshipful wife, Molly, seated next to him, lovingly wiped perspiration from his face. He remembered his initial powerful speech at Copperfield so clearly—he knew now that his locution strongly set the tone, the direction, for the many improvements and reforms he made at the school during the last six years of his employment.

He was pleased with the synergy, the sustainability, the high level of professionalism exhibited by his assembled administrative team...

Dr. Phil was on the porch of his lovely, and paid for, Lake Fargo cottage. *What a perfect spring day*, he thought to himself. Even though their cabin was small [8400 square feet], Dr. Dolly was glad he had convinced his wife Molly to build a spacious porch. He enjoyed taking naps in the shade and watching people walking along the paved path situated between his cabin and the lake. *Hmm. It isn't very warm today. Why am I sweating so much? I don't remember putting on a long sleeve shirt.*

He saw baby stroller after baby stroller pass by, each being pushed by a wholesome and excessively attractive young mom in a white skirt and blouse. And he saw so many elderly persons riding three wheeled bikes, jangling their bells and tooting handlebar horns. *Strange, I have seen ten or twelve hot dog stands roll by—who is eating all those hotdogs? Oh—I see some are owned by the Blue Cross—perhaps it is a benefit concert.*

And I didn't know horses could be ridden down the Lake Fargo Partnerships Path, either…I thought the HOA had rules against such obvious personal freedoms!

Overview
Copperfield Community College District [CCCD]
Hamilton County, North New Mexico

[To provide a meaningful and appropriate introduction to this study of CCC, the following is excerpted from a successful grant application written by former CCC Chief Grant Writer, Alberto Fuentes, an Argentine citizen working legally in the United States.]

Copperfield Community College [CCC] provides post-secondary service to a geographic area larger than the nation of Ukraine within the borders of North New Mexico. The District is nestled in an area known for chili farms and racehorse production.

The District maintains three campuses—The Main Campus in Hamilton City, North New Mexico, a store front in Stockham, North New Mexico, and Industrial Bocker Campus in Rozwhel, North New Mexico. [The Main Campus is never referred to as The Main Campus by CCC administrators. One of their many slogans is Copperfield Community: One College, Three Campuses. The Main Campus is generally referred simply as CCC.] Nonetheless, the Main Campus is the Main Campus. [Ask anybody who works in the Copperfield Community College District!]

Copperfield Community prides itself on being a Higher Education Leader in North New Mexico and the Great South East Mid-South West. A significant portion of CCC enrollment comes from its Nursing Assistant, Butcher Training, Custodian Specialties Preparation Institute, Advanced Mortuary Science Institute, Meter Loop Construction Facility, Russian Motorcycle Repair Training, Home Beer Brewery Facility, Police Academy, Fire Academy, Cosmetology Department, Massage Therapy, Senior Citizens Book Clubs, and Developmental Education Departments.

Over seven thousand students attended CCC recently—our three percent semester-to-semester student return rate ranks in the ninety-seventh percentile nationally for community college retention. Three thousand of these students are in at least two online classes and four thousand students have dual enrollment status at local high schools…. Nearly eighty percent receive federal funding or in-house Dean's Grants—only about four percent have ever written out a check for tuition. [But the book store—well, that is another matter.]

CCC serves a diverse student population of developmental education students, students supporting their families on minimum wage work-study jobs and federal aid, working class adults hoping for a better life, athletes from out-of-state and out-of-nation [who aren't quite good enough to get the universities' attention but completely fill our residence halls], socialist activists, displaced revolutionaries, housewives who need time away from their kids, traditional-type students who don't really have the money, ability, or inclination to attend Hamilton State University—and the growing successful cadre of technically-oriented students who take advantage of our excellent vocational programs, move forward in life quickly, and get great paying jobs soon after leaving CCC—and then contribute fully to the betterment of society.

CCC has world-class championship athletics teams that no one in Hamilton County has ever seen play. Coincidentally, no Hamilton County resident has ever played on a CCC athletic team [except for one kid from Rozwhel who became an MLB all-star].

CCC's excellent faculty and staff are here to adequately serve the needs of our students. Many of them couldn't find jobs at universities or high schools but are quite happy to be here because of the salary and benefit package—especially the retirement plan.

Most of the faculty members do not hold doctorates because they believe further education in their disciplines will make them unsuitable teachers in the community college environment.

Even so, fifty-four of our faculty are enrolled in an Ed Leadership Program because they, too, want to become CCC administrators and earn large, comfortable salaries for attending boring meetings and out-of-nation conferences, and eventually purchase lake front property.

Our administrators are fiery protectors of an increasingly artificial, decision-tabling, and ultimately bizarre community college culture—and have managed to convince our faculty and staff that organizational theory and management are more important than academics…

Most of our faculty members are excellent cooks and are well-versed in topics concerning hummus, meat balls, pasta salad, quiche lorraine, tarts, malabi, chocolate, and other numerous menu items suitable for potlucks and snacks.

They are excellent curriculum facilitators but are discouraged from creating creative curriculum which might impede our institution's strategic vision.

Our secretarial staff can demonstrate superior FreeCell [and other computer solitaire games] skills and has read every vampire novel ever written. Most of the staff members here, below the Dean level, are former students—we are very proud of our *Grow our Young-uns* philosophy!

Many of our students love CCC so much they take five to nine years to complete one semester certificate training programs.

The College continues to wisely outsource many of its custodial and maintenance functions.

Certainly, we will promise in this application that we will one day internalize the cost of the proposed grant program. But since we are constantly changing presidents and other top-level administrators, we probably won't keep our promise.

Nonetheless, CCC will be able to use pop-culture corporate language and period-relevant buzzwords to explain how the grant project performed. And we will continue to apply for [and receive] additional funding…

History of the Copper Coin

The Copper Coin is the unofficial—and never publicly acknowledged—off campus hangout for CCC staff and faculty. *The Copper Coin Tavern*—now part of The Fountain Plaza strip mall—was once anchored by the famous Three Coins in a Fountain Fine Dining and Spirits [cocktails] restaurant long since closed. This establishment was named after the *Julie Styne/Sammy Cahn - Four Aces* million seller and 1954 Oscar winning film. The resturante' originally opened in 1965 with the development of the college and surrounding bedroom community. A full-sized roman motif [and splashing] fountain graced the entryway.

Early on, many college co-eds were known to have "skinny dipped" in the fountain—after hours—in an attempt to capture the romanticism portrayed in the 1962 Italian film classic *"La Dolce Vita."* Three Coins closed in 1975 after the owner and operator, Gino Gorgatto, returned to his Sicilian roots with the wife of the restaurant's once-famous chef, Salvatore Ragusa.

So, the Fountain Plaza strip mall now houses Fountain Pharmacy, Dave's Dry Cleaning, Ted's Taco Tuesday quality fast food, and the Copper Coin Tavern which was established in 1983. The name of the tavern was said to have been dubbed by locals after the Three Coins had closed operation. Evidently, the stained copper rust spots embedded within the crested reservoir of the under-maintained fountain served as a point of reference. The Copper Coin acquired part of the original Three Coins Bar and relocated it four doors west of the original restaurant's location.

The bar is a staple of Copper Coin's ambiance, with a solid oak top, golden copper rail, and nine of the original bar stools with copper gold foot rests. Four high-back red leather button pleated booths were also salvaged from Three Coins—each capable of seating six comfortably. Rumor has it, when sitting alone in a booth, a patron can hear *Sergio Franchi* crooning ["*O sole mio!*"]—and detect the potent aroma of fragrant fennel in fresh Italian sausage.

The Copper Coin did receive a feeble attempt at national Cultural Significance recognition. Bob Zontarg and his Little Colorado River Band penned a song called Ode to the Copper Coin which was heard by a few patrons [eight or maybe nine] during the band's three week stand at the club a few years back.

Ode to the Copper Coin [in the key of C Major for three guitars and a tenor voice]

Copper Coin in the prime time
Aahaahahh
Not sipping white wine
One guy was crying, and cradled the phone
Channel Three on the table
Wasn't hooked up to cable
She was wearing cashmere—I should have gone home
Her name was Nina
She was a dreamer
I spoke to her eyes
Our hearts were bare
She played a few CD's
The kind that intrigued me
She sat down beside me
I felt so alone
I know that you're hurting
But I'm really not flirting
My boyfriend is Hansmuth
Our love is bound
My old face was hairy
The moment was scary
She danced through the door way

The barkeeper frowned
Copper Coin in the prime time
Aahaahahh
Not sipping white wine
One guy was crying, and cradled the phone
Channel Three on the table
Wasn't hooked up to cable
She was wearing cashmere—I should have gone home

[Just For the Record—Players of the Little Colorado River Band—B. Zontarg, Rhythm Guitar - R. Jenkins, Steel Pedal Guitar - M. Carroll, Bass and Vocals - J. "The Master" Sego, Lead Guitar and keys - J. Kompento, Drums - AV Allen, lighting - L. Johnson, Security]

Dr. Phil Dolly President of Copperfield Community College

…Woke up, fell out of bed—Dragged a comb across my head—Found my way downstairs and drank a cup—And looking up I noticed I was late—Found my coat and grabbed my hat—Made the bus in seconds flat—Found my way upstairs and had a smoke—and Somebody spoke and I went into a dream…

"A Day in the Life"—Lennon/McCartney (1967)

How my fortunes have changed, thought President Phil Dolly as he parked his Cadillac in the **Reserved for President** parking space at Copperfield Community.

Back in the fall of 2005, the Board of Trustees at North East Central Community College, his former institution in Payson, West Dakota, let him go.

Dolly continues to reflect on his departure even to this day. *Hard to say what happened. Enrollments were shaky, but we had good feedback from our stakeholders. I developed and opened some new storefronts in the county. The staff was well-liked, I think—there was some grumbling because we recruited most of our athletes from out of state or from east Africa.*

I had us actively—and I thought positively—involved with the Highbrow Learn-ed Commission—maybe that letter they sent the board questioning our dual enrollment policies had something to do with me getting canned.

I know a big issue was that I changed the focus at NCCC[T] from being a predominantly occupational education focused college into what I thought best—a higher education transfer course provider—a Higher Education leader. Well, that was a tough county to work in.

Dolly enjoys driving to work and pulling into the CCC main campus every morning.

Each day he proudly passes through the massive gateway arch—sort of a cross between the Parisian Arc de Triomphe and Saddam's triumphal Hands of Gleny Arch in Baghdad. [This strange bit of grand but grotesque architecture was evidently donated to the college by a wealthy (yet obscure) South American back in the 1960's...]

He noticed Dean Paxton Preston pulling in—making a wide circle with that gleaming silver Lexus. Dolly had to keep an eye on Preston—Paxton and his wife were very ambitious. The Dean had been hired just before Dolly and came to Copperfield with a glowing recommendation from Dr. Leonard Sushy, his dissertation chair. ["Dr. Preston's study of community college parking lots is one of the best I've ever seen!"] Dolly knew the alumni from Toledo at Arlington were very powerfully networked—and he also knew he would have to survive at least five years at Copperfield Community to become fully vested in the state's retirement plan.

Dolly reminded himself to make a note in his journal about Paxton's increasingly obvious ambitions...

Dr. Dolly noticed, with an inward smirk, that Preston was checking his Blackberry—probably looking for online career development guidance from Dr. Sushy.

Dolly had heard that Dean Paxton stopped at the Hamilton International Airport once a week, on his way to work, just to get his shoes shined.

Certainly, Dolly should feel good about his status at Copperfield. He had been the number two choice [as he learned later]. After conducting a national search, the CCC Presidential Search Committee had decided on the acting interim President—former Copperfield Community VP of Instruction Hans Goeber—but, most unfortunately, Goeber received a DUI while driving home after celebrating the news of his permanent hire—and the arrest and mug shots had not been pretty. Police records indicate he had said to the arresting officers—

Keep your @^%%$$$% hands off me, you !! [_][*&^%$—don't you know who I am? Ya, I am the eight hundred pound gorilla the universities fear. You @*[$[]#]# cops vuld never make it through the academy at my college!

The event, of course, caused great turmoil in the community and institution. Dr. Goeber's mug shot, complete with blood shot eyes, showed up in the local paper—and in the *Chronicle of Post-secondary Education* and *Bowling Stone-Ed Magazine*. The community stakeholders were mortified! Dr. Goeber claimed to have sipped merely two glasses of white zinfandel, but blew point-three-five on the breathalyzer! The Board called on Goeber to resign before he signed his new contract.

In a heartfelt and lachrymose statement released from his jail cell, Goeber announced he would resign, spend more time with his family, attend therapy and counseling, and help the "healing process" at Copperfield Community however he could. [He also denied vigorously the rumors he had been having an affair with a former female adjunct who was now tending bar at the Copper Coin Tavern.]

The next day, the Governing Board President called Dolly and offered him the job. He and his wife Molly were on the next flight out...

~ * ~

This morning, just before he got out of the car, he loosened up his belt a notch. Dolly stood 5' 7" and weighed two hundred thirty pounds [Five more than last week, he discovered on the scale this morning.] He was concerned about his weight, of course, but the rigors of his position, the burdens of leadership, precluded him from being physically active. He did, however, play in the annual Copperfield Community College Foundation Golf Tournament each April, May, June, July, August, and September.

This morning, like every morning, he checked in with his secretary, Rebecca Bitterluck-Fallingflat. Becky had also been the previous president's secretary and was actually quite relieved when Goeber failed to nail down the job. Bitterluck-Fallingflat did not like Goeber's arrogance. [And she also suspected Goeber had been "carrying on" with Dr. Preston's secretary, Nina.]

"Good morning, Rebecca."

"Good Morning, Mr. Dolly—I mean Dr. Dolly. Today, you have a meeting with the Partnership for a Green Copperfield Strategic Planning Group at nine AM, a late lunch with your wife at Moo Moo's tentatively scheduled for one PM, and a meeting with the Hamilton County School Superintendents about dual enrollment increases [Dolly groaned inwardly] *at 2:30 PM.*

"I have those enrollment printouts you requested from the Finance Office too. Glen Keynes called a few minutes ago. He seems anxious to talk with you—something about academic and vocational enrollment trends…"

"Oh—you probably should walk through the student lounge—the Copperfield Men of Diverse Colors Club is having a pizza sale to support this month's Stop White Female Domestic Abuse Celebration—Oh, and a student named Jann Bryde came by to complain about Dr. Chick, but I told her to go through the normal due process Copperfield Chain of Issues first—you know, Chick then the Chair then the Dean then the VP then the Ombudsmen… Plus—that legislative work session scheduled for Friday afternoon has been cancelled for now."

[Her phone began ringing—sort of—it sounded a bit like Lady Gaga.]
"Thanks, Becky."

He heard her answer the phone as he walked into his own office… *"Yes, please mail it to me—that's **R-e-b-e-c-c-a B-i-t-t-e-r-l-u-c-k** hyphen **F-a-l-l-i-n-g-f-la-t**—no, just one **t** at the end. Yes, that's **R-e-b-e-c-c-a B-i-t-t-e-r-l-u-c-k** hyphen **F-a-l-l-i-n-g-f-la-t**." The address is…What? Oh—**F-a-l-l-i-n-g-f-la-t**." Yes, flat as in Nebraska!"*

Dr. Dolly shut the door.

Hmm, he thought after considering the meeting coming up with the Superintendents, *I'm not sure, but I think the Superintendent from Leucadia Unified may be making more money than I do. She always sits in the back of the room with a superior smugness on her face.*

Dolly noticed the trashcan in his office hadn't been emptied overnight. This was a small detail, but he would have to talk to the Custodial Management Quality First Team Now! [CMQFT Now!] about this oversight. Dolly was convinced the appearance of a college has a tremendous impact on stakeholder satisfaction and future market penetration, as well as brand recognition and sustainability.

Dr. Dolly, thinking of the Men of Diverse Colors Club pizza sale, had a fleeting recollection of the old bar pizzas he used to relish back at the Nose Guard Pub in Payson back when he was president at NECCC. *Ach, those were some good times…*

Ach, I guess I'd better call Moo Moo's and get a reservation. Molly just loves Moo Moo's.

Glen Keynes, Institutional Research

Glen Keynes's office was neat—perhaps strangely so for a man in his position. Things were kempt and tidy—nothing out of place. A few loose-leaf folders were arranged efficiently on bookshelves. He had two laptops and a combination laser printer/copier on a sturdy grey fifties era metal table. [He noticed once—from a still sharp black paint stenciled ID number on the back—it had come from an Organization of American States surplus store.]

On this desk, he kept an "enshrined" eight by ten photo of Derek, his pet Chinchilla—the picture was taken in Big Sur country a few years back.

His personal life is organized, too. He keeps himself well-manicured [even a pedicure once a month] and crisp—every day he wears a long sleeve plaid shirt and an appropriate tie—either red or blue in color. His wife [a lovely and kind woman committed to Glen and their model-like spotless home] makes three trips to the dry cleaners a month. He drives a nice late model Del Fugo SUV—and has it detailed every third Friday.

He has one cup of coffee in the morning [frequently from a pot made the previous late afternoon—never from pricey Moonbuck's!], and eats three apples a day—worms and all—topped off by a cup of wheat germ late at night. He keeps a few bottles of water on a shelf for guests.

Glen is an accomplished musician, and plays the Rams Horn in his church ensemble. He is president of his HOA, and is certainly a well-respected member of various service organizations [including Rotary, Chambers, and Tigers Club].

He is known as the "go to guy"—and he gets things done right the first time. His reports and presentations are accurate, readable, and concise. He is much different than Alberto Fuentes, his former grant-writing colleague, who was fired for incompetence and fraud.

Glen gets up at four AM every morning—rain or shine—and runs six miles. He had been the lacrosse coach at Homer Lipscomb College, North East Newark Campus many years ago. At age forty, Glen is trim, fit, and focused. He is on top of his game.

Glen is constantly in communication with the world of academic research. He reckons he receives over eleven emails each day from the listservs and organizations he and CCC are connected with professionally. [He also reckons he receives two hundred fifty in house emails each day detailing pot lucks, lost dogs, pet ducks, baby showers, prostate exams, mammograms, student organizations, doughnuts, diversity celebrations, software upgrades, must-read vampire novels, muffins, lost keys, staff garage sales, and lake front condo rentals.]

When a visitor comes to his office, the first things he or she notices are the two personal messages Glen has written on four by six cards—both propped up on his desk and clearly visible. One reads—"*Your Crisis is NOT my Crisis*." The other reads "*No Time for Emergencies Today!*" [Strangely, they have been crumpled up a time or two but still look fairly new and functional.]

Sometimes Glen [MBA Case Western, BA Philosophy from Dartmouth, AA from the Louisiana, North East Texas Partnership Religious Seminary], a man who understands educational research and statistics, knows it is best to remain quiet when he hears a dean or VP make some offhand [and usually inaccurate] or rambling reference to a statistical test.

He has become painfully aware some administrators don't know much about research or statistics—despite their titles, vocabulary, and doctorates. Glen has learned to meet with such administrators privately to discuss their plans to analyze or even request data. This helps to avoid public embarrassment for his superiors—and he knows how defensive administrators can become when challenged.

Community colleges do not invite diversity of thought, he sighed to his wife once after a really tough week. *For the most "eclectic" of higher education intuitions, these colleges have a knack for being insular, close-minded, and defensive, and their senior staffs often behave almost like adolescents—apparently out of touch with reality but acting like they know more than anybody.*

Glen is a very busy man. He is in constant contact with the college's tech people, the Highbrow Learn-ed Commission, the new grants writer, MyPEDS, the registrar—and most of all, Dr. Philip Dolly, College President.

He knows Dr. Dolly prides himself on being an expert on the community college movement—Dolly constantly touts the community college position as a leader in higher education. Dr. Dolly believes the time is ripe for CCC to begin offering BA degrees—one of the more controversial community college trends. Some community colleges offered BA degrees in technical or occupation areas—like Fire Science, Police Science, or Nursing. But Dr. Dolly was convinced CCC was capable of offering BA degrees in general academic areas and maybe even MA degrees, too.

[Glen has heard rumors that Dolly is thinking about putting the college up for sale to some big proprietary online institution.]

Glen usually likes Phil Dolly—and knows Dr. Dolly is able to constantly redefine himself and make comeback after comeback in the profession. Dolly's ability to parrot buzz word after cliché after buzzword during meetings was, well, quite impressive, and gave a clue about the man's staying power—though Dolly had worked at several institutions previously....

But grave new challenges awaited CCC in the future. Some were manageable—perhaps some were not. He was concerned, of course, about the rumors—rumors that the governor of NNM was about to cut fifty percent of community college funding.

But that wasn't his only worry....

CCC, like many institutions, has seen a trend upwards in vocational enrollments the last decade. But the current upward spike—well, it was just stunning! The truth of the matter was that Glen didn't want to share this information with Dr. Dolly. The bar graphs he had prepared pretty much told the story.

How could Dolly continue making all those speeches about Copperfield's role as a higher education leader, a community college that even Hamilton State feared, when academic enrollments were trending down and vocational enrollment was flying high? Copperfield Community College, in Glen Keynes's mind, was most accurately a post-secondary institution—or to use the pejorative phrase from an earlier time—"grades 13-14."

[And while he wasn't prepared with data sets or the gumption to tell Dolly today, Glen also knew that fifty-six percent of the "academic" enrollment came from non-transfer development education courses in reading, arithmetic, and GED prep. And thirty percent of that came from dual enrollment at the high schools.]

During the last few days, some very strange letters had begun appearing in the local newspaper from a group calling itself Movement to Reform Community Colleges Now. The incendiary pieces were sure to be read and discussed by the CCC community. Not good.

Industrial Bocker Campus

Located in the nearby town of Rozwhel, the district's Industrial Bocker Campus [IBC] operates on a shrinking budget and lower-than-anticipated student enrollment.

The Occupational/Vocational Community Skills Center was originally developed in the 1970's to train "vocational" students in welding, industrial arts, auto mechanics, and air conditioning repair. Industry certification issues, employer dissatisfaction with certificate completers' "hands-on" work knowledge, low-student "placement in employment" numbers, and industry slowdowns [due to demand, change, and economic factors] hastened the steady decrease in enrollment. A combination of factors contributed to overall student dissatisfaction with the educational training they received on the Rozwhel campus. Students now refer to IBC as *"I've Been Conned."*

Professor Julia Flowers

Professor Flowers had just finished her phone conversation with CCC's childcare service. She would have to let her Chair, Dr. Seemy, know, once again, that she would miss her office hours because of a child-related issue. Her eldest son, Ezekiel, had developed a fever at the childcare center and, well, he was being sent home. Her husband, a sharp dresser and successful computer game developer named Trevor, was currently in Argentina dealing with a client, the flamboyant and flaming Bustaglio Calliente [Trevor was trying to get a Spanish translation down right for his company's successful new educational video game, **Earth Destroyer Mission Deluxe Version 34.6**]. So Julia would need to pick up the sick lad herself then stop by her mother-in-law's house for her other children.

She loved her husband Trevor so much. Trevor was a looker—sort of a cross between Val Kilmer and Tom Cruise [circa *Top Gun*]. He wore the cutest Italian open toed loafers and suspenders and starched shirts, and was a whiz around the kitchen. She had described him to one of her colleagues: *"Trevor is so cute. He will spend a whole Saturday making trips to the grocery store, trying to find the right ingredients for a special soup. And he will stand there all day, stirring the pot, stirring the pot, and checking his smart phone for messages from clients."*

"He always sends me flowers on my birthday, Valentine's Day, Ukraine Day, Mother's Day, Columbus Day, Christmas Day, Martin Luther King Day, and on each of the kids' birthdays. He sends the cutest cards. He makes a lot of money too. With his first bonus check, he bought me a BMW convertible [the license plate reads 'My Princess'!] And he is convinced we can retire in three years and travel the world. Except..."

Well, except for Ezekiel, Brunhilde, and Serpentine, their three kids. Lovely children all—they are ages three, two, and one. Zeke wasn't planned, and then Brunhilde and Serpentine seemed necessary to fill the quiver.

Julia and Trevor had met in the corporate world—gazed into each other's eyes over cubical walls, attended global networking conferences together, sipped Moonbuck's over laptops, and dreamed of trips to China and Vietnam, Churchill Downs, just hiking, loving, coupling, dreaming. No one denied they looked good together—certainly they were one of the most handsome couples at CCC.

The women around the campus, when they met Trevor, were most impressed. *"Mas Caliente! He's a keeper,"* said Elena Vasquez. *"Wow—GQ!"* gushed Dr. Seemy. *"I hear he makes a lot of money,"* noted Dr. Dolly's secretary to Dr. Preston's secretary, *"but those shoes have gotta go!"*

Committed Libertarians, Julia and Trevor know they are smarter than the average bears and have big plans for the future—even though they are upside down by 400,000 dollars on the fifty-year-old fixer-upper house they bought just a few years back. *["Trevor says we will still make a killing on this house—he is so smart."]*

Julia had worked her way up from the adjunct ranks to get the full-time position at CCC. She is trim, attractive, and business-like. Her courses were delivered efficiently and professionally. She had frequently taught overloads and taken on many extra paying responsibilities, but with the birth of her three children, she had to cut back on her work at CCC. Trevor was frequently away on business, or playing video games, or playing paintball in the desert with his friends. *["He works so hard,"* she told Nina just last week —*"he really needs—and deserves 'Trevor time' time by himself…"]*

Besides teaching and mentoring the Responsible Fatherhood Young Men's Group, she only serves on the Program Review Committee, the Interactive Television Committee, the Curriculum Committee, and Safety First at CCC Committee, Salary Committee, and the ongoing Mission Statement Review Committee. Life has been much easier since she cut her committee load in half.

Professor Flowers always wears crisp business clothes [and even dons special maternity business suits when appropriate]—strangely enough, she almost always wears ballerina slippers.

Her red hair is long, silky, and luxurious. Sometimes her students think the green eye shadow she wears makes her mysterious looking—sort of like a gypsy or a half-size red-headed Cher...at least those students who still remember Cher.

At the office, she is very private, but sometimes has long soul-tearing and tearful conversations with one of the other Communication Division instructors, Jack Frost [Spanish Instructor]. Jack is much older, in a committed relationship, and safe.

Frost rides a motorcycle, writes medium-grade poetry, and stays more or less aloof from the day-to-day CCC buzz. His thinning hair is always a bit oily from tonic—and he typically smells like a whistling sea captain.

Frost seemed to understand her concerns with her children, their impact on her career, and the torrid love she felt for her husband. In many ways, Frost was like a college girlfriend—someone she could talk to, someone helpful and not threatening, reassuring and supportive. She always felt warm and comfortable in his office, and hugged him tightly when she left. Sometimes, on tough days, she clung to him for a moment or two and felt, well, better.

He was so confident—so manly—so different than—much of the world. He thoughtfully supported and acknowledged the frequent potlucks, bake sales, pancake feeds, and vampire novel discussion groups at CCC but seldom attended such events.

Sometimes Jack and Julia would have lunch together at the Copper Coin and, while conversing, she would touch his hand to make a point, then a faint smile would cross his face, and he would stare out through the window and sigh. At such times his heart hurt—but this discomfort might be caused by enchiladas and frijoles or the torrid *Gusto con Hobgoblino* salsa served at the Copper Coin.

[She was sometimes uncomfortable at the Copper Coin, though. The large, boorish, overtly socialist bartender, Henry McDougal, frequently made eyes at her. *Crazy old communist*, she thought more than once.]

She heard McDougal whisper, once, *"Ach, lassie, you're quite a looker, ye be, yass, quite a looker."* She immediately texted her husband to see how his day was going.

Julia had been in the corporate world [credit unions], and she knew how things should be done.

Each night after work, when her hubby was not traveling on business, she would tell the loving and immaculate Trevor about the failings and negative issues she associated with CCC.

[He grew tired of this, but knew she needed the job to keep health insurance coverage for him and their growing family. Plus, Trevor enjoyed telling his hip and clever game-designing colleagues that his wife was a professor. But he didn't tell them where…]

~ * ~

She told Jack Frost, once, she hoped her kids all grew up to be nerds and made lots of money someday.

"Trevor and I are going to be sure they don't play sports, don't ride dirt bikes, scooters, or ATV's, and don't turn into writers, poets, musicians, dancers, artists, chefs, skaters, cowboys, or teachers. We want them to have real futures."

That was another one of those times Jack smiled and looked out the window. He carefully watched her walk away and sighed, mumbling something poetic in Spanish. Dr. S. Chick, wandering down the hallway, thought he heard Frost say, *"Vuelva usted mañana."*

She was committed to balancing her life as mom, Professor, and wife to Trevor. She had learned to accept the perceived inadequacies of the CCC administration. But the students were another matter.

She cornered Jack Frost on campus early one morning, just after her 8 AM class.

"What's wrong with these people? They're half asleep. They can't follow instructions, can't read, can't write, can't come to class, and have the lamest excuses! Some of them just aren't college material—they need to get their own lives in order before they try to go to school. I may just stay home with the kids. When I try to teach online, the server is always down. When I teach regular old classes, I have to interact directly with the, the, the students."

"You can't imagine their bad hygiene. And the tattoos! And the piercing! I've got one student who looks like a homo sapien pincushion! Why do they all wear black? And the cell

28

phones—buzzing, ringing, texting, searching, downloading who knows what? It's more of an appendage, a security blanket, a baby's pacifier!"

"My textbook order is all messed up. I've got Leslie's old office now, and the A/C is just too cold in there. I'm on four committees and serve as an advisor to the Respectable Fatherhood Men's Group [RFMG]! I only get $70,000 a year to put up with all of this!— Jack! Jack! Are you listening to me, Jack? I may have to drop out of the Ed Leadership program at the University of Topeka, too; Trevor wants me to spend more time with him!"

"Plus"—she nearly sobbed this out—"I may be pregnant again!"

"Jack—Are you listening to me? Frost? Are you in there?" Jack just smiled and looked out the window. "Uh, Congratulations," he said, with only half-hearted gusto. [Scowling, Dr. Preston was walking towards them, down the sidewalk, and so the pair parted.]

~ * ~

Just before heading home that afternoon, she stopped by Jack's office. Frost was on the phone—his tone was pained. "Yes, I'll pick up a gallon of milk. Yes, I'll put the trash dumpster away. Yes, I'm sorry I washed your sweatshirt with the towels. Yes, I should have been born on a different day so my birthday doesn't interfere with your mother's. Yes, I'm sorry I spend most of my salary on the house payment and don't have more to spend at happy hours. Yes, I'll…"

Somehow discomforted herself, she headed out the door and went over to pick up the feverish Zeke…

As he watched (through the window) Julia's curvy form move away and towards the parking lot, poet Frost thought out loud to himself—

I wish I could make the speech, I wish I could make the universe stop moving away, I wish I could stop the cosmic sameness that throttles me. I wish I could tell you, Julia.

And he closed the door, got on his bike, and headed over to the grocery store for milk.

~ * ~

Later that same evening, when the kids were in bed, when Trevor [who had unexpectedly returned from South America a day early—*and in a strange moody state of mind,* she thought] had dozed off in a chair, still wearing his suspenders and Van Heusen shirt, smelling gardenia-sweet and manly, with his finely-sculpted face turned slightly from the lamp, Julia's thoughts turned back to Jack Frost.

From Frost's phone conversation—both what she heard and what she imagined—she knew he was taking another beating from home. For some odd reason, she felt pity or concern for him. But come on, she thought, he seems happy with his life. Poor old Jack. Always a bit scruffy, shows up to work on a Harley Davidson motorcycle [I think he said it is an AMF Retro Dino Moto—whatever that is], and wears a backpack.

He writes all those crazy poems about bitter love, broken dreams, shattered hopes, and what he swears are harsh realities. He spends so much extra time at the office—always grading papers, always meeting students, always volunteering tutoring help in the language lab.

Always so stubbly, too. He should probably see a dermatologist about his sun-damaged face. And that crazy Vitality hair oil [pah], and that Old Rice Aftershave, and those silly old hard-toed janitor shoes. He's just so, so—blue collar! And how many wives has he had? And his girlfriend! Oh my!

Silly old Jack, she smiled to herself. She threw an afghan over Trevor, kissed his perfect cheek and loosened his suspenders, and wandered down the hallway in the dim glow of a burnished metal horse head nightlight. Slipping off her ballerina shoes, she changed into a nightgown and hugged the chilly pillow, and dug her green polished toenails [with superbly crafted butterfly diatomic images—"*Mariposa mas fina,*" Frost once commented quietly—but she had overheard him] into the crisp cotton sheets.

[The sheets had been expertly laundered—and the king-size bed had been made—earlier that morning by Julia's trustworthy housekeeper and confidant, Manuella Vasquez.]

Silly old Jack, she thought. *You just don't have IT. Those Janitor shoes have got to go!*

CCC Police Safety Public Report for
02-17-11 to 03-16-11:

02-29-11; Theft: A student left his backpack unattended in the restroom of Copperfield Hall and it was stolen.

02-24-11; Criminal Damage: An unknown suspect damaged the vehicle of an instructor [*Dr. S. Chick*] in lot E.

02-25-11; Harassment: A former student reported being harassed via her smart phone. Her only connection to a possible suspect was her former Vampire Novel 103 classmates at CCC.

02-26-11; Harassment: A student reported being harassed via texting. [Rozwhel PD is also investigating.]

02-26-11; Harassment: A student reported harassing text messages from a former friend in South America.

03-02-11; Criminal Damage: An unknown suspect damaged the hood of a socialist's car in lot E. The student was then chased down the alley by a bat-wielding, pipe smoking, and as yet unidentified *socialist militant*.

03-02-11; Lost pet [duck]: Reported by retired faculty member [*Hose*]. Duck later found swimming in neighbor's swimming pool…. HC PD looking into possible pet licensing violation pursuant NNMS 265-876.R2.

03-03-11; Criminal Damage: An employee *[Bob Zontarg]* reported the tires on his vehicle intentionally punctured by 20 penny nails while parked in lot E.

03-04-11; Toxic Waste Report: An adjunct faculty member [*Keegan*] reported soap suds from a student car wash fund raiser were entering storm drain in violation of NNMS 123-123.b6

03-04-11; Drug use/marijuana: A non-student *socialist*, wearing a bright red arm band, was contacted regarding being observed smoking a pipe that appeared to look like that used for smoking marijuana. The subject, a legal alien, admitted to smoking marijuana earlier in his career, but not inhaling, but via consent search was found to have nothing illegal on him except for some Scottish tobacco. He was banned from the campus. On 03-x5-x0 at 1-24 hours the subject was observed on campus during a public safety drill/exercise. He was arrested. Hamilton PD took disposition of the arrested *socialist.*

Medical assists: 12
Information: 55
Illegal parking: 2
Suspicious activity/person: 2
Damage: 1
NNMRS traffic violation: 1
Vendor Policy violation: 1
Vehicle accident: 1
Vehicle repossession: 1
Trespass warning: 1
Lost pet: 1
EPA violation: 1
Socialist **arrests 1**

Kat Van Dorn, Professor of English

Professor Van Dorn is feeling pretty good about herself. In her second year of teaching at Copperfield, Kat is recognized as a strong faculty member, a good committee team player, and an active participant in community events. She received her Master's in Rhetoric and Composition from Hamilton State University three years ago, graduating cum laude and confident. While at HSU as a graduate student and full-time instructor, she served as an editor of the college's Literary Journal, helped organize their annual international conference on writing, and published several articles in national peer reviewed journals including the *English Journal, College Composition and Communications, The Rhetorical Quarterly,* and *Feminism Today.*

At thirty, her teaching experiences are rich. She has taught on Interactive Television, online using both Web CT and Blackboard course management systems, and in traditional face-to-face situations. When eligible for a sabbatical in five more years, she hopes to complete her dissertation in Rhetoric and Composition at the University of Hamilton, located in Santa Rey, eighty-nine miles to the south.

Kat had concerns about "pausing" in her academic career to teach at a community college. But several considerations influenced her decision to apply for the then-open position at Copperfield. She knew a stint of teaching in the community college classroom, working with emerging and developing writers, would give her experiences that could not be duplicated in the university—either as student or instructor.

Plus, as a committed academic professional, she knew very well that teaching writing at any level can be rewarding, helpful, and contribute to her knowledge base about methods, activities, and internal and external classroom learning processes.

Finally, she needed a job, and the community college full-time position paid far better [three times as much!] than what she could receive as a Master's level instructor at Hamilton State U.

Her university colleagues had warned her about the teaching/learning environment at the community college—and she had received many good-natured jabs from them following the interim President's DUI arrest.

Still, she was convinced her work was important at Copperfield, and her vision, purpose, and intellect were clear and focused.

"Kat," her doctoral advisor and long-term friend Dr. Haller from U of H said to her three years ago, *"I hope you are making the right decision to take the position at CCC. I know the pay is attractive, but you will be spending much of your time involved in non-academic activities at CCC. There will be many days when you feel like a cashier at Sticky Mart—and you may be treated like one, too. Please, please don't desert your dissertation."*

"Be careful your pedagogic and academic sensibilities do not, uh, change too much. Protect, my dear, what Matthew Arnold would call your 'buried life.' Please, be brave, my child," she said, tears welling up in her eyes.*"* [Dr. Haller turned away, wiping her eyes, then embraced Kat and wished her well, wished her the best.]

This reaction, and advice, had startled Kat momentarily, but she did not allow Dr. Haller to dissuade her from her decision, nor had she allowed her ensuing time at CCC to modify her behaviors, interests, or academic endeavors.

During the past three years, she had maintained a detached, objectivist, clinical eye on her surroundings. The emics—and etics—of community college life were entertaining, to say the least.

Old Doc Roz, bearded friend, would-be poet, and grandfatherly confidant, Chair of the Rhetoric Division at HSU, had benignly sent her one of the articles he had published years ago about community colleges and middle class values.

"Read this, my dear. You may find it enlightening as you descend into the maelstrom of community college life! Somehow you must prepare for the intellectual erosion, the whimsical culture that awaits you!"

Kat smiled, remembering that moment, and considered how the old man's academic career had been built on Op-Eds and newsletter articles. But, she thought, at least he wrote. And, he apparently wrote some gangbuster pieces back in 2007 or 2008—but not much of merit since then.

Well, not that this new non-academic life was perfect. She was uncomfortable with the Professor title given master's level teachers at Copperfield—even though she had a significant publication and presentation record.

[Strange, she marveled. *At Copperfield we have a Professor of Plumbing and two Professors of Custodial Science. I wonder if they have written scholarly articles about soldering flux, Teflon tape, or broom handle durability.]*

She was amazed at how much energy the faculty at Copperfield spent on meetings—daily meetings about quality initiatives, constituency labor concerns, union meetings, salary negotiations, golf tournaments, strategic planning, organizational learning, wellness exams, potlucks, and even baby showers.

Kat reckoned she spent sixty percent of her on campus time at college restructuring and reorganization meetings.

There is so much talk about critical thinking among the faculty, she whispered to herself, *but it is much like an advertising campaign, or ideas for a web page. I wonder how many of the faculty members truly understand the liberating nature, the egalitarian qualities, of a great books curriculum or the liberal arts?*

Coming from an intensive and fruitful academic environment at a Research I University, she was often overwhelmed and obfuscated by the stress and anxiety evidenced by the CCC faculty in terms of their teaching loads, overload pay schedules, and office size.

[*They acted so much like "labor,"* she found herself thinking more than once. *Or like* young-uns!]

If these faculty members are modeling higher education learn-ed behavior for first generation college students, why are they dressed so poorly? All the flip-flops, cargo shorts, smocks, sports bras, t-shirts, unkempt hair, and baseball caps! Why do these professionals choose to dress like baseball fans at happy hour?

Why do faculty members, once they become administrators, begin to dress professionally? Who sees the students first? Even the secretaries dress better than the faculty.

The daily dose of management meetings, quality initiatives, and outcomes assessment usually seemed far removed from her students' actual learning needs.

While she would never voice her feelings publicly—or in the faculty lounge or hallways or offices like so many of her colleagues at Copperfield— she had many questions about the actual competency and intentions of the administrators, especially the President and Dean Preston. [*Pleasant enough men, they talked incessantly, but in actuality did so little,* she thought to herself.] She often marveled at the proliferation of dean and vice president positions the last few months at CCC, and she wondered what many of these people would do—or how they would be perceived—at a major university such as HSU.

[*She heard, in her mind, old man Roz laughing again—"Ha Ha Ha!"*]

Why did all of these administrators hold or seek a doctorate in leadership? Why was the Ed Leadership doctorate a necessary "union card" for entry into an upper level "leadership" role in the American community college?

Based on the age-old academic model she understood, university administrators came out of academic departments, beginning their careers in academia as educational experts, seeking the terminal degree became an essential pathway to knowledge acquisition. They were academicians and scholars [teachers] in a subject matter discipline who earned entry into higher education based, almost entirely, on their academic insight and discipline expertise.

Grounded in the principles required for scientific inquiry and truth finding, these professionals thrived because they knew "something." They had a thorough understanding of subject matter—scientific methodological approaches—based on theoretical models or frameworks and experimental practice. Having intellectual depth and understanding of theory frames used in inquiry, they also possessed a deep comprehension of complex organizational approaches to problem solving and arriving at a measurable level of truth.

She knew the most successful demonstration of leadership could be seen in any number of history's prized leaders. Included were those in the military, in politics, in business, and in religious orders. True leaders— Soldiers, Generals, Princesses, Kings, Queens, Senators, Judges, Presidents, Governors, Mayors, CEO's CFO's, Ministers, Priests, Rabbis, Bishops, Popes—well, their leadership success did not require doctoral coursework, degree accomplishment, credentials, self-centered networking, or weekend seminars at a golf resort.

Was it possible for paper work to provide leadership?

Why was the non-academic doctorate apparently a requirement for community college "leaders"?

She was baffled sometimes by the posturing, the posing, and the corporate nomenclature surrounding, simply engulfing, daily discourse at CCC. The alleged "myths" and "misplaced" and "inappropriate" stereotypes of community college culture she had heard about on the "outside" seemed painfully, and sadly, accurate now that she was an employee. *"I will never go native,"* she whispered to herself, after a painful reorganization meeting—at which Dr. Dolly huffed and puffed about higher education leadership. [She knew Dolly had written nothing—except for clandestine and probably accusatory notes in his ever-present journal—presented nowhere, and had been fired from his last job.]

She daily found several on the administrative team naïve in their understanding of complex issues—and they often used words, almost like junior high kids, at the periphery of their knowledge base. She considered composing an article discussing the role-playing, the scripted behaviors she found among community college administrators. *But who would publish such a thing? And who would read it? These people want to hear success stories, not criticism. I wonder if they ever read anything—or write anything. They are experts at copying and pasting, and recommending someone to "take the lead" on projects! And they always seem so defensive.* She was simply amazed so little community college criticism or reform literature had ever been produced.

Anthropologists would be stunned if they conducted an honest, scholarly ethnographic study of this place! Copperfield Community culture was so insular, so protected, so, uh grades 13-14.

"*Property taxes,*" once quipped gruff Doc Roz while he stroked his Walt Whitman beard. "*That's all that keeps 'em solvent,*" he said, as he walked off to light his meerschaum pipe." [*Another memory—she could still smell his Captain Bleak tobacco as he wandered down the literature building hallway.*] "Remember, my dear, in America— *everything is the opposite of how it seems to be. Those two year colleges are disguised social service agencies!*"

Still, Kat loved her students—loved teaching. She was highly respected and had a tremendous work ethic. She was quick to lead when called, and exhibited the highest levels of professionalism. She was an old time professor—dedicated to her discipline and the academic life. In some ways, at the young age of thirty, she felt overly mature, overly serious, in the daily circus of Copperfield Community.

She had learned to grow silent and contemplative at meetings, but to volunteer to "take the lead" on writing or research projects. At HSU, as an instructor, her committee work had been focused on academic activities—at CCC, the committees seemed to be focused on responding to threats or warding off threats—external or internal, real or imagined.

Her academic weltanschauung had thus far preserved her from embracing the apparent foibles of Copperfield culture.

Kat was surprised to learn few faculty members ever applied for grants—and still fewer tried to publish articles or even Op-Eds. *"I'm here to teach. I'm not interested in that publish or perish mentality,"* she overheard Dr. S. Chick say at a department meeting. She knew many had made "best practices" presentations at local conferences or regional community college conferences—and they were to be commended for this—but she was surprised so little scholarly work was produced, or attempted at CCC.

She observed that part-time adjunct faculty represent eighty-seven percent of the Copperfield teaching staff—and teach an equal percent of course sections. *How can that be?* she wondered—before learning that most full-time faculty rarely taught the designated fifteen hour course load. It seemed paid release time for administrative committee work, faculty senate roles, online course development, mission statement re-writes, and division reorganization initiatives always superseded the necessity to actually teach.

She had also discovered seventy percent of the CCC Professorship held the MA as their highest degree, but only one besides herself was working on a PhD in an academic area. Fifty-four were in a cohort pursuing Ed. Leadership degrees from the University of Topeka, hopefully to prepare themselves for careers as Deans, VP's and ultimately Presidents [at CCC and beyond!]. *The union card for community college leaders!*

Kat was pleased to learn she had won a BISON [Big Institute for Staff and Organized Normalization] award for teaching excellence, but her joy was tempered somewhat when she learned seven other CCC faculty members also received their BISON plaques. [Her happiness was further dampened when she received word from Dean Preston there was travel money for BISON, but not for the National Combine of English Teachers [NCET] national conference, where she was scheduled to make a presentation on embedded tutoring]. In her usual even-tempered way, she simply murmured to herself, *"Well, I've got a lot to learn about community college culture."*

Kat sometimes wonders if the administrative staff—with their generous salaries and inflated egos—could grasp the irony of the school's name: Copperfield Community College. Dickens's novel, *David Copperfield*, she mused, was about class-consciousness and the wide gulf between social classes in Victorian England. Well, she considered, we can certainly observe class distinctions at CCC! She wondered, also, how many faculty members or administrators in the district had ever read a Dickens novel—or even the local newspaper. Or their mail.

Kate decided to re-read an Op Ed piece written by the old gent, Dr. Roz. She worked carefully to neatly unfold it from between the pages of her paperback copy of *The Oxford Companion to English Literature*. [The article is provided in its entirety below.]

John Updike, Grace, and Community College Middle Class Ethos
by
Dr. Jeffrey D. Roz (2006)

How would one distinguish the cultural differences, in general, between community colleges and universities? Certainly one could consider faculty credentials, administrative staff preparation, academics, focus of service, "learning readiness" of students, missions, vocational training—the obvious and usual. Community colleges do an ample job of preparing their students for the next steps in their lives. They provide a valuable entry point for a richer participation in American society and can potentially accelerate a student's quality of life, both on the job and in the soul.

However, I believe a fundamental difference has to do with a social or class distinction criterion: I believe that community colleges' aspirations may be to prepare their students for entry *into* the middle class, while universities have aspired to pull their students *out* of the middle class. I am no economist, no political scientist, and no sociologist. I am just a steady observer of community college riffs and phrasings.

The dialectal response to community "middle class" composite cultural needs, economic needs, training needs—and response to university demands for changes in academic articulation matters—keeps the community colleges flexible and "organically" [as in nineteenth century romantic philosophy] reactive.

What about novelist John Updike? Well, he was, of course, fascinated by the middle classes [the "middle"]. Updike once said,

> There is a good deal to be said about almost anything. The idea of a hero is aristocratic. Now everyone is a hero or no one is.... My subject is the American small town, Protestant middle class.... It is in middles that extremes clash, where ambiguity restlessly rules.... What we need is a greater respect for reality, its secrecy, its music.

This, I believe, represents a partial conceptual framework behind much of his work. [For a great introduction to Updike, read the "Rabbit" tetralogy.]

So, how is the Updike view of the middles related to community college philosophy?

I have said in another place that community colleges have not developed a theoretical framework since the open door policy of the sixties, but I suspect I may be incorrect.

Perhaps community colleges have become the protectors of the American middles.

Though it was probably never intended, community colleges have evolved into places of great tension—tension between developmental, academic and vocational demands, tension between traditional and online course offerings, and tension with local "stakeholders" over staff salaries, travel expenses, baccalaureate training, and bond elections.

The middles at the community college struggle to obtain training, to prepare for further schooling, to live and to love. [Perhaps in the middle of the tetralogy, Updike toyed with the idea for a novel called *Rabbit Earns His Associates Degree at Copperfield Community College!*]

The emergence of "work force development," supported by ancillary academic programs, appears to be the actual driving force behind community college post-secondary education "market share" positioning. Is this altogether bad? Poverty is not good.

My notions of the middle class have both material and intellectual undertones. I sense that twenty-first century middle class America cares far more about their material well-being than their intellectual pelf.

Surely, the American middle class is becoming more expansive in its demands for goods and services. Nowadays, a "small" house is 2200 square feet and can likely have a swimming pool [especially here in North New Mexico]. Once, a family of four shared a bathroom. Each child now expects one for his/her private use.

The trickle upward of buying power and the all-encompassing "religion of stuff" appears to be thriving, no matter what one thinks about the economic situation. Hard work and accelerating salaries drive the economy.

The idea of the community college [a priori] was certainly poetic, certainly beautiful, a metaphor for entrance into prosperous—and intellectual—American middle life. The post WW II individual American experience has centered on the development of a [seemingly] nourished and materially satiated middle class. What do ELL training, GED training, and massage therapy training have in common? They are all entry point activities to a better "quality" of life.

However, most of the "stuff" we harbor in our homes and hearts has done little to improve the "core" quality of our lives. The entire system would collapse [has just about collapsed!] if all mortgages, auto loans, and credit card debt were called in tomorrow. What would *we* do without our Ipads and our video games? [Save money, think, and reflect more? Spend less time filling in the bleakly lonely portions of our lives with idle talk? Stop listening to the same old songs we've heard a million times before?]. One can take this axiom to the bank: the more things one possesses, the more one is possessed by those things.

Sadly, the middle's intellect seems to be now vigorously centering on Diskneeland fantasies, Caribbean cruises, summer blockbusters, and happy hour [where the "middle" really expands!].

This is what fascinates me—and why I consider Updike. A standard of living, making a living, is not mysterious. Economists have carefully studied the

41

relationships between behavior and the economy. The Institutionalist school of economics, for example, sees behavior as part of a larger social pattern influenced by current ways of living and modes of thought.

But knowing *how* to live may be the greatest secret of all. I am not a moralist or an Emersonian, but the relationship between outward success and inner grace has a Calvinistic flavor—and can be traced to the American Puritan experience in the 1600's.

Wealth without sensitivity, without reflection, creates a kind of tyranny in personal, domestic, and global understanding. What should the "middles" intellectual values reflect? How should vocational, a-vocational, and intellectual meaning offered by American community colleges trisect for the "ambiguous" middles?

How many times do community college instructors hear the phrase— "Oh, I'm just taking these classes [English, math, history—insert name of academic courses] to get them out of the way"? Many of you nod in gentle agreement; you are empathetic to the view that coursework of any kind is simply preparation for the world of work and ownership—a rite of passage into the middles. The place where you, too, live and function.

Those of you who work in academic disciplines at the community colleges should continue your most important task: promoting how to live and how to improve the quality of the intellectual life—not just how to make a living. Poverty of spirit, I believe, is the worst kind of destitute.

Remember the "Rabbit!"

Let's rethink the kind of music we make in the middles—and in "middle" education.

Elena Vasquez, Career Counselor

Elena Vasquez enjoys coming to work every day. She parks her Civic carefully in a shady spot each morning and looks forward to a Moonbuck's from the newly refurbished on-campus food mall. Always nicely dressed, she considers herself a role model for the young—and not so young—Latina women at Copperfield Community College. She is poised and successful.

"Vaya con Dios," she says cheerfully and sincerely to Professor Van Dorn when their paths cross in the parking lot.

In fact, there is nothing Elena loves more than her job, except for her six-year-old son Xavier. He is the joy of her life and his birth motivated her, once a single mom at seventeen, to finish her GED, attend community college, go on to the university, then enter the helping professions.

Sometimes she thinks for a moment or two how different her life might have been if her Austro-Hungarian boyfriend Fitzgerald Aba-Novák had not run off with the Pennsylvania-Dutch girl who did nails for a living. But only for a moment...

Her office is nicely decorated. She has good Scandinavian furniture—comfy chairs, a modern Norwegian love seat, a desk, and bookshelves—she purchased with her own money. She is very proud of her professional niche, and sees accurately her future is wide open at Copperfield. She works hard and she has much to be proud of.

Her door has nicely crafted sayings by positive thinkers and motivators from all walks of life. Under her nameplate on the door, a colorful banner reads *"Bien venidos."*

In a corner she keeps a refrigerator, a microwave, and a coffee pot. Usually she has some interesting tea bags and some cheesecake, or perhaps a bowl of fruit for her guests. Of course, she always has several packs of gum available for her students—and Kleenexes, too.

The walls are tastefully covered by framed posters portraying significant women of color, including representations of Zapatista women, a photograph of Harriet Tubman, and a new lithograph portrait of Sonia Maria Sotomayor.

Elena Vasquez serves as board member for the nearby Chapter of Chicanos Por la Hungria. Some of her colleagues at the college think the organization is too political, but she points out that her connection to the group assists the institution's role as a Workforce Development Center. She is also certain her board membership helps to strengthen Copperfield's stature as a North New Mexico Students First Serving Workforce and University Transfer Institution [NNMSFSWUTI].

Elena stays very busy during the day. She typically counsels or advises three or four students each morning before heading off campus to meetings in the afternoons. Besides being a Por la Hungria Board member, she also attends the local Latina Women's Initiative group meetings, leads focus groups for the Strategic Planning of the Copperfield Master Plan, attends the town's *Stop Domestic Abuse of Men Now [SDAMN]* group meetings, and volunteers for a billboard and highway sign paint and repair group.

She drives to classes for her doctorate in Education Leadership program a few miles away at the downtown University of Topeka campus. She is close to completing her coursework, along with the other fifty-three members of her cohort.

Elena is excited about being able to put ABD [all but dissertation] after her name. This will be a great source of pride to her and her mother.

She is considering volunteering time at a no-kill animal shelter, too. She loves dogs [especially German-Hungarian Shepherds] very much.

She also volunteers some time at the local county jail site to work with female offenders.

She is busy—very busy. *"I don't know what I'd do without my smart phone calendar,"* she exclaims in a tinkly corporate voice. *"Madre de Dios! I love my phone so much."*

She is well-known and appreciated in the local community—by Anglos, Hispanics, African Americans, Asians, Native Americans, Pacific Islanders, and all other closely commoditized and demarcated ethnic and demographic groups.

Elena tries to go to the gym early every day or two to work out. She is also one of the co-advisors for the CCC Men of Diverse Colors Club. [This week she has to order buffalo chicken wing-flavored pizzas for one of their fund raising activities.]

Elena does a good job of filling her performance reports, attending campus meetings, and networking. She has an eye on a Deanship in a year or two. At twenty-eight, she is nearly ready to assume the responsibilities of such a position at the community college.

She would like to have Dean Paxton Preston's job after he becomes a Vice-President. She sees him as quite ambitious, a community college career man, a friend, and mentor.

Strangely, sometimes her heart flutters when he walks near her. His dress shoes are always so nicely polished, his hair is perfect. He cuts a smart figure speaking to his Blackberry, or eating cheesecake in the Café' Bistro Con Carne Salad Copperfield, or gazing at her quietly during those long strategic planning meetings on Friday afternoons—but Elena also knows he is married to a....[She mustn't think of such things—such notions only confuse her—besides, there is Dashika!]

Other parts of her are conflicted, of course. She spent a year working as an interpreter in Honduras. At times she has Marxist sympathies and is sensitive to the incessant capitalist exploitation of oppressed working classes and minority groups. [She took down an antique-store-purchased poster of Che Guevara, but the decision to do so pained her deeply.] Yet she loves to buy stocks and bonds and is trying to start an investment club with some of her Career Advising colleagues.

Still, Elena enjoys reading articles posted at *The Hob Fob*, a British Marxist-Socialist online Journal, but she is afraid the IT people might report her for inappropriate computer use. She keeps a stack of *vampiro* novels in her office. They are written in Spanish and were gifted to her by Jack Frost, the Anglo Espanol Professor.

Her own family has difficulty accepting her statuesque and amazingly-intelligent significant-other, Dashika. Elena knows her powerful connection to Dashika is at odds with her strict Catholic upbringing. [Her nana will not even acknowledge Dashika and either leaves the room or averts her eyes when Dashika stops by. Elena wishes her family could accept the fact she is somewhat-nearly romantically involved with Dashika, a blue-eyed, blond-haired, athletic, shiny-toothed white woman.]

A self-professed liberal, an emerging proud and confident Latina professional woman, she voted Obama. She has assertively struggled with her state's border policies and taken umbrage with Hamilton County Sheriff Jose' Arroyo's apparent racial profiling—though she learned recently that one of

Dashika's distant family members [her cousin Earnest Smith], while sneaking across the border into West México, was thankfully saved by Arroyo's desert water bottle program.

She loves to eat menudo with her family on special occasions, [her Aunt Manuella Vasquez also makes fantastic albondigas!] but Elena is charmed by French cuisine and bistros. She senses, on one level, her newfound desire for European food may be a positive symptom of an emergent acceptance of diverse cultures and her willingness to fully embrace other peoples. She is a strong proponent of multiculturalism.

Yes, she enjoys watching hockey too and even attended a High Tea party [with scones, lemon curds, and chocolate dipped strawberries] at a University of Topeka faculty member's home recently.

She has her sights set on a nice town home in Paradiso Valley and is considering having the dainty rose tattoo removed from her shoulder blade.

Still, she does not appreciate the Anglicization of her heritage. [The very sight of Del Taquito Steeple restaurants angers her and brings color to her pretty cheeks.] She tries to speak Spanish as much as she can so she does not lose this powerful connection to her culture.

But Elena is also very careful to use the corporate meeting speak [*Absolutely! Stakeholders! Sustainability! Awesome! Robust! Green Jobs! Ipad training! Brand Recognition! Leadership!*] that will advance her own prosperity within the district—the largest community college district in North New Mexico.

Elena is capable, professional, and well-liked at CCC. She is intellectually gifted, genuinely kind and caring, and strives to be helpful at all times.

Sometimes she is concerned the pictures taken of her on the beach in Mazatlan' will surface somewhere and cause her grief.

Of course, Elena was doing nothing wrong, but she was clad in [what some might consider] a revealing one-piece white swimsuit. That particular spring break, she was on a social networking field trip with other doctoral students and for some reason, at the time, Elena thought it might be cute or personable to pose while leaning sweetly against a palm tree.

46

She cannot remember who took the pictures or gave her a towel later. Thinking back, she remembers little about the social networking trip or the flight home but she did earn three credits—and an A—for the course.

Dr. Dolly's Morning

Dr. Dolly was not very happy this morning; the red message light on his office phone was blinking, and that was never good news. More than six dozen messages had been left, each munificently colored with discontent, anger, and outrage.

[Summative White Paper Report of Telephone Messages Contained on Dolly's office phone]

1) Faculty complaints were legion concerning the CCC bookstore lady and her numerous errors when ordering textbooks for classes—and then further faculty complaints had been voiced over the proliferation of non-academic merchandise taking precedence within bookstore (i.e., magazines, candy, granola bars, food items chips, pretzels, nacho chips, non-academic romance novels, satire novels, vampire novels, video games, music and video DVD's, CD's, Ipods, clothing merchandise, etc...);

2) Dr. Dolly received the disturbing news that copyright infringement officers were coming to visit campus over potential textbook copying violations;

3) He also learned National Science Foundation [Washington D.C. based] investigators were coming to review grant dispensation in relation to reported violations of student scholarship monies going to faculty members who were not associated with teaching science or math—the focus of the grant, and;

4) Some secretary called to warn him about the erroneous publication of a local escort service's telephone number in CCC's latest distributed marketing materials.

Dolly's immediate response was necessary in regards to the campus marketing materials. Apparently the college had inadvertently listed a dating service phone number on a fundraising letter sent to potential CCC Foundation donors. People who tried to call the committee were instead offered "Live, one-on-one talk with a local girl looking for fun" for $2.99 a minute.

A college spokesman [William-Henry Ireland] later said a typographical error caused the letter to contain a toll-free 800 number rather than Copperfield's (404) area code.

[Surprisingly, the rather large retirement community near the college, who typically register for life-time learning classes and are consistent donors to the college's annual scholarship fundraising drive, did not issue a single complaint over the phone number mishap.]

The Hamilton County Woman's Book Discussion Group

Few would believe the HCWBDG was actually a front for the MRCCN [Movement to Reform Community Colleges Now] organization. But they were. Oh sure, they read Oprah's books, contributed to Green Peas, and met for Moonbuck's coffee on the mister-system equipped tropical rain forest motif patio, but such benign activities were a front for their true purpose—to get rid of Dolly.

They had a steadily increasing-in-volume dossier of information about the President and his activities in Hamilton City. In fact, they actually possessed several videos [soon to be posted on Lube Tube] of Dr. Dolly's adventures at the Nose guard Pub in Payson West Dakota, from many years ago.

Moral and steadfast, they saw through Dolly's shenanigans. Lately, the Blue Hats [as they have become known because of their colorful self-identifying and branding demographic headgear] have been discussing Marx's *Communist Manifesto*.

The chemistry of this group was strange and their reasons for disliking Dolly varied. Some were students who had not met with success at CCC. One was the ex-wife of a CCC football coach. Another had waited too long in a class registration line. Another got sick eating pizza at a fundraiser. One felt jilted because she couldn't make the cut at a CCC Foundation Golf Tournament. Strangely enough, another had recently moved to the states from Brazil or Argentina or Ecuador or some such place and spoke very good English.

But these rank and file members were merely pawns, easily swayed by the mysterious and angry masterminds of this sinister, clandestine organization.

What kind of information had they compiled on Dolly? Using wiretaps, private investigators, news clippings, and published board-meeting minutes, they had determined—and documented—the following examples of Dolly's incompetence, fraud, and buffoonery:

1. Dolly's apparent ignorance of CCC's revenue sources surfaced during his speech at a Rotary meeting (and then published in local newspaper). Dolly: *"We receive a very small portion of our revenue from local property taxation. I am not concerned about falling home prices affecting the college operations. I'm more concerned with the state's portion of nearly 60 percent of our budget influencing the services provided to our students…also tuition and fees account for only 2 percent of our revenue. This is an area I believe we should consider during our debates."* [Actual: Property tax 42 percent, Tuition and fees 21 percent, State General Fund 14 percent, other sources: 23 percent].

2. Dolly's campus-issued cell phone records indicated several improprieties. His non-school related business—and clearly personal calls—overextended his contractual plan minutes and cost the district an extra $906 during the previous three months. This raised an initial flag of suspicion by the accounting budget office at CCC.

3. CCC's directory and city discount coupon book [10,000 copies printed and distributed], personally endorsed and approved by Dolly, contained advertisements for a suspect dating service and the All Nude Cabaret near the county line.

4. Faculty and administrators at CCC incurred charges of nearly $290,000 in international travel expenditures for "educational global experience." These costs were found to be an abuse of CCC's travel funds—all approved by Dolly.

5. Local hotel and cognac expenses billed [under Dolly's name and CCC account] totaled $4,682 during the weekends Dolly claimed to be at a regional strategic planning and mission statement conference. His phone bill at the hotel included out-of-country calls to [54] (11) 5777-4533 totaling $638. Dolly was seen at the conference during daytime hours only. He traveled in his own vehicle.

The conference actually was located 154 miles from the local hotel where he was registered.

6. Accreditation issues were surfacing that described the over expenditures of instructional funds [$1.34 million] used for CCC's VISCAM [virtual intelligence smart classroom application mode]. What was the actual verifiable number of students impacted by the three-year pilot program? Thirty-four.

7. Finally, Dolly's expenditures for a new twenty two million dollar registration and budget focused software program [SCUD] had come under careful scrutiny. The package was purchased from one of Dolly's former UT-A classmates [one Hector Bianciotti Jr., now a consultant with Softer Brain Software from Toledo, Ohio]. Besides the high initial cost, there were several other issues: 1) The annual site license is $6.2 million; 2) Dolly forgot to budget money for training, so no one knows how to work with the software, resulting in still further high dollar consultant costs; 3) During system conversion, registration information [including info needed for state audits] from years 1999-2009 was hopelessly destroyed; and 4) the software doesn't work very well anyway.

Guitar Bob Zontarg, Custodian Specialist V

Custodian Specialist V, Bob Zontarg, was developing a throbbing ache behind his eyeballs, and it wasn't from the glasses of beer he'd put away down at the Copper Coin last night.

After attending a college required Learn-ed College Action Seminar, he was more confused than ever. Dean Preston [*What an arrogant s———— that guy is*] thought Zontarg to himself while hearing the presentation the Dean had made to the assembled custodial and maintenance staff. Bob was now even further convinced Dr. Preston enjoyed listening to himself.

"There are thirty six and a half principles of the Learn-ed College. The Learn-ed College, according to Sister Mary Union-O'Leary—the leading authority on this topic—and I have heard her speak many times at many conferences—the last one in Honolulu back in May—or was it in Salzburg in April, simply means everyone here at the college, including the

Custodial Specialist Team and Maintenance Technicians Quality Improvement Hosts, has a role to play in facilitating student learn-edness.

"You might think, as a Landscaper VII or Restroom Use Control Technician VI, you are far removed from the education of our students. You may consider yourself to be only underpaid and overworked janitors, grass cutters, speed bump paint striping technicians, or gardeners. Not so. Not so. CCC students are watching you—and you have many opportunities to model good learn-ed practices—yass, you are limping learners yourselves. Each day, each hour of your employment here at CCC, you have an opportunity to model this life-long limping learn-ed behavior for our students. Whether you are putting on a pair of gloves, lighting up a smoke on break [in a CCC GB Policy 956 B.1 Revised statutes designated smoking area of course], drinking a cup of Moonbuck's coffee, or driving a golf cart to your next job site, you are modeling learn-ed behavior!

"Now, as part of CCC's ongoing Task Implementation Improvement Initiative and our refocused commitment to the institution's 2010-2015 Strategic Goals Implementation, your supervisors will be indicating, on your performance evaluations, whether you are emergent learners, needs improvement learners, or subdued learners. We are piloting this proposed needs-based job performance rubric for spring 2012.

"This is all part of our latest quality initiative. As we move closer to being a Totally Infused Learn-ed College [TILC], your pay scales and raises will be tied to student assessment, our strategic outcomes, and success. I might remind you, quoting loosely from the CCC Human resources and Policies and Procedure Manual": A class category is a recognized and perpetually shifty standard which describes or characterizes a group of jobs manifesting a social structured work class. Any job description of a class specification [i.e., Landscaper XXIIV or Restroom Use Control Technician VI] is never finished or complete [*You will work like DOGS!*], in terms of detailing the duties of any particular position within the class.

"Of course, your input is desired and we encourage you to participate at the next Strategic Focus Group meeting—Oops—got another meeting to go to—you fellows can go back to work. Remember, we are a Learn-ed College!

"Oh, and by the way, the rumors we are planning to outsource the twenty seven positions included in the Maintenance Technicians Quality Improvement Hosts employee group are simply not true. We have had conversations with several outside companies in the Maintenance Technicians Hosts industry, that is correct, but we are simply making an effort to

determine where our pay schedule fits in with national standards and job task expectations. This is part of our ongoing Human Resource Self Study and Quality Initiative Action Plan [HRSSQIAP]. Be watching the **My CCC Employees First!** *web page for further info! [But not during your scheduled work hours!]*

"Oh—*be sure to fill out the evaluation form in front of you. We need to complete, close, and strengthen all institution feedback loops to continue improving our Quality Improvement Credit scores. Dr. Dolly is really planning on a Bullridge National Quality Award this year [despite that idiot Goeber's fiasco, he thought to himself]—let's all do our parts.*

"Remember, we are One Copperfield! Onward to Excellence! Student Success Guarantees our Fiscal Success! Learn More to Spend More!" [Looking just a bit out of place, temporarily forgetting the other CCC marketing slogans, the Dean picked up his materials and left the room quickly. *Great meeting,* thought Dean Paxton to himself.]

Zontarg wondered if this speech had something to do with the Doug Jackson incident.

[Maintenance man Doug Jackson worked at the K-6 elementary school for 15 years prior to coming to CCC. Last term, Jackson had offered the college maintenance staff's "power washer" for use by the Student Young Leadership Club members, who were hosting a campus car wash on a Saturday to help support club travel to Washington D.C. Somehow, the power washer water wand got stuck at full force and student Alexandria Garcia lost control of the 20,000 psi sprayer. The handle wand spun out of control and struck two cars and the bumper of a soaped-down Del Hugo SUV before being smothered by Ricky Espinoza, a former high school wrestler. An occupational education student by the name of Donald finally stopped the out-of-control snake. Eventually, the gas generated two-wheeled pressure washer was shut down by pulling the spark plug wire. Nobody knew where the on/off switch was located. Copperfield had to pay owners for repairs to the three vehicles, including paint chips and minor dents. The expense was well in excess of what it would have cost the college to send all twelve of the students on the Washington D.C. trip.]

Zontarg heard groans, coughs, and murmurs of disbelief among his fellow workers—and he thought he knew what they were grousing about. *What* *in the *&~$%#@ did student grades have to do with mowing the lawn?* These administrators gave him a gut ache.

Most of 'em weren't smart enough to change the oil in their own cars. And they were always coming up with some crazy scheme to reorganize or evaluate or stir up the college. They couldn't even figure out how to use their own smart phones! *What was wrong with these people? H——, they came and went almost every year. What the h——was a Learn-ed college? Did the students care if this was a Learn-ed college instead of a Teach-ed or a Mr. Ed college?*

Bob thought back to the good old days—before the DUI laws were so tough, before random drug testing. He would usually buy a six-pack of good ice cold beer to drink on the way home. This gave him something to look forward to every day after work. Light beer and pork rinds. He thought back to those big beer parties out in the desert. Back then, he thought, work was fun.

Now we gotta worry about kids' grades. What are these kids supposed to do at college? They just want to party and send text messages and tie up the college's computer network downloading music. Seems like the more we worry, the less we get done. It seems like the kids are more interested in their Ipods or smart phones than going to class, anyway.

All of these d——-meetings about how we are supposed to improve our performance take away from the time we need to do our work! All these meetings about Customer Service and Learn-ed colleges! Just let me get back to work! Geez, Preston, what is wrong with you, anyway?

Bob has been at CCC for nearly 34 years, and back in the old days there had been some good parties. One of the English faculty members owned an empty lot about a mile south of the campus. Sometimes they'd have great "lot parties"—all the maintenance guys and professors were there. They had bratwursts, beer, hamburgers, and a big fire in the winter. Always a keg. Sometimes a dean would even stop by and smoke a cigar.

Everybody had a lawn chair, and there'd be a boom box, and they would drink and eat and have a great time.

Huh. Couldn't do any of that anymore, thought Zontarg. *Now they'd arrest us for having a fire, or drinking in public, or they'd tell us the music was too loud, or "That's not part of the Learn-ed College" or "You're not setting a good Go Green example." Ha! What a bunch of girlie men, anyway. And there's too many women working here. All these potlucks and quilts and baby showers every d—- day. Baby showers!*

And Bob used to enjoy smoking anytime and everywhere. There were ashtrays in every office back in the 70's. Now, he has to walk over into the vacant field across the highway to smoke to avoid arrest or use one of the designated smoking areas where he felt like a criminal for lighting up a smoke. [He thought that big-bellied Chief of Police at CCC had it in for him, anyway.]

There's even some new regulation about how we can't ride horses to work if we want.

Nope, just no !*&~*&^ fun anymore. Every day somebody gets fired, or quits, or goes crazy.

But not me. Not Guitar Bob. And that's because I still got my band together. We can play both kinds of music—country and western.

Barry Woodwurd, Counselor.

Mr. Woodwurd works steadily and without ceremony. He might have had a career in minor league baseball but chose instead to provide academic and career counseling to community college students. After working at an intemperate Alaska college for a few years, he came to CCC without fanfare and has flourished in a steady work-centered kind of way.

He belongs to a few organizations—and attends a conference or two every year or so—but would always prefer to help students rather than spend time networking or hobnobbing.

There is not much to say about Mr. Woodwurd. He does not draw attention to himself, or find self-definition in community college culture, or compete in the parking lot.

He would tell you he has an analog, rather than digital, orientation to the universe, and he finds the increasingly self-aggrandizing worlds of Facebook and karaoke mildly painful and misguided.

He reads the *Hamilton County Democrat* each morning before heading to CCC. Sometimes he rides a bicycle to work. Sometimes he drives his car. Sometimes he walks. Barry waves to retired Professor Hose when he sees him sitting on his front porch, quietly resting with Wilbur the Duck. [Mr. Hose never waves back but stares blankly off into space. Sometimes Wilbur quacks and smiles.]

Barry has a full life outside the community college, but he gives his workday complete and uncompromising attention.

He is a favorite among the CCC staff and students. If something needs to happen, he will get it done the right way without questioning or complaining. Never a windbag, never needing attention, he just works effectively with integrity and vigor.

He converses with Elena Vasquez when appropriate or necessary. He respects her obvious high energy and unwavering commitment to community college culture.

Typically, he meets with seventeen to twenty students per day. He has posters of Jackie Robinson and Carl Yastrzemski decorating his office. "Great men," he shrugs. "They were great players too."

Western Columbia University educated (MA, Student Personnel), he is sharp-dressed, charming, some would say handsome, and too often self-deprecating.

Mr. Woodwurd can almost always be found in his CCC office working with students.

Sometimes he can be found, after work, shooting a few baskets with his colleague, Mr. Allworthy, over in the gym.

Married and happy, he does not gossip, seek status, or complain. A true communitarian, he is at peace with himself and his decisions.

An intrinsic steward rather than a self-professed leader, Mr. Woodwurd does his job well then goes home to his family and friends. Quietly.

Mr. Allworthy, Professor of Philosophy

Professor Allworthy was feeling creative this afternoon. After grading a disencumbered stack of PHI 101 essay exams, he thought he might return to the draft of his nearly-completed novella.

[His students, nice enough people, just couldn't differentiate between Descartes and Plato.]

Mr. Allworthy, MA Philosophy, Hoping College, was actually quite happy to have a job teaching anywhere. He had been a part-time instructor at CCC for eleven years now.

During that time, he had successfully aborted three PhD in Philosophy programs (*Too much reading and writing. If I'd worked on an EdD, I'd be a VP by now!*). Even so, he had cheerfully maintained his forklift-driving career at the all-night discount furniture warehouse in Hamilton City.

Cynewulf Allworthy had conducted a nicely-stylized academic ritual this past winter when he ignited, in the family barbecue grill, the emerging-yet-marked-up draft of his dissertation on Descartes. He felt quite at ease during this cathartic moment and even felt great joy as his kids came out and cooked chocolate graham cracker S'mores over the curling Cartesian flames of his life's ambition. [*Well*, he thought, *that may be the end of my academic career, but I've still got my book. I just know it will change our lives*]. He recited Frost's "The Bonfire" as his tome incinerated and the kids went back inside.

Mr. Allworthy was more or less supported by his wife's plastic pot and pan business. Typically, Alice made in-home presentations three nights a week. Her thrift-store clothes were clean, and she was a good worker. She had sold bowls and lids to nearly everyone who worked at CCC, and she felt oddly connected to the wives of Dr. Dolly and Dean Paxton. [The wives found Mr. Allworthy's wife to be a bit chatty and odd. They couldn't understand why Alice's husband didn't want a full-time job at the college. Or why he didn't have one. But some rooted sense of *noblesse oblige* kept them buying spatulas and mixing bowls from her—especially near the holidays.]

Back to the professor.

He was on to something with this novel—and it was big. [Not the biggest, but big!] In his readings of Descartes, Mr. Allworthy had become fascinated with philosophical dualism. [Sidebar: by dualism, we mean the following. Dual (two kinds of) realities exist: 1) An individual's conscious perception of reality and 2) Reality as it exists apart from an individual. Others might call this subjectivity and objectivity.]

Well, Allworthy had this notion his book would be a best seller in academic circles because he had come to grips with an amazing fact. At the community college there is no philosophical dualism. All consciousness blends into the pursuit of a singular approach to intrinsic meaning. His colleagues find value, worth, and a level of contentment in simply being community college employees, participating in an artificial intelligence created in some ancient and vast cosmic void or conference. The single mindedness confounded his Kant-like sensibility. The college had only one modality, one purpose, one vision. What was it?

In the true, or intended, platonic subordination of the community college, diversity and stewardship would flourish. Idealism, truth, and beauty would be balanced by several Aristotelian commandments: "Thou shall devote the utmost powers to a common social welfare...above pleasure, money...shall ponder and revere the universal laws that bind ...use just so much of tools that service requires. Thou shall endure hardship...remain steadfast until habit becomes second nature. You shall find a few friends and hold to the social welfare that is the task of man."

What had Allworthy learned? Social welfare had been replaced by ambition! Selfish ambition had become the singular modality! CCC was in violation of its true purpose. Philosophical duality had been replaced by philosophical compost. Yass. The syllogism was plain as day to our philosopher.

Allworthy's book, his satire, his novella, was an attempt to construct meaning out of this chaos. He looked at the clock and realized it was time to retreat to the propane-scented palace where sweaty workingmen mesh with machines. Here, within the vast chamber of crated commodities, he could decouple from Dostoyevsky and dabble in Descartes' Meditations.

But he was filled with warmth—in the novel form, his ideas could be articulated—and perhaps cut a broad swath of moral, social, and economic righteousness. Because he was able to clearly recognize the lack of philosophical duality at the community college, he knew his own core being was healthy and vibrant.

Alice called out, "*Don't forget your lunch pail, Cynewulf dear.*" His son, *Caedmon*, hugged him, and the squire went out in front of their brownstone apartment to catch the 9.40 PM Downtown bus. Redeemed.

Poster Seen Everywhere on CCC Main Campus

"EARTH DAY" *Event!*

The Men of Diverse Color Student Organization at Copperfield is celebrating Earth Day by collecting Toxic Debris! Bring Toxic Items to our Collection Bins Just Outside Room 211.

WE NEED:

Used cell phones

[What happened—many student and faculty cell phones were reported either missing or stolen and placed in bins set up for the drive. A student contest among Student Council members had offered "free pizza" for the winning contributions.]

Used eyeglasses

[What happened—Dr. Seemy's office was ravaged by student groups looking for all her old eye glasses. Seemy has decided to file a formal complaint with the college and has retained legal counsel.]

Empty printer ink cartridges

[What happened—all campus-wide printers became inoperable due to ink cartridge thefts.]

Our Cheerleader: A poem by Carl Wermanski

The cheerleader is magnificent.

She is lovely and sculpted—perhaps the perfect female form.

Her moves are silky and sensual—she is conditioned and coy and represents something significant…

Why is she dancing before the masses?

The cameras capture her figure, her smile, her golden hair.

She wiggles and rotates, kicks and yodels
Why is she dancing before the masses?
Why are the women watching her?
Why are the men watching her?
The steady *boom chukka boom* from the stadium speakers
Keeps her prancing…
Does her performance affect the outcome of the game?
Do the shirtless painted fans in row 76 hope to capture her attention?
Does she plan to marry a player someday—or open her own dance studio?
Is she dancing for herself or someone else?
Why is she dancing before the masses?

CCC Athletics and Issues

Carl Wermanski [aka coach "Ski"] is the Defensive Coordinator of the CCC Football Team. One can immediately recognize Coach Ski, even from a distance. He is a somewhat large fellow with a habit of repeatedly tugging on the "sans-a-belt" waistband which circumnavigates his comfortably trite black nylon shorts. A set of heavily squatted quadriceps expose and amplify a three inch scar over his left kneecap. His legs gradually morph into matching rutabaga-shaped calves which truncate into ankles rooted in black, well-worn, serrated-soled sneakers.

His sizable sloped shoulders are mal-aligned into a bullish neck. Visible hair sprouts from beneath an athletic department-issued grey t-shirt with the Copperfield Fighting Gaucho tautly embroidered over his left pectoral. Coach Ski's sparkling blue eyes, small facial features, and gregarious laugh often disguise his aggressive coaching style. Married to wife Marie for twenty-three years, Coach Ski has one college-aged daughter [Susan] who attends an out-of-state private university, and an eleven year-old autistic boy named Brian.

Coach Ski is well-liked by nearly all Copperfield personnel and students. He is a regular at the Copper Coin Tavern and enjoys bantering and discussing politics with Henry McDougal, the Copper Coin's second shift Barkeep.

On this particular Thursday afternoon, Coach Ski appeared a bit irritated. One could tell by the way he wore his Copperfield baseball cap which was tightly pulled over his buzzed flat top. He had just finished meeting with the head football coach, Curtis "Spike" Raymond, and Spike's young assistant wide-receiver coach, Thomas Tiller ["T.T."]. The two were currently walking in silhouette behind the computer commons building, making their way back to the coach's office in south gym—the opposite direction of Coach Ski. They were easy to identify. Spike stood a portly 5'8" and T.T. was a lean 6' 5". Coach Ski would often refer to them as Toulouse- Lautrec [because, when seen together, they created a comically haunting image].

[Spike played backup line-backer on the 1982 Hamilton City High state runner-up squad led by quarterback Danny "Dusty" O'Brian. Dusty went on to play at an NCAA Division II program and later had served as an assistant offensive line coach for a number of NFL teams. Spike supposedly still "keeps in touch" with Danny. Spike's ex-wife Barbara left him years ago because, as she claimed, "*He treats football as if it were his life…and his marriage as if it were a game.*"]

Coach Ski didn't much agree with the head coach's approach to recruiting and maintaining players' eligibility. Ski was reviewing the just-departed head coach's meeting in his head.

Spike*: I'll tell you what, this kid can flat out run. Gotta have this kid—we've made the Southwest JuCo Mega Conference South East Coyote Division [SJCMCSECD] of Eastern North New Mexico playoffs for six years running [all but one of the five conference schools miss the playoffs]. I'll tell you what…my daddy use to say…'don't tell me how rough the waters are, just bring home the ship.'*

Look, I don't care how you do it, just get Marcus eligible, this kids D-I material…. What about the sixteen credit hour online weekend course out of Florida you used to get Darnel eligible last year, T.T.?

T.T.: *Coach that school is no longer in operation. I checked their web page and it's gone. I think they may have accreditation issues.*

Spike: *Hey, Ski! What about the online digital-friendly school with a Nevada P.O. Box…ain't that where Dr. Hendersand got his Doctorate before retiring two-years ago? How 'bout the religious academy in Texas—don't they train Preachers or Rabbis or something? H——, the kid only needs thirty-six credits!*

Geez, thought Ski, *this coming from a guy who thinks the Passover is a no-huddle shotgun snap offensive formation.*

Just then, Coach Ski crossed the path of Developmental Reading Education Instructor, Colleen Jasper-Rutger. She typically leads her campus-conquering stride with a stainless steel coffee mug [*monographed with Professor J-R*]—slicing her pathway through parked cars, students, staff, and open campus space. Today, however, having just returned from the Summer Language Institute Plan for Undergraduate Participation meeting (SLIP-UP), she was clutching a folder close to her chest, zombie-like, plodding along and gazing vacantly toward her cubical asylum, dreaming of retirement, failing once again to construct any meaning from the two hour meeting she just endured.

[Ms. Jasper-Rutger created the "Read-Meal" program at CCC—where students who are enrolled in developmental (<100 level) Reading and English courses are provided complementary food (pizza) and soft drinks. All her course sections maintain the student enrollment necessary to continue the program each semester. Her classes fill and the students stay glutted by Mafia Mick's pizza.]

"Hello, Colleen!" said Ski. *"How are things?"*

"Oh well, Coach, you know CCC. Another day, another meeting."

"Hey, I understand Carl is making progress on his global connections with distance learning. I know some members of our coaching staff hope it's up and running by fall."

[Colleen is married to Carl Rutger, TLC (Teaching Learn-ed Center) director. Mr. Rutger wishes to expand distance learning by offering online courses in Tibet to further CCC's higher education presence on a global scale -- also to grandly increase FTSE dollars and fatten up his own resume so he can get a better job, more respect, and a bigger office somewhere else].

Currently, a not fully-operable forty foot diameter satellite dish sits on top of the TLC building, waiting on district approval and a private partner funding source. The TLC is the most expensive building (by square footage) on campus. Originally wired and cabled for once state-of-the-art transmissions, the TLC is now a relic of outdated features representing more of a museum piece than a technological showcase—however, it is still referred to by President Dolly as *"The top state-of-the-market technologically sound institutional facility in the greater South Mid East North South West."*

"Well Coach, I'm not really sure what's holding up the process, but Carl is a determined soul."

[*Sidebar:* Opposed by Dr. Dolly, external stakeholders hoped to change the facility's name to "Technical Learning Center"—and are willing to use a paid sponsor's name affiliation to make it happen. Local business leader Jake Spencer, owner and operator of Jake's Diesel Motor Maintenance Repair Shop, has offered to fund the project. Jake does service work for two major "long-distance" trucking firms and has a marketing firm working on a radio and TV promotional piece. *"Jake's supports truckers and Copperfield Community College with TLC long-distance service"*—is the proposed advertising slogan.]

About this time, Ms. Tina Pendergast, Copperfield Community College's head tennis coach, was coming from the direction of the north parking lot. Almost immediately ending his brief conversation with Colleen, Coach Ski turned and headed toward CCC's food court.

Colleen: *Hello, Tina. Why…you always look so healthy. How do you remain so thin?*

Tina: *Thanks, Colleen. Nerves, stress, and inflammation. Ha!*

Coach Tina Pendergast was nicely tanned, and she sported a white visor with short straight hair cut a perfect one inch below ear lobe length, exposing small gold and diamond tennis ball earrings. She was wearing a powder-blue tennis short/skirt combo and white tennis shoes with the popular Nietzsche swoosh.

Tina: *I'm heading for a cup of Moonbuck's—do you have time to join me?*

Colleen: [After checking her smart phone scheduler, Facebook, Twitter, her professional home page, and sending three texts, thumbs twiddling like mad, facial expresses changing from joy to pain, bells ringing, horns honking, whistles shrieking] *Yes, sure, sounds terrific. Thanks, Tina.*

After claiming their $9.50 [each] lattés, Tina and Colleen were joined by Art History Teacher Jill Grendhall.

[The ladies found a table on the patio upwind from Prof. S. Halstead (CCC Mortuary Sciences) and Prof L. Jensen (CCC Electricity Department). The two old friends were illicitly smoking and reminiscing about the good old days when they rode around in a 1965 Impala terrorizing rural East Nebraska, drinking beer, and hunting ducks. Jensen was mumbling something about how he "missed building meter loops for York People's Power."]

Jill was a proponent of the arts and served on a committee charged with exploring the possibility of offering a liberal arts curriculum at CCC. [Sidebar: She couldn't stand her low life, beer-drinking, oyster-breath colleague, Dr. S. Chick.]

Tina to Jill: *I see you're registered for my one-hour tennis class again this term, Jill. I hope you are able to play in the club tournament this summer—we'll have some good matched competition. You should consider joining the class, too, Colleen. It's really great fun.* [Side bar: Coach Pendergast actually does not like Colleen or her nerd husband Carl. *Technology,* she once whispered to a well-built date at the movie theatre, between bites of popcorn, *has empowered the ignorant!]*

Colleen: *Oh, I just wish I had the time, with classes and committee work, and well, Carl and I are going to Tibet this summer on a Himalayan mountain climb. It's part of the professional development funding Carl is taking advantage of to prepare for CCC's global curriculum initiatives. Most of the trip's expenses, I think around $26,000, will be picked up by CCC.*

[The three continue discussions concerning tennis and the condition of the tennis courts.]

Tina: *I have often argued with the football coaches and athletic director concerning this matter.*

Why is the football field so well-maintained and nurtured year-round when only four home games are played there each season? The tennis courts, which are used almost daily by both the college and the local surrounding community, have not been re-surfaced for better than a dozen years. Coach Ski's wife, Marie, takes my tennis class; she knows the condition of those courts.

Jill: *I've had conversations with the athletic director concerning intercollegiate athletic purpose at a two-year institution. I have diligently emphasized life-long learn-ed benefits for* *all—and continuously questioned the minuscule number of students participating in "intercollegiate" activities. The community college is the only educational entity which dedicates so much time, facilities, effort, and money to benefit so few team sports participants—I have argued for the consideration of offering an expanded intramural program to increase participation, lower costs, eliminate coaching budgets, and better embrace the Greek model for athletics and health components for life-long learning. I even suggested they offer football field use to local youth soccer programs, year-round, and allow community members to walk or exercise around the narrow gravel path surrounding the field.*

[Just then, Dean Preston materialized, and, apologizing for the interruption, asked Jill if she was heading to the Strategic Conversation for Higher Education Measures Excellence [SCHEME] meeting, already underway.]

Jill: *Oh yes, Dean Preston, I am. Are you heading there now? I'll walk with you.* [The pair exits left.]

Tina: *Well, Colleen, I have to get going myself. I sit on the Dual Enrollment Action Division [DEAD] committee which meets at 11:00. And today, at 3:30, is a special session for Teaching Higher Education: Going Above Post-secondary [THE GAP], of which I'm also a member.*

[After bidding Tina adieu, Colleen departed for her office cubical, considering how Preston reminded her of a fluttering humming bird, nervously hovering in a spot or two, then instantly zipping off to another meaning-free, walking-dead meeting already in progress.

Dandelion Kind
(a poem by Sebastian Dominick Pelligrino, 1924)

Sunshine a pleasant sight
Golden flower bright and yellow
Fuzzy stem, green tiny leaf
Make a cool summer tea
But you are still a weed to me
Dress salad with bitter scent
Oil, vinegar, peppered spice
Flower, though, soon will pale

Blow and drift and no longer be
But you are still a weed to me
Wheat stacks sway oh-so-proud
Dictate the fading flower's fate
Shed no more that grey top head
As steward of land and seed
Be gone you pest!
Indeed, indeed…just a weed

Dean Paxton Preston
Career Choice Self-Efficacy

Each morning, when Dean Paxton Preston pulls up his black with red trim dress socks, he admires the long-eared rabbit tattoo on his left ankle and thanks God he graduated from the Education Leadership Program at University of Toledo at Akron [home of the Jackrabbits]. He nearly weeps as rich memories of his alma mater come sweeping thought his consciousness—Friday nights watching their legendary football team, dancing the Toledo Two Step with Barbara, barbecuing rabbits at grad school parties, and fully embracing UTA's consummate focus on professional networking, speech making, conference attendance, and corporate policy emulation.

Every morning, Dean Preston gazes at Barb [known to some of the CCC faculty as Botox Barb], now his lovely wife, still sleeping in their king-sized bed, and wonders, in amazement, how this charmed life came to pass. All those years of struggle, sacrifice, meetings, retreats—not to mention the production of his forty-seven page dissertation ["One of the best I've ever read," commented his advisor, Dr. Leonard Sushy]—a study focusing on the use of speed bumps in community college parking lots. [Dean Preston had considered creating some spin off articles from the dissertation, but he also secretly knew he didn't like writing, didn't like the effort required to publish such scholarly work.]

He thinks of the Ethan Allen furniture gracing his home [all 5600 square feet of it]—of their cabin in Santa Rey, of his Lexus with the custom wheels [Barb agreed with him about the wheels, "Honey, you earned them!"]. Too busy at the office to perform the mundane tasks of domestic life, he retains a weekly pool service, monthly landscapers, an on-call scorpion exterminator [the bug man, his wife calls him strangely and almost affectionately], and a bi-weekly house cleaning service for his wife.

His salary, six figures now, is more than he ever dreamed he would earn. He is so proud of their children—Iva, a freshman at the land grant State University of Arizona, and Currier, a high school junior at Broomy Prep [who Dean Preston hopes to send to UTA!].

Sometimes he is overwhelmed by his good fortune—he had been a shop teacher at Leucadia High School when he learned about the eighteen month combination online and summer residency Education Leadership Doctoral program at UTA. Except for the two weeks of residence required in Toledo, he was able to complete his doctorate courses online—from the privacy of his own home [the old home they lived in before he became Dean of Instruction at Copperfield Community].

His wife has always told him he was very smart—and he must be smart—the classes he completed really didn't seem difficult to him. [He sometimes wondered why he didn't have any homework.] He learned many valuable skills, though, including attaching files, chatting, and dancing. Producing the extensive forty-seven page student interview-based dissertation on speed bumps, though, well, that was tough. All those peer review sessions, all those Moonbuck's coffees—and then he paid some old composition professor [*I think his name was Doc Roz*] $2500 to edit the grammar. *But that was money well-spent!*

Now, nearly every day, Dean Preston is giddy as he helps plan CCC's strategic mission. He has grand purpose in life—besides a very large salary.

Just a few years ago he was earning $37,000 a year as a secondary school shop teacher. Now, thanks to his training, his education, his strategic network of mentors and professional affiliations, and the strong recommendation of Dr. Leonard Sushy [noted motivational speaker, presenter, Toledo Two Step dance instructor, and community college scholar], Dean Preston stands poised to become a Vice President in a year or two. He is a highly trained, sophisticated, first generation administrative career professional, an executive with newly found and developed intellectual capabilities.

Dean Preston does not always agree with the President, Dr. Phil Dolly. But wishing to prosper in community college culture, Dean Preston has learned to be subservient, to agree with the president in principle, to be a Team Player.

Preston did quite well when Dr. Dolly assigned him the task of chairing the committee to rewrite Copperfield's Mission Statement. Dean Preston asked Glen Keynes, Institutional Researcher, to take the lead on this matter. A day later, Keynes had distributed copies of a document with several mission statement variations the committee could choose from. After a lengthy twelve minute debate, the best fitting statement was selected. Preston was very pleased with the committee's work. [He had arranged to have bagels, melon, hummus, grapes, and Moonbuck's served at the committee gathering when the final mission statement version was being crafted—he had learned, back at UTA, food was very important to decision making.]

[Side bar: Glen Keynes chuckled for days about this later because the committee's choice of the best fitting mission statement was actually a closely paraphrased version of the Pioneer Elementary School's mission statement!]

Dr. Preston [when they travel, his wife always signs the resort registry as Dr. and Mrs. Preston] gets along well with most of the faculty—except, perhaps, with the very bright biology professor, Dr. Deuce Darling, the eccentric art teacher Dr. S. Chick, and the talented, yet seemingly not ambitious, Professor Kat Van Dorn from the English department.

Preston often wonders why a man of Dr. Darling's abilities and pedigree [PhD in Big-Petroleum, North Central Oregon State] would be teaching at a community college. Darling, a truly academic man, had to be approached carefully in meetings and discussions. [Darling was seldom impressed by Dean Paxton's hazy knowledge of statistics or research methods.]

Dean Paxton, who was politically a Machiavellian and clearly sensitive to current time group think [He was a Team Player and knew even more buzz words that Dolly—"*Branding!—Stakeholder bifurcation!—Video capture!*"]—was also suspicious of what he saw as socialist or Marxist leanings in Dr. Darling. [Although Preston's own academic background and dearth of reading habits precluded him from accurately understanding socialism or Machiavelli or Marxism on any level!]

Dr. Preston finds the young Career Counselor, Elena Vasquez ABD, most charming and, well, pretty. At another time in his life, he would have been overcome by his attraction for her. Not now. Her culture, tattoos, accent, and warm personality would have been most interesting to him when he was an undergrad. But not now, no. He has heard rumors fetching pictures of her are posted somewhere on the internet, but his moral compass and sense of professionalism and his career future compass would never allow him to investigate such rumors. Not now. He simply enjoys interacting with her—and her fresh ideas—at meetings and college sponsored luncheons and sometimes on long walks around the campus.

Each morning, Dr. Preston checks Facebook to catch up on news from his UTA colleagues. He scours the internet for position openings, salary comparisons, and webinars that might help his career prospects.

He will never forget the best advice given to him by Dr. Sushy:

"Remember, Paxton, nothing—absolutely nothing—is as important to you as your career. Nothing. Now go get 'em boy. Yee Ha!"

The Multimedia Data Display Outdoor Event

The Student Academic Advancement Team [SAAT] was scheduled to meet outside the Staten Conference Center and Administration Building at 10:00 AM. [*The center was named after Mr. Michael P. Staten, who once owned a thoroughbred horse that had placed in the Kentucky Derby. Just prior to Michael's passing, legal dealings were completed to fulfill his wishes in donating a parcel of land to the college. The Dourine Staten Conference Center and Administration Building now sits on the original plot of gifted real estate.*]

SAAT regularly meets to discuss and share developments concerning student issues which limit academic achievement.

The audiovisual needs of this particular meeting required a projector capable of broadcasting data results. A group of student ambassadors, who shared a common interest in film making, had assisted the faculty team in producing hip and jazzy components for the presentation by synchronizing 226 decibel-level techno-music and color sequences corresponding to data slides.

Allen Finckle, the college's audiovisual engineer, was busy connecting wires, securing public address speakers on tripod stands, and duct taping cords and aluminum stands housing a set of portable screens. Finckle, known simply as "AV Allen," was struggling with speaker feedback screeching as he hurriedly adjusted a tuning knob located near a complex [and puzzling display] situated on a large electronic panel.

AV Allen had been at Copperfield for nearly six years, having previously worked as an assistant sound man with a now-defunct local rock band known as "The Legends." AV Allen's claim to fame was that he once worked as a roadie securing equipment needs over a two-month period when the Legends served as a back-up act for the once- popular band Uriah Heep [their famous hit song was "Easy Living."] Other than that two month apprenticeship, AV had taken a technology and media course at a nearby tech school, and then an eight week circuit connection course at Copperfield a few years back.

Some of the students at CCC thought AV Allen's voice sounded like Mr. Ed's, the talking horse of old-time television.

AV's long pony-tailed motif—tucked under a black Jethro Tull bandanna—was bobbed slightly. After muting the speaker feedback, he returned to the tape job required for this student/faculty theatrical [and gauche] depiction of data. Customary at any outdoor Copperfield event is the ever-droning musical compositions chosen by AV Allen to "entertain" him, and others, during set up and dismantling the AV paraphernalia.

The weather had thus far cooperated with this special outdoor SAAT event, which was scheduled to last only a bit more than an hour. Sociology faculty member Norine Hedlund arrived at 9:47, trailed by three of the student ambassadors responsible for the "artsy" component of the presentation.

Two of the students were each carrying boxes of five dozen or so mixed variety donuts, while the third wheeled a cart holding three jugs of orange flavored juice drink, two large bags of sixteen ounce Styrofoam cups, and a large brushed stainless steel urn of hot, steaming, thick, leftover Moonbuck's coffee.

A table covered with a plastic white cloth was set up near the portable projection screens to display the goodies and beverages.

Food [lots of it—healthy and otherwise] and loud [usually inappropriate] music remain staples for any Copperfield event, regardless of its location, time of day, or purpose.

At ten minutes to the hour, Glen Keynes presented Ms. Hedlund with an updated student headcount report just issued by the district IR office. He briefly noted the data rich reports, the primary indicators of college effectiveness, along with FTSE figures. These data could come in handy if Ms. Hedlund was asked data-specific questions after the multimedia extravaganza. Glen then took a seat near the back and muddled through a manila envelope he held in great protective fashion.

By meeting time, the Staten outdoor facility was filled with secretaries from nearly all the VP's offices, one student worker from the computer commons, three occupational education office workers, Dr. J.T Hunniplact, an adjunct Psychology instructor, one student affairs support staff member, and Mr. T. Callahan's Communication 101 class of twenty-five eager students. Absent was Career Counselor Elena Vasquez, although she sponsors the student ambassadors. She was off campus—occupied with her duties as an active Por la Hungria Board member.

Fifteen Anthropology students also joined their Instructor, Eileen Keegan, on the south lawn to view the data show. Adjunct Instructor Keegan (aka "Vegan Keegan") enjoys holding class outdoors, whenever possible, to take advantage of the "natural" light. Well-liked by most students, Keegan's organic natural style compliments her tall and angular form, high cheek bones, clear jaw line, and broad unbroken smile. With little or no make-up, she is refreshingly handsome.

Ms. Keegan is an avid supporter and life-long activist for the "green" movement. She had participated in the first Earth Day in 1970 and was hooked. Really hooked. With lifetime memberships in an array of eco-friendly clubs and organizations, she displays photos and mementos which celebrate her environmental avocations within her adjunct cubicle.

Her organizational affiliations support and embrace everything from aardvarks to zebras, oil shale, snails, gales, hail, tornadoes, and whales—from volcanic ash to recyclable trash. Keegan's office space is a museum—holding a complete "rainbow" sample of ribbons and wrist bracelets representing every awareness movement, foundation, and organization over the past decade (all of these items are recyclable, of course).

She shops only at the "Granola Gondola Natural Food Co-Op," and either makes her own clothes (preferring natural dyes from roots, juniper, or pomegranate berries and turmeric) or purchases trade-free organic items from "Heady Eddy's Apparel and Smoke Shop." "Vegan" only wears hemp—hemp skirts, hemp pants, hemp shirts, hemp shoes—and carries only hemp bags.

Recently, Keegan had been campaigning for the development of a "people's garden" for homeless Hamilton community members. She attempted to secure a hectare or two of Copperfield land just east of campus. The plot would grow organic and sustainable grains, fruits, and vegetables—seeded, cared for, and harvested by local needy neighbors. Lap-top Dave agreed to offer his church as a food distribution location. And Copper Coin second shift bar-keep, Henry McDougal, volunteered to supply non-mechanized soil preparation—using vintage Quaker farm equipment powered by a team of grass-eating, organic-fertilizing, two-ton plough horses. Dolly vehemently opposed the idea and personally assured it would not happen. [He was overheard saying, "*We don't want any of that low-class, low-income, trailer park trash anywhere near this campus.*"]

Ms. Keegan has been an adjunct instructor at Copperfield for nearly eight years—and during this time has had only one dissatisfied student. Seems a cattle rancher's son, Homer Pile, discontent with her philosophical position on the beef industry, defaced the P.E.T.A. sign gracing her classroom by scratching "*People Eating Tasty Animals*" under the acronym.

Dean Preston arrived nearly twenty minutes late after being "tied up" in a hallway conversation discussing the falling property values at his summer lake house with his education planning consulting partner, Thomas "Red" Happle. They both had earlier attended the monthly meeting of the campus budget task force to "iron out" meeting minutes and verify time changes for the next scheduled session.

Preston stood to the side of the musically-infused and color-merged data report session, laughed, applauded hysterically, and left after ten minutes [with a chocolate frosted doughnut in each hand]—rushing off to the [in-progress] graduation requirement meeting which began at 10:30 in the Teaching Learn-ed Center [TLC].

Around 10:45, while a distorted Richard Strauss' "Also Sprach Zarathustra" audio from Stanley Kubrick's *2001 Space Odyssey* accompanied dancing enrollment numbers, a wind gust toppled one of the portable tripod speaker stands. The speaker tore through a viewing screen and then unceremoniously crashed into the table cloth-accented food table. Fortunately, no one was struck; only the two large bags of sixteen ounce Styrofoam cups were damaged.

Then, suddenly, earth-toxic cups were freely sailing through the mall, cart-wheeling and dancing, flock-bombing like sparrows around a stockyard filled with feeding cattle.

Thinking of the potential catastrophic environmental harm the displaced polystyrene could cause, Chad "Clean Boy" Chummy, a student from Ms. Keegan's class, began chasing the blowing cups. While sprinting past the food table, his foot caught the terra-bound corner of the flapping plastic tablecloth, knocking the brushed stainless steel urn of coffee to the ground. An ebony tsunami, a tide of burning, steaming, yet still tastefully aromatic Moonbuck's coffee [and three sprinkle-topped donuts] splashed to the patio floor of the Conference Center.

Mother Earth groaned

The data show was over.

Emmie Seemy, EdD, Chair, Communications

Dr. Emmie Seemy seemed likeable enough. At sixty-four, she could have retired several years ago. But the job, Reading Professor AND Chair of Communications, gave her substance and meaning. Her days at CCC were pleasant—her faculty seniority afforded her a bit of eccentricity that was accepted by both her younger colleagues and senior administrators.

Dr. Seemy's signature motto at the bottom of her emails read:

Never Quit! Never Yield! Never Give Up!

She didn't really trust anyone, though, and kept an eye on all correspondence, meeting minutes, and the activities and behaviors of everyone around her.

Dr. Seemy was quite a character, that's for sure. She wore [very large] black-framed glasses with sequin designs embedded throughout the thick frame and earpieces. She dyed her hair jet black and kept it in a sixties era beehive. Dr. Seemy typically wore old-fashioned rhinestone cocktail dresses [even short ones that showed her age-knobby knees].

Her clothes always smelled like smoke and perfume—that hot, rich, blanketing Las Vegas smoke and Chanel Number 5 perfume odor permeating gambling houses and strip hotels in the seventies.

She drives a Lincoln—an old eighty-three Lincoln still in terrific shape [except for dog hairs on the back seat].

Dr. Seemy used to have two great big dogs; large, spit-drooling Dobermans she would bring to school with her. They would lounge in her office and were quite the topic of discussion around campus—the dogs were loved and hated, admired and feared. Students generally liked the great beasts, but then, Castor, one of the pooches, bit a student named Gerald Ladmo. The college settled for an undisclosed amount out of court. She had to board the dogs after that instead of bringing them to CCC.

Dr. Seemy had smoked for decades—and quit only after *it came down from the hill* that smoking was no longer legal. She had smoked Virginia Slims through a long, black sequined cigarette holder—when grasping the cigarette holder, and leaning forward in her chair, she had the aura of a thirties or forties Hollywood actress—poised, debonair, and strangely distant.

"You never know what's coming down the hill," she often said to her secretary, Belinda Bean. [The hill, depending on what day it was, could represent the district offices, the governing board, or state legislative policy].

74

Oh, Dr. Seemy could tell you stories about the college, and about her own past, that you probably wouldn't believe.

Her zenith had been in the seventies. Some things—like the wet t-shirt contest at a Columbus Day party in 1978 she'd like to forget. And the near affair she had with that guitar-playing janitor back in 1983. *Thank God Rudy* [her husband and a local judge] *never found out about that,* she says to herself at least once a day. She and the long-haired Zontarg [who she now made an effort daily to avoid] ended up in a hot tub together at some Christmas party—Bob had been playing his electric guitar while in the Jacuzzi [somehow without getting shocked]. At that moment, overcome with some girlish passion [and fueled by seven or eight tequila shots], she dove into the water headfirst and…

But she had survived all of those silly times in her youth, and now had great wisdom, based on her experiences, to share with her students and younger colleagues. [She wished she could develop a better relationship with Prof. Flowers—the young lady seemed troubled and distant.]

"Dr. Seemy," Belinda interrupted, *"Don't forget you are responsible for the menu assignments at next week's division meeting. I've heard Professor Powers wants to bring runzas, Professor Banks is bringing barbecue ribs, Professor Zhukov is bringing potatoes of some kind, and Professor Smithers is bringing that funny green dip with the red onions. Do you know what the tutors are bringing? What about the Spanish instructors?"*

"Wait a minute, Belinda. What is a runza?"

"Well, as Professor Powers described it to me, it is a sort of hamburger roll— something that is popular in Nebraska."

"Oh. Well. I'll send out a reminder email and see if I can get the menu completed. I hope Maria Gutierrez makes tacos. Those foreign language tutors are so good at making tacos!"

Seemy had a loyal following of students. They were typically single moms, about thirty-five years old, whose husbands had left them for one reason or another. These gals enjoyed sitting in Dr. Seemy's office and discussing their personal lives with her—and Dr. Seemy enjoyed their company. Many of these women were smokers, overweight, tattooed, and possibly community college lifers.

The sisterhood they formed gave Dr. Seemy a sense of completeness, of calm, of fulfillment. *But for the grace of God, she often said to herself, I could have been one of them.*

After one particular hour-long near therapy session with a just-deserted young woman [whose new boyfriend from New Mexico, Reginald, had left her to join the Mongols Motorcycle Club], Dr. Seemy told her, directly and with power, *Never Quit! Never Yield! Never Give Up!*

Back in the early eighties, Dr. Seemy developed a print module-based developmental English and reading program. During those years, she spent thousands of dollars of department instruction money printing off copies of various exercises and assignments [frequently violating copyright laws, if the truth be known]—the idea was that students who needed help with basic grammar, mechanics, spelling, word attack, and comprehension skills could sign up for "auto-lab" then get some credit for doing "individualized" work at their own pace.

The program was reasonably successful but lost impetus as online instruction, different articulation agreements, and accreditation issues manifested themselves in the 1990's.

However, Dr. Seemy obviously learned a great deal about various pedagogies and course management systems. Now, as part of her teaching assignment, she manages to teach twenty-two overload classes *["They are quality courses,"* she told Dean Preston only last week] online each semester. With these extra classes [anything above five classes or fifteen credit hours at CCC is an "overload"], she is making some serious money—far more per annum than Dean Preston or her husband the Judge. Overload pay at CCC is $750.00 per credit hour.

[This gives her $16,500 extra each semester—on top of her regular full-time nine month contract of $92,000 and Chair stipend of $15,000. Dr. Seemy, who has an EdD in Adult Basic Education from an unaccredited online university, an MA in Special Ed from HSU, and a BA in Elementary Ed from Cal State Fillerburg, is earning 140,000 dollars per year—second in the district only to the President, Dr. Phil Dolly.] Her husband, who has a JD from

Northeast San Pogo State, earns $84,000 as a municipal judge in Hamilton. And who says an education doesn't pay?

Henry McDougal, Second Shift Socialist Barkeep, Copper Coin

McDougal was a tough character. In the dead of the North New Mexico winter, he could be seen wearing a tank top and shorts, puffing on a pipe, a red wool beret tipped to one side of his baldhead. He has an anchor tattooed on one arm and his family coat of arms on the other.

Few of the patrons in the bar know he was formerly Comrade "Fightin' Boy" McDougal of the North Scotland Militant Socialist Movement [NSMSM], a violent social reformer who got his kicks fighting Capitalists at football matches and who marched in Glasgow every May 1. He was known as a bit of an enforcer—he loved to smash heads and property, and he was also adept at writing scathing anti-capitalist articles in the local socialist newspaper.

He still keeps a duffle bag filled with ball bats, brass knuckles, machetes—the tools of his trade—in case he is called upon again.

Ach, those were the good old days. I miss those dear times with me friends and colleagues. We really had a chance to show them exploiters what we wuz made of, he thought to himself. But things got a little too hot for him in Glasgow—he had heard MI Five or Scotland Yard or somebody was looking for him on a murder warrant *[I had nothin' to do with tha' Irishman, tha' mad rocket, for sure—ach, but they wuz huntin' me down like The Big Grey Man of Ben MacDhui!]*, so he left his wife [and six kids] a farewell letter and caught a steamer to Ellis Island.

After kicking around in New York [and mostly neglected by soft and over-fed American Socialists], he decided to give the West a try—and his in-depth knowledge of Scotch whisky, ale, and his big arms, helped him land a job at the Copper Coin [eventually]. He was initially hired on as a bouncer, working when the Coin hosted live bands, but he finally moved up the working ranks and now he slung whisky and beer for a living.

Now, McDougal was an educated man—he had taken a Degree in Economics at the University of Stirling—though it took him six or seven years because of small-offense jail terms. [Mc Dougal was also said to have studied rhetoric with Professor Hugh Blair.] He was well acquainted with the ways of university faculty members and principals. But this lot from the local college was just amazing to him. They didn't tip "*worth a dom*," but he heard they made all kinds of money; they crept around like criminals, and generally came across as a bunch of bampots! [Sidebar: Scottish vernacular for confused people.]

They didn't want to talk about football or even American sports—they were always looking for donations, trying to get him to sign partnership agreements, and giving him advice about how he should become a lifelong learner.

He had tried to start a Socialist Students' Union group on the CCC campus, but those *"d—- Capitalist exploiters"* in charge of the college would hear nothing of such a student group.

Many of 'em wouldn't even buy a belly washer but would sit at the bar with a glass of water ["with lemon and a straw, please"] and try to sell him raffle tickets, recipe books, or advertising space in the college catalog. [He did once buy a city discount coupon book from some adjunct faculty member, and found the online dating advertising section interesting. *Ach!*] None of the CCC people seemed particularly bright—he tried to talk to one Dean or Principal about Hegel, trying to strike up an interesting conversation one afternoon when the bar was near empty, but the poor fellow was thinking he said bagels and asked if the Copper Coin had any cream cheese.

He kept his eye on Julia Flowers [*Oh lad, she's a looker—with that red hair, sure she's from the Scootland, I thought I saw her once walking near Bowness-on-Solway near Hadrian's Wall—ach she is a beauty—and I hear she's married to a* gowk *video game player. Ach! And she sneaks around with that old, gnarly, nearly bald-headed, sun-beaten Spanish teacher, too—with her three wee ones at home—oh lad, there is just no justice in the world or for me heart, not a shred of heart justice lad. The bleedin' capitalists have ruined the world, they have, and me heart, too. Ach. And the Ipod has kilt live music, it has...]*

Dr. Salinas Chick, Humanities Faculty

Dr. S. Chick was not happy. He was still fuming over some comments made by a blogger on the *Times Greater Education* website. Chick had responded to an article [a nostalgic view of old time professors and their non-materialism], and challenged some of the piece's assumptions. Chick thought the author of the piece was unrealistic and removed from the economic realities of teaching and working in the modern world.

Another blogger, irreverently referring to himself as "Don Quixote," defended the article's author and challenged Chick's comments. Why this bothered Chick so much was a mystery to even him, but it had affected the humanities instructor for weeks.

[Lately, Dr. Chick is dreaming of a large Englishman who rides a snorting horse and chases him through the college parking lot, shouting profanities and poking him in the backside with a lance.]

Divorced and fifty-two, S. Chick is not a pretty picture. Slumped and tired, his youth left him long ago. His paunchy little belly and cookie cutter baldhead are not attractive.

Most of his students find him stale [but seemingly knowledgeable]. Chick wears the same attire—clean slacks, clean white shirt, and sport jacket— every day. He is never ruffled, never emotional, never "amped up" about training opportunities or district-wide initiatives. Typically, during his classes, he fixes his eyes on the exit sign above the classroom door while he lectures— avoiding all optic content with his students—even those who infrequently raise a hand and ask a question. He drones on with facts and figures which seem only connected to distant times and places.

He eschews committee work and interactions with his students outside of the classroom, although he does maintain his office hours religiously. ["*No reason to get the chair on my back,*" he said to a colleague once, as she happily left campus for a lunch meeting during her office hours.]

Chick is probably the last faculty member at any community college in America who doesn't teach online [or make more money on extra assignment contracts than from his regular salary].

Even so, he enjoys reading articles on the internet and commenting.

But he was not prepared for the Don Quixote attacks.

He and his former wife [Marcy] never had any children. They had maintained several large dogs. ["*She loves those d—- dogs more than she loves me,*" he told his divorce lawyer.] They had come together gradually and hesitantly, following a series of interactions after A.A. meetings ten or so years ago.

Their lives had been built around some shaky and foolish sense of an academic future—both held sporadic one-semester appointments at different proprietary schools before he landed this full-time job at Copperfield Community.

His ex-wife holds an MA in psychology and usually found work as an adjunct instructor here and there at the seven local community colleges. When he obtained a full-time position first, back in 2004, she flew into a jealous rage and left—left him for a bug exterminator [who played second base on her weekend recreational softball team].

Chick holds most of his colleagues in near contempt and socializes with none of them. [Although he has made halfhearted attempts to flirt with Nina, the Dean's secretary—a bouncy and curvy red head of forty-plus who found herself sans spouse recently.] Chick sometimes stands near her desk, drumming his fingers on the countertop nearby, trying to find something clever to say. Sometimes he sits in a chair in the waiting area and pretends to read the latest issue of *Community College Bleakly* for a few minutes, meanwhile gazing at her longingly [when she isn't looking].

S. Chick's colleagues roll their eyes when they see Chick come into the room or hear him speak at meetings. *"He is so out of touch with current community college best practices,"* Career Counselor Elena Vasquez was overheard to say when she was fielding a student complaint about Chick.

Chick holds a doctorate—most of his colleagues at Copperfield do not.

[Sometimes he wakes up at night wondering what kind of degree Don Quixote possesses.]

He sees the deans as buffoons, the faculty as even bigger buffoons, and senses affection only for the clerical [especially Nina!] and maintenance staff.

S. Chick's office is an untidy, hopeless mess. There are stacks of unopened student evaluations, reports, and handbooks [dating back to 2004] in the corner behind the door. A cardboard box containing a few gifts and knick knacks form his students collects dust bunnies in another corner. Cardboard boxes, many containing personal items, are stacked precariously in a third corner. [These boxes were stashed here temporarily back in 2005 when Marcy left him and they closed up housekeeping in the big rental over in Shindler City]. He has never taken any of the boxes over to the studio apartment where he has spent the last four years.

On a hook on the inside of his office door hangs his wrinkled and moldy one-use graduation gown [with hood and robe] which he wears each year to graduation.

Scores of old journals, newspapers, textbooks, and notebooks ramble off the bookshelves and tumble to the floor.

The custodian, "Guitar" Bob Zontarg, empties the trash can each night in Chick's office, and sweeps the two or three square feet of open floor space, but he is afraid to touch the boxes or folders scattered on the linoleum. He thinks old Chick is crazy. [Chick thinks Zontarg is crazy too.]

Chick has toyed with the idea of coming in some Saturday to clean the place up, but the thought of coming back to the office on a Saturday is simply too painful. [Reclusive Chick watches classic black and white movies all weekend when he can—and orders in pizzas and Chinese].

He occasionally reads a Zane Grey novel or works a Sudoku puzzle. But the stressful nature of his work keeps him pretty "low key" on his days off.

Chick enjoys his privacy—and is quite smug about his tastes in food and drink. Friday nights he typically enjoys a bottle or two of cold, cheap beer and a can of smoked oysters [eaten with toothpicks or plastic fork]. Patting his belly after such a meal, the satisfied Chick smiles and thinks out loud—*"It's good to be a man!"*

When his wife left him, she also took the large dogs. The departure of the dogs provided Chick with a window of opportunity to procure a new pet or two. Now, he keeps six neutered Siamese cats—named Archimedes, Achilles, Ajax, Argus, Agamemnon, and Hector. Chick is not good about cleaning out the litter box [es] and a prominent feline odor can be detected in his apartment. Chick does not notice the smell, and he has no visitors except the pizza and Chinese food delivery people....

But Chick, deprived of human affection and social interaction, loves his cat family very much. He has difficulty telling them apart, but is very fond of "five A's and an H," as he refers to them collectively.

Chick is convinced some shrug of the universe, some inscrutable curse, has kept him back—kept him back from his academic career, from relationships with women, from financial success.

Chick drives a fifteen year-old faded green Toyota pickup. The odometer has rolled up about 226,000 miles. Most of those miles were put on back when he was an adjunct. Sometimes he would drive a hundred miles a day to different campuses just to eke out a living. The paint is bad on the old Toyota, but the engine is still good. Chick often purposefully parks his truck next to the Dean's silver Lexus LS10. The Dean has big oversized wheels on the car—those big chrome six spoke wheels. The car is always immaculate—always has that just-detailed and hand-waxed look. Chick thinks he is making some kind of statement by parking his old truck next to the Dean's shiny new Lexus. But Chick himself isn't sure about the nature of the statement. Someday Chick will have to buy a new vehicle, but he dreads that day as much as death itself.

Chick doesn't know it, but he received his full-time appointment mostly by accident. When he was interviewed, he didn't have a PowerPoint presentation. He had merely rambled on during his teaching sample, trying to explain the difference between impressionism and expressionism, using some nearly illegible notes on a lined yellow legal pad. His droning voice had nearly put the committee to sleep. He was rated "Number Four Candidate" out of a group of four. But events turned his way.

The committee's Number One choice learned she was pregnant and declined the job offer—besides, her husband was an executive for In-tell and she really didn't need the money. Then, HR discovered that number Two had manufactured his transcripts and work history [he was a fraud]. Number Three accepted a better paying job at a local high school. This left Dr. S. Chick. Time was short, budgets were tight, and the interview committee members were busy with other committee work. They didn't want to reopen a national search and screen all those applications again.

The committee had some concerns about Chick's credentials too—he held a Doctor of Arts degree from the American Ethnic University of South

Honduras. The unofficial transcripts were a bit smudged. Four of the five committee members had never heard of a Doctor of Arts degree [Three of the five thought all doctorates were EdD's].

Oh—the chair of the committee, then interim—Dean Goeber, had hoped they would land a new Humanities professor who had a recent degree in Ed Leadership. He felt such people were highly trained in the area of organizational management and were better suited to the newly emerging models of community college theory. But after further review, they learned that Chick had received a legitimate MEd in secondary school art education from Southern New Mexico State College back in 1984.

They offered the job to Chick. He accepted. A week later, his wife left him for the bug man, and he moved those cardboard boxes into his office. Chick's penultimate career achievement cost him his wife and his dogs.

Dr. S. Chick was then a Professor of Humanities at Copperfield Community College... He doesn't own a cell phone or an Ipad, but he has a platform and a place in post-secondary education. And he is able to steal at least a glimpse of Nina daily.

Skeeter Smith, Men's Baseball, CCC Gauchos.

Coach Skeeter Smith leaned over and spit into an empty Styrofoam coffee cup—the sixteen ounce size. His phone was ringing, and the caller ID let him know it was Coach Billy Jones from Leucadia High School.

Billy coached the boys varsity baseball team for the Leucadia Fighting Coursers.

Skeeter: *Hmm. Well, I gotta take this call.* He spit into the cup again and answered cheerfully. *Good to hear from you, Coach. Looks like your squad is gonna take the Skypipe Division again this year* [Leans over and spits into his empty Styrofoam coffee cup—sixteen ounce size].

Billy: *We're hoping our bullpen holds up, Skeeter. [Spits in his own twenty-two ounce empty cup] With prom coming up, we're afraid we might lose a few of them to arrests. [Nervous laugh.] Now coach, I'm wondering if you've thought anymore about that prospect I* *was telling you about—our short stop, Ritchie Cummins [Nervous laugh].* [Spits in his own twenty-two ounce empty cup].

Skeeter: *Coach, I talked to our athletic director, Jorge Anno, about Ritchie. We were quite impressed with Ritchie's on base percentage [.670], his batting average [.540], and the forty-six RBI's he's batted in the last four games.*

But Coach, we just can't use him. You know that Copperfield Community is committed to winning the Southwest JuCo Mega Conference South East Coyote Division [SJCMCSECD] championship every year—and to be frank, we just can't use local players. [Leans over and spits into his empty Styrofoam coffee cup—sixteen ounce size]. *What has happened is that, you know, most of the SJCMCSECD community college teams have rosters filled with Korean, Honduran, Japanese, Costa Rican, Argentine, French, Jamaican, Cuban, Puerto Rican, Nicaraguan, Russian, and Canadian players.* [Leans over and spits into his empty Styrofoam coffee cup—sixteen ounce size].

We just can't use our local boys, no matter how good they are in high school, against them teams and win. [Suddenly Coach Skeeter feels just a twinge of good old American "beer and hot dog at the baseball park" guilt.] Well, h——-, now I suppose you can send him up here, and we'll take a look—that's the right thing to do—but I sure can't guarantee no scholarship [Leans over and spits into his empty Styrofoam coffee cup—sixteen ounce size].

Billy: *Coach, I'll tell him you'll give him a look.* [Spits in his own twenty-two ounce empty cup]. *Now coach, I don't mean to get political or anything, but shouldn't a local college be helping with the development of local athletes too? [Really nervous laugh] I mean, our boys are playing well and do well, but we haven't seen a local ball player make your roster since 1979—and that kid went on to be an MLB All Star [Nervous laugh].*

Skeeter: [Glares at the phone—doesn't like where this is going....]

Coach, why don't you bring him out here personally and I'll talk to him. By the way, I think we're going to be looking for a part-time batting instructor for the Intro to Varsity Baseball PE class. The regular part-time pay is $675 per credit hour, but our coaches get $1000. And this is a four credit hour course, so I believe your pay would be $4000. Would you be interested? Oh—can you speak Spanish? Poquito? Si? Mas grande, mi amigo!

I'll put in a good word for you with Jorge. I know he appreciates the hard work you all have done down there at LHS.

[Leans over and spits into his empty Styrofoam coffee cup—sixteen ounce size]

C'mon out to practice next Friday—bring your boy and we'll talk about the coaching job, too.

Billy: *I've always wanted to be a JuCo coach. [Nervous laugh.] I'll see you Friday, Skeeter, and I'll bring Richie along—if he can make it [Nervous laugh.].*

Both hang up—both open up new cans of chew.

Billy to himself: *Man, wait till I tell the wife I'm gonna coach JuCo!*

Skeeter to himself: *Well, h——, it's the least I can do.*

His secretary, the eight-year work-study, Chow Zee Tong, brought him some paperwork.

Chow: *Coach, here are the attendance and revenue figures for the season so far.* [Chow leans over and spits into the empty Styrofoam coffee cup—sixteen ounce size.]

Through twelve home games, a total of 288 paid fans have watched the Gauchos play. That's an average of twenty-four people per game. At three dollars a ticket, that's a total of [works on calculator], uh, $732. And since the health department closed down the concession stand, we aren't making any money on food and drinks. Jorge wants to talk to you 'cause the light bill for the stadium was $1600 for last month. [She leans over and spits into his empty Styrofoam coffee cup—sixteen ounce size].

Skeeter: *D——-! We gotta raise ticket prices [Really Nervous laugh.]!*

[Leans over and spits into his empty Styrofoam coffee cup—sixteen ounce size].

JB O'Connor, Student

JB had just left the Student Success Center [housed in the Teaching Learn-ed Center] at Copperfield Main.

He had taken a battery of academic placement, career guidance, political party proclivity, student government group and organization interest inventories, and TB tests.

He had spent about twenty minutes with a lady counselor [d——-, she's hot!] making course selections and was now walking over to the Business Center Complex to pay his registration fees.

JB had come to this venerable institution of higher learning for various reasons. [But mostly because his dad told him to go back to school or else...] About two days ago, he quit his job at the Sticky Mart and thought he might like to lounge around the house for a while. That same afternoon, while he was home watching the TV and drinking an ice cold beer, his dad, John, strode into the house and told him he had to get another job, or join the military, or go to college, or get out of the **!%$^@!** house.

Basically lazy and not suited for menial labor, JB had been out of high school for two years now and had never really thought about going on to school. But, none of the armed services wanted him because of his inability to read, so college seemed like a good possibility.

Soon after, during a family council, once the shouting and screaming ebbed, his dad encouraged young JB to attend CCC and find himself. *"JB, you can get the easy courses out of the way, and we can save some money in case you want to go to a college someday. I know that CCC is far cheaper than a regular college;—I think they charge $350 a semester compared to HSU's $2600. Look, if you'll enroll in four classes, I'll pay the costs and you can stay at home. Then someday, when you decide to go to a real college, we might be able to afford it."*

Despite JB's documented reading problems [and his poor showing on the math placement test], the lady counselor [*d——, she's hot!*] had urged him to enroll in Art History, History of World Civilizations, Calculus, and Anatomy and Physiology. [*She knew these classes needed enrollment or they might be cancelled—leading to faculty complaints about her advising practices and ability*]. "You can do it, JB," she said, shaking her pretty fist in the air above her head. *We'll MAP out an ASS* [Academic Support System] *for you and make sure you get free tutoring as often as possible from our peer, para, online, embedded, and virtual tutors. You will love it here at CCC. Chiclet?"*

His dad had given him the $350 he needed for tuition. With receipt in hand, only three hours later, JB was enrolled. He went to the bookstore to pick up the four textbooks he needed for his classes. JB was a college man just like that. [He thought about buying a CCC t-shirt but knew they weren't considered cool in Hamilton City.]

After walking past stand after stand of cinnamon tea blends, vampire novels, coffee cups, key chains, rulers, stuffed horses, sunglasses, movie DVDs, flash drives, candy bars, paper-thin one-use graduation gowns, CCC logo shirts, get-well cards, and Go-Go Green Posters, he found the ten foot by ten foot section reserved for academic text books at Copperfield Community College.

After scrutinizing titles and course section codes, he picked up the books, checked the prices, and called his dad.

"Hey Dad, I'm down here at the book store. Yep, things are going great. The counselor is HOT. Yep, you were right—the tuition was $350. But I'm gonna need some more money—I had to buy four textbooks—they've got CD ROMs and stuff—and the total bill is $846.71 [that includes tax!] for the books. Dad? Dad? Are you still there?"

Dr. Deuce Darling, Biology Professor

Dr. Darling has few career prospects at the community college. He is well-educated [PhD, Big-Petro, North Central Oregon State University], an excellent teacher [rave reviews semester after semester], and an intellectual participant in his discipline [published articles in peer-reviewed journals, ongoing research projects].

But he does not wish to be an administrator—he could not join the network of inaction, leadership puffery, silly career machinations, misspent energy, endless discussions, tabled decisions, and self-centered speeches.

He loves teaching at CCC—following a rather itinerant career, working in industry, tramping through the petroleum fields of Saudi, the Ukraine, and the Governor of Alaska's back yard.

Yes, I met the Governor. A charming woman. We went horseback riding together near Wasilla—and enjoyed a glass of a fresh Alaskan zinfandel following. Just a lovely day—such a personable lady. She invited me to hike in the De Long Mountains with her family. Yes, I am looking forward to the event. And, oh my, can she ever cook salmon!

He is a large man, easy going, but with a piercing and analytical mind.

Deuce has a large, healthy shock of jet-black hair, and forearms that could crush a mustang—or a fiscal miscreant. He is feared at the college and in any lunchroom or buffet line.

Dr. Darling has an appetite. He can eat seven or eight plates of Chinese buffet [including sushi, lo mien noodles, sweet cakes, octopus, and egg rolls] and then build a hot fudge sundae for dessert. Several times a week...

Darling is a connoisseur of fine wine, the arts, and beautiful opera singers. He maintains season tickets to the Hamilton County Symphony [V. Ross, director], the Hamilton Zoo, and loves watching Rocky Stevens European adventures on PBS television. He loves the Democratic Party, but is open-minded, fair, and has a work ethic that could not be challenged or criticized.

He enjoys visiting with "offbeat characters" such as the old socialist barkeep down at the Copper Coin, the Scotsman McDougal. [Dr. Darling leans left, but not that far left.]

However, just as much as he was loved by his students and fellow faculty members, Dr. Darling is feared and loathed by the administrative staff—Dr. Phil Dolly especially.

Darling, sensing the growing autocracy of Dolly's presidency, had spoken out about the "*culture of fear and abject lunacy*" which was developing at CCC. [Darling found Dolly's half-baked scheme to sell CCC especially revolting]. Via Dolly's cronies, the "word" about Darling's grumblings got back to the president, and the CEO made a note about the professor's comments in his journal.

Darling really infuriated the administration when he commented, upon hearing about yet another administrative "retreat": "*No wonder we never get anything done or move forward," he was heard to say. "The administrators are always at retreats. Always retreating!"*

Then he further alienated himself with the publication of an article dealing with community colleges and negative media relations.

He himself was always moving forward, always producing. When a committee gave Darling an assignment, he completed it—thoroughly and without complaint or whine—in two days. When he was asked to serve on the salary committee, he did such complete and compelling research on comparative salaries and benefit packages nationwide that CCC gave its employees the best raise they had seen in a decade.

When asked by a now long-gone VP why he didn't pursue an administrative role, Darling looked him straight in the eye and said, "I can't be around you people. I like to get things done and I have no agenda except my students' learning and my personal integrity. Why would I want to be an administrator?

"Even you people call it the 'dark side.' What's so dark about sitting at meetings and drawing large salaries? Why don't you call it the bright side? I have bright students…"

Dr. Dolly feared such men—"*a university wanna be*," he said when discussing Dr. Darling with Dean Preston.

Darling's success with the wage increase issue had infuriated Dr. Dolly— the president had acquiesced to the committee's demands and gave the faculty the same percent pay raise increase the administrative staff received—for the first time in twenty-two years. *But why is the man working here for 50K a year, Dolly wondered, when he could be making real money back in the Big Bio oil fields? Something is fishy about Darling; something just doesn't make good horse sense to me. I don't know of any way we can get rid of him—he's not really a threat, but his factual and logical approach to decision making really irks me. He just doesn't fit in our world. "Has he ever used that crazy science logic on you, Paxton?"*

Wilbur the Duck

Quack.   Qurrrrk   Qrrrrkkk!   Quack   Quack   Qrrrrrrrkkkk   ! Qrrkkkkkkbedodododod ! Quack!

[Wings flutter, feathers fly]. *Quack! [Richard—the water is too cold in my wading pool, Richard…]*

Laptop Dave, Student

Laptop Dave could be seen at the campus Moonbuck's, or on a patio, or on a bench, nearly every day at CCC. He always had his laptop and a Bible with him—and a cup of Moonbuck's Supremo Iced Coffee. No one knew for sure if Laptop Dave was enrolled in any courses at CCC. Rumor had it that he was a preacher, or a musician, or maybe a left wing politician of some kind. His car had several dents and was without hubcaps. The tires looked very iffy, but he kept the interior clean.

Before he was banned form the CCC campus, the bartender Henry McDougal could frequently be seen discussing politics with Laptop Dave— usually on a bench outside the administration building. The pair would be shouting, waving their arms, and sometimes arguing about Christian Democrats, Arizona's immigration problems, emics and etics, the value of female companionship, socialism, and Intelligent Design.

Dean Preston and Elena Vasquez, when walking and talking together, always greeted Laptop Dave. And he always cheerfully and graciously acknowledged their hello.

[*"Such a nice student"*, cooed Elena into Preston's left ear, the one without the diamond earring, one late afternoon.]

Laptop Dave, a man of great patience, has five daughters—all young women now—all beautiful and intelligent. Seven or eight presidents at CCC had made inquiries about Laptop Dave's identity and purpose. Laptop Dave has outlasted them all.

Richard Hose, Retired Faculty Member

Mr. Hose retired from teaching at CCC two years ago at the age of sixty-one. The former accounting professor now lives a very solitary life. He and his wife dwell in a two bedroom bungalow not far from CCC Main Campus.

Mr. Hose does not visit Copperfield, though he is close enough to hear the fireworks explode during the football season when the CCC Fighting Gauchos score.

Mr. Hose enjoys crossword puzzles, milk and crackers, chain smoking, and reading comic books. He once owned five different suits [one for each day]. Now he wears only pajamas and a bathrobe. He rides around in a Lark scooter, though he is quite capable of walking.

One time, about a year or so ago, Ms. Hose took her husband with her grocery shopping. While she searched for fresh fruit and canned meat, Mr. Hose sat on the Lark taking up space in the greeting card and magazine aisle, looking at comic books and the covers of motorcycle magazines. A crazed kid pushing a cart with a Parkinson-obsessed front left wheel collided with the Lark displacing Mr. Hose from his throne.

Mr. Hose does not go grocery shopping with his wife anymore.

Mr. Hose made a mistake when computing his retirement pension. He retired one year too early, and this error will cost him 646.40 dollars per month for the rest of his life.

Sometimes Mr. Hose sits on his back patio and feeds the birds and squirrels. He is always too hot in the summer, too cold in the winter, and too dissatisfied in the spring and fall.

His wife, Myrtle, cooks and cleans and does the laundry. She is not happy with her life, but she has Mr. Hose to take care of now.

Certainly Mr. Hose had a career at CCC. He graded many papers and attended [by his computation] 16,453 meetings during his seventeen years at the college. He was never able to pass his CPA exam, and has trouble doing his own taxes.

But he is quite able to measure out appropriate quantities of birdseed for his feathered friends and squirrel buddies. *"Come to Daddy,"* he says every morning to Snappy the fancy pigeon.

He also maintains an old but pristine collection of Green Stamps.

Some days Mr. Hose just stays in bed, or watches Oprah, or reads from his gaggle of old *Tubby* and *Lu Lu* comic books.

Mr. Hose is neither happy nor sad. He had a career at CCC then he retired. Now, at sixty-three, he has nothing much to look forward to, and he cannot really pinpoint any grand moment from his past life.

Mr. Hose has a pet Duck named Wilbur. Wilbur is white. Mr. Hose keeps a collar and a leash on Wilbur [who spends most of his days quacking around in a small wading pool]. Sometimes Mr. Hose takes Wilbur for a walk around the house while riding in his Lark.

Mr. Hose's wife smiles at this and knows it is good for Mr. Hose to have a loving companion like Wilbur.

In their frequent conversations, Mr. Hose questions Wilbur about what he likes to eat, what temperature he likes his pool water, and why he doesn't lay eggs.

Last Friday, he asked Wilbur if he had ever taken a course in Cost Accounting.

When answering Mr. Hose's frequent questions, Wilbur smiles and speaks without guile or excuse. He is a kind and good-hearted duck, and Wilbur has become Mr. Hose's best friend.

Mr. Hose sometimes considers calling his old friend Jack Frost, the Spanish teacher, but doesn't.

Mr. Hose holds but one fond memory of Jack Frost, a memory still reverberating from a certain poem his colleague had written after a party. [Both men had been invited, but only Frost attended.] Mr. Hose keeps the memento in a Fats Domino forty-five record sleeve: *Jack Frost at the Birthday Party.*

Frost had come down the still-chilled mountain to attend this warm-air birthday party.

He had hoped the band would let him sit in—he knew three or four chords.

But it didn't happen.

Now the tired party was just about tapped out. Frost was sitting on a PA speaker, sloshing down the last of a warming amber beer, gazing across the patio at a lovely dread-locked woman.

Same old Frost delusions—He was lonely, she was lonely, nothing would happen.

He was an outlier—didn't know the buzzwords, didn't spend more than he made, had never watched the right TV shows—he belonged back up on the Rim in his travel trailer.

Nimble Frost was listening to the Suburban males—hollow puppet— mannequins—talk about their softball teams, their hot dogs, spicy wings, and droid contracts. Their women were panting about computer programs and the next potluck.

Corporate culture clinging was so chaotically common—Frost's analog world was a fossil.

Water bottles, cell phones, endless talk about sports, jobs, and coupons—what they knew and loved—was nothing. [But they understood clearly how to chill by the pool...in an organized matrix]

Back to the party...

The rockabilly band—hip young guys with sideburns and tats—was packing up. The way-cool bass guy asked [politely] Frost to move.

Frost got on his Sportster, found his way to a diner, drank four cups of coffee, and rode back up the mountain, chilling at Mt Ord, frosty at Christopher Creek, snug in his travel trailer...

Frost, the secular saint, had returned to his monastery.

Still at the diminishing party, the lovely dread-locked woman thought of Frost but turned

her adoring attention to a soft-looking thirty-five year old market-making bald-headed guy who was wearing flip-flops, tribal tats, sunglasses, cargo shorts, and a Dallas Cowboy jersey. He was loud and proud.

And she felt oddly comfortable with the clone and was relieved old Frost was gone.

~ * ~

Some days Mr. Hose just stays in bed and reads *The Hamilton Democrat*. He laughs at the letters, cartoons, and editorials directed towards the college and the President, Dr. Dolly.

Mr. Hose thinks of all the students he taught then realizes he can't remember any of their names or faces. Like zebras, they passed before him, part of the community college experience, a world he carefully managed for seventeen years.

Sometimes he wishes he would have been a Sticky-Mart Greeter.

Some days Mr. Hose just stays in bed and wonders what he did with his life. But just for a minute. There are always birds and squirrels to feed. And Wilbur.

Gert, CCC Student and Mother of Four

At 10:30 PM, Gert poured herself a shot of cheap tequila and got out her art history book. Her four kids were finally asleep. Gert is thirty-six years old.

You might say she had been a bit of a party girl back in her late twenties. Gert had been quite happy with her routine—back then she had worked at Sticky-Mart, loved playing darts at the Copper Coin Tavern, could dance on the tables after a few beers, and looked terrific. She was a karaoke queen—and batted .370 on the softball field. Her nickname had been *The Fly*.

Her parents wanted her to go on to college, or cosmetology school, after she finished her GED, but she would hear nothing of it. Gert had boyfriends [lots of 'em], backstage passes to almost every rock concert in Hamilton City, and some great legs.

She even worked as an exotic dancer for a few years, but after a snake bite gave her an infection, she quit. [She had also been startled to see her old funny dad in the crowd one night, boozy and leering, paying one of her big, bouncy-bosomed friends for a lap dance.]

Now, fifteen years later, she was holed up in a twenty-six foot travel trailer with her kids, living on welfare and aid to dependent families, worried about her snake-sized varicose veins and bleeding gums, and desperate to get a job. Her looks were gone, her teeth hurt, and the kids were always hungry.

Recently, one of her community college teachers, Dr. Seemy, told her [actually, shouted at her in a high pitched voice] to **Never Give Up!**

Gert enjoys speaking to Dr. Seemy about her troubles—she wants to be like Dr. Seemy someday and have money and brains. [Gert has started wearing black sequin framed eyeglasses in homage of Dr. Seemy].

Gert is about done. She has no idea why she needs calculus and art history and chemistry to be a massage therapist, but someone at the college, some big wheel, some Dr. Elvis Perkins or Patches or Paxon or somebody, changed the requirements, and now she is having big-time trouble finishing her thirty credit hour [now forty-one credits] certificate.

Gert couldn't study. *I'm just too tired. I don't know if I can take another hour of class with that Dr. Chicken, either. That guy is a total bore.*

This was her second try at art history, her third try at calculus [after taking five pre requisite math classes over seven years!], and her first attempt at chemistry—which she was failing. She was tired of tutoring, tired of being poor, and, well, just plain tired.

Gert had spent nearly eight years working on what should have been a one-year massage therapy program. *How can it be?*

Thank God I've been receiving Bell Grants, been able to get school loans, had confederate and institutional work-study jobs, and renewable Men of Diverse Colors Club scholarships—or these last eight years would have been really tough.

Pushing through the door, Gert lit up a smoke [with filter] and gazed at the stars, listening to some Harley Davidson motorcycles booming through the dark and humid Hamilton City Night.

On the slab next to her trailer squatted her 1989 Del Fugo four door sedan—with three flat tires, a shattered rear windshield, busted transmission, faded smiley face decal, and frozen motor. Nearly fossilized in rust, it had nurtured her sense of financial inadequacy for years now. *And I can't pay the rent money tomorrow, either.*

About six minutes later, her oldest child, carrying a brand new vampire novel and a can of house-brand soda, hungry and unable to sleep, found Gert, passed out, propped up against the trailer, cigarette still burning in her fingers, snoring, and drooling.

T-RUN—Transfer to Real University Now—Issue

Yet another problem for the CEO at CCC manifested itself. A representative from the Southeast New Mexico University [SENMU] transfer office, located on the Copperfield site, was disciplined by Dolly [verbally berated and threatened, actually]. Word got out and Dolly looked bad again. What happened? Well, SENMU's program "Transfer to Real University Now" [T-RUN] published the following transfer "fact sheet" information in *The Hamilton Democrat.*

[The ad as it appeared in *The Democrat…*]

T-RUN Program Opportunities—Need justification for transferring before earning Community College AA degree?—Despite claims by Community Colleges that it is "cheaper" to remain at Community College, please consider the following, which is based on an actual CCC student transcript.

Typical Community College Academic Progress towards achieving the Two Year Associate in Arts Transfer degree:

Year One
Semester One—12 hours
Semester Two—12 hours
Year One Total—24 hours

Year Two
Semester Three—12 hours
Semester Four—12 hours
Year Two Total—48 hours

Year Three
Semester Five—12 hours
Semester Six—12 hours
Year Three Total—72 hours

Year Four
Semester Seven—12 hours
Semester Eight—12 hours
Year Four Total—96 hours

Year Five
Semester Nine—12 hours
Semester Ten—12 hours

<u>Year Five Total—120 hours</u>
*Assumption—Full-time enrollment considered
 12 hours
*Assumption—No remediation (developmental)
 course work necessary
*Assumption—All courses taken, successfully
completed, and recognized as university "trans-
ferable units."
*The typical community college student profile,
 according to national data:
   • forty-five percent of all American undergraduates attend community colleges;
   • thirty percent have a household income below $20,000;
   • eighty percent work full or part-time while taking classes;
   • thirty-five percent are parents or have dependents; seventeen percent are single parents;
   • only thirty-one percent of all community college students who intend to earn a two-year degree – actually complete their program in 6 years!

Why Spend Five (or more) Years to Achieve a Two-Year Degree?

Consider the Many Advantages of the **T-Run**
 Program Option!

[Dolly was very angry—he wanted the SENMU on-
campus presence removed, but changed his mind
after being informed they paid Copperfield a
 handsome yearly office rental fee—which more
than made up for the apparent slander against CCC.
But Dolly apologized to no one.]

Daily Email Posts, CCC

Because of numerous programming activities at the CCC Residence Hall Complex during the last few hours, CW Post hadn't checked his emails since earlier that morning. After watching the CCC horse bareback riding teams complete in the CCC Annual All Cowboys and Diversified Non-Cowboy People of the West Rodeo, CW slumped in his chair and collected himself. *I'd better see what's going on at CCC,* he thought, and opened up the inbox. *Here we go...maybe someone's got food left for lunch.*

[The emails are compiled chronologically, as received, by subject heading below...]

Re: Lost Dog

Condo for Rent

Strategic Planning Focus Group Meeting Cancelled

FW: Goodies in the Admin Office

Single Parents Club Bake Sale Room 261

Re: Muffins left over from Dean's meeting in Dr. Preston's Office

Re: Free VaVaVoom Samples

Free OSHA Training on April 9

Has anyone seen my lost Pet Duck Wilbur?

Health Fair - TODAY! Chips and Soda Provided Free!

Ladies Saddle Club Meets this Wednesday at Rodeo Grounds!

Tough Questions for Community College Leaders Online Seminar Room 320

Traditional Heterosexual Woman's Club Meeting Today! Potluck!

Re: Ultimate solutions for student Customer Service issues

Re: Copperfield Men of Diverse Colors Pizza Sale Today

Recall Last Email Concerning Copperfield Men of Diverse Colors Pizza Sale Today

Soup is On in Room 272

Thank You, Wilbur has been found at Home!

Re: Last Chance for Muffins in Dr. Preston's Office

MEd in Ed Leadership Cohort starting NHU!

RE: Radioactive Materiel Missing from Science Lab

Quack! Scrawwkkk. Quack!
Women's Basketball Golf Tournament this Weekend! Potluck!
Men's Baseball Golf Tournament Next Weekend
EdD in Ed Leadership cohort starting U of Topeka!
Golf Team Golf Tournament three weeks from today!
Dealing with Difficult Customers
FW: Dealing with Difficult Customers
Administrators! Learn to Use Your Smart Phone Meeting Today!
Budget Coupons for Mazatlan Travel Available
Pizza Night at Copper Coin Lounge!
Pumpkin Brioche for sale 50 cents in culinary!
Has Social Networking Let You Down?
Customer Service Training Today
Lost Cell Phone!
Android Phone Training Today Free Pie for first 10 Students to Register
Learn to Manage Problem Students in Your Courses webinar
CCC AA in Ed Leadership Planning Committee Tuesday!
Re: This Friday is Green Day
MEd in Ed Leadership begins for UH
Plain old American Luncheon This Week…
Pancakes in Faculty Offices!
Highbrow Learn-ed Commission Lunch Today!
Free Colonoscopies This Week at Sticky Mart!
Recycle Club Meeting today!
The Earth is Flat Meeting Today
Re: Lost Cat
Re: Lost Chinchilla
On Site Flatus Analysis/ assessment Project This Week!
Don't forget to Carpool this Week—Potluck Available
Re: Email etiquette committee meeting
RE: Bring your aluminum cans to school for recycling Thursday!
RE: Recall Bring your aluminum cans to school for recycling Thursday!
Student Helpers Needed to Celebrate Women's History Month!

Cesar Chavez Luncheon this Week!
Sustainability Team accepts electronic device donations!
Native American Heritage Luncheon this Week!
Italian American Luncheon this Week
FW: Plain old American Luncheon This Week...
Recall Plain old American Luncheon This Week...NO interest!
Disknee Institute Luncheon This Week!
RE: Bring your aluminum cans to school for recycling Friday
Free Massage at Massage Clinic
EdD in Ed Leadership Starting at HSU
Socialist Students Group Study Meeting Room 211 Cancelled
Pizza Night to Celebrate Needy
Celebrate the Lunar New Year: Year of the Duck—Free Food
FW: You're invited! 2011 Copperfield College Latino Film Festival
FW: Copperfield CENTER FOR RESPONSIBLE FATHERHOOD Meeting Cancelled!
Today: Film on Maternity Care System 2 PM Room 211
Tech Institute E-Learn-ed Delivery System - undeliverable emails
Re: HOT STONE MASSAGES FOR STAFF [FILL-IN TODAY]
FW: Nominations Past Due for Mentor of the Month Award
RE: Have you sent a quality note this month? 345 in the series...
Women's Month Quote # 172
Wii Club Meeting Cancelled due to power outage!
Car Raffle and Glee Club Meeting at CCC- Bake Sale
Quiche Recipe Book for Sale in Bookstore now
Warning! Malicious Community College Novel now circulating!
CCC Bookstore closing—Closeout sale on all Recipe Books!
Harms and Showboat Book store opening in old CCC Bookstore location
Vampire Novels on Sale Today!
Earth Day Luncheon
Copperfield Corpulent Couples Club - Dinner Party registration
International Students Golf Tournament This Week
American Horse Association Fund Raising Bake Sale Thursday!

Public Safety Report for 03-17-11 to 04-06-11
Relay For Life Lunch
Earth Day Raffle
Leadership Training For tomorrow's VP's
Has anyone seen my Vampire Book?
Re: Found Lost Dog
Volunteers needed for Dunk Tank!
Seminar: How to write better Emails!
Healing Racism Event!
National Library Week Celebrating Week Today
Healing Xenophobia Event
Computer Solitaire Tournament this Tuesday Afternoon!
Healing Copperfield Event!
I have an extra Vampire Novel….
National Hairbrush Celebration Event Next Week!
National Healing Celebration Week!
CCC Year Books Available
All Free Massage Appointment Times Filled
Car Keys found
Graduation Singer Auditions.
Associate Students Blood Drive in Room 305
One More Free Massage Available
On Site Prostate Project
FW: On site Hemorrhoid project!
Tiramisu- layered dessert / slice $1.10 / Chef's Room!
Recall on All Student ID's Issued Last Week
Good running Mini Van for sale
FW: On site Hemorrhoid project!
FW: Lost—One Vampire Novel
Ciabatta-a rustic loaf / $2.50 per loaf—Today in Culinary!
Uganda Athletes Meeting Today in Room 305
Room Change for Uganda Athletes Meeting
Re: One muffin still available Dr. Preston's Office

Doughnuts for sale in Admin building!
Re: Has Anyone Seen my Keys?

Wow, thought CW to himself. *Fewer golf tournaments than usual! Huh. I was hoping to find a potluck for lunch—looks like I might still be able to get a muffin over in the Dean's office. Sure aren't many emails this morning. But I was only gone two hours…*

Father John, World Religions Adjunct—CC with a Splash

Father John, adjunct faculty member, wearily slumped over the rough and cracked steering wheel of his rusty old Ford Bronco after his Tuesday night World Religions class. He smashed another cigarette butt into the debris-laden ashtray and sighed deeply.

In many ways, the night had been typical—the heating and cooling systems had worked in opposition all evening—making the room, at times, unbearably hot—and then nearly Arctic-like when the a/c unit kicked in. [He had mentioned this to the custodial staff and learned the controls to the unit were located seventy-two miles away at a technology device controls center at IBC over in Rozwhel]. "*Sorry Father—we've been looking into this for fifteen years!*"

A howling wind outside blew leaves into the classroom whenever someone opened the door. Fluorescent bulbs flickered with minds of their own.

Students had straggled into the class late and had been disinterested in his lecture on the Dao. But tonight, something had somehow been different. One of "God's Marines," Father John, a Jesuit, was up against a difficult foe. He was beginning to realize the enormity of his task at this community college. A few weeks into the semester, he has begun to fully, completely, see his situation. Ach, laddie, the picture wasn't pretty.

Tonight, the college servers were down, his email was inaccessible, and only one light worked in his classroom. Plus, he could hear pounding music coming through the wall from the Music Appreciation class next door.

[Then his class got started late because the door was locked. Fortunately, Finckle, the AV man, was walking by, coming out of the Music Appreciation classroom—and he opened the door for Father John—although this task was not within his span of control].

And then, well, his students always presented him with challenges.

There was Rudy, a big strapping red-headed young man with tattoos and a billy goat beard who worked as a welder in the day time and dozed off during class. He'd been in the navy. The demands of his daily life were simply wearing him out. He was a good husband, a good father, and he was just plain tired after working all day.

Oh—and Mary—a single parent at nineteen—who texted openly with gusto [with a furrowed brow and pursed lips] off to nowhere. She clearly believed in learning by physical osmosis—that by simply occupying space, her learning and career needs would be met. She was quite pleasant, but not really interested in academics. A mortuary science student, she was in this class because *"I have to take a humanities course to get my certificate."*

And Conrad—well, an apparently former fine specimen of a lad, once a great tailback on his high school football team, whose academic career had nearly been destroyed by late night partying at the clubs—he often came to class looking haggard and drawn—and he never made it through the evening session without sneaking out the door to smoke.

Father John was from Nabob County—part of the Albuquerque diocese. He had convinced the Bishop of his plan to teach one class at CCC and to have the adjunct salary donated back to his home church, San Rafael, for the food bank. The trip to Hamilton City was nearly 170 miles one way—and difficult in stormy weather, but Father John was able to stay overnight at the rectory of St. Thomas Aquinas Church nearby. He knew that Copperfield had a reputation for academic excellence—he remembered reading Dr. Phil Dolly's opinion piece in the *Duke City News* about CCC's future as a higher education leader.

Well. He had seven students remaining in his course [from the twenty-two originally enrolled], and no one was passing. They didn't do their homework, didn't study for tests, and never came by to see him before class. [He had made arrangements with Dean Preston to occupy a small office in the Teaching Learn-ed Center just for that purpose.]

Father John cared deeply for his students. He just wished he could do more to help them alleviate their personal problems so they could focus on school.

Jesus, Mary, and Joseph. I need the patience of Job.

Another of his students was Ricky, evidently a very bright student who was clearly not ready for an academic course such as World Religions, but one of the advisors had convinced Ricky he could succeed.

Cynthia, a rather heavy but pretty young woman of twenty, talked all class, and her vocabulary was quite good, but she had turned in no work. She was active in CCC student government and friends with Conrad.

Trevor was a high school senior, a dual enrollment student, who drew stick figure cartoon pictures [with flair].

Still, there was Kimboo, a very pleasant, charming, and intellectually-gifted African woman from Nigeria who simply could not speak or write English. Father John had sent several emails to the Helping English Language Learners [H.E.L.L.] program director about Kimboo's situation, but had as of yet received no replies.

Father John had recommended, to his students, computer programs, the tutoring center, online tutoring, and private conferences—all to no avail.

Well, I think I'll stop off at the Copper Coin Tavern on the way over to the rectory and consider this situation further! At least I'm raising some money for the food bank!

Father John ended up having a great time at the Copper Coin. He argued politics for a while with the Scottish socialist bartender, McDougal [*a good Catholic but a bit off the beaten path*, thought the Father]. He sat down next to Coach Ski at the bar—the CCC football defensive coach was sipping a Canadian Club with just a splash of water, and enjoying a pitcher or two of good cold draft beer after a late practice.

Coach Ski asked if the Father could bless the team. "*No, lad, I'm a Jesuit. You'll need a Franciscan for that!*" They laughed together. When Ski learned Father John was a Fighting Irish football fan, he bought the cleric an Irish whiskey or two. Before long, they were arm and arm singing the Notre Dame Fight Song.

[Three hours, three whiskeys, and six pints later, Father John called a taxi.]

Father Francis, parish priest at St. Thomas Aquinas Church, had received word from the Copper Coin barkeep that Father John would be arriving in a cab around one-thirty AM.

When the taxi driver delivered the weary priest, Father Francis led Father John to his cot and tucked him in. He seemed to understand the situation. *"Well, John, laddie, 'tis not the seminary ya be teaching at."*

Father John, tired, a bit tipsy, but apparently repentant, whispered something—*perhaps he is praying, thought Father Francis. Sure he wants forgiveness for such a night!* Father Francis bent over, but the words escaped him.

Father John raised himself up on one arm and whispered something again, still not quite audible to mortal man.

The moment was eerie. Suddenly, crickets stopped chirping, mists rolled into the room through the open window, and the numerous luminous, glowing votive candles stopped flickering. Time itself seemed to stand still as the priest tried to speak.

"Please, Father, speak more loudly," the parish priest further encouraged Father John. Then he leaned even closer to hear, nearly falling over onto the cot himself.

With a smile on his face, Father John [his old hairy, hoary face barely visible in the dim room, his red and rheumy eyes gleaming with fire] began chanting in a sing song voice—

Wake up the echoes cheering her name...

Wake up the echoes cheering her name...

"What's that now Johnny? Wake you up when—oh, lad, God Bless, ya, John, you *are at Copperfield now, not Notre Dame,"* said a laughing Father Francis. *"Get a good night's rest, boy, and come to confession tomorrow."*

[Sidebar: The cost of the taxi ride home and the subsequent next-day towing expense of Father John's rusty Bronco, negated his semester's salary contributions to the Albuquerque diocese.]

Jack Frost, Espanol Professor

Mr. Frost did not appear troubled on the exterior. But inside, he was nothing but churning emotions and agitated feelings. One of his former colleagues, the now-retired Richard Hose, said of Jack: *"He's like a duck—calm on the surface but paddling like h—-underwater."* His poems, which his few readers would probably judge "fair to middling" in quality, revealed his uncanny ability to capture the sadness, and joys, of brief moments in life. Jack was an observer, not a participant. He carefully protected his experiences and opinions and had an unspoken disdain for much of life. He kept his poems in a large, old, crinkled manila campus mail folder. He had experienced as of yet no academic or financial success with his metered efforts. His lack of publishing success disappointed him, but he was not surprised.

In Frost's mind [and experiences], life has dealt him one disappointment after another. He had been married twice—his first betrothal lasted five years and gave him six children [now all grown and more or less alienated from their erratic and *pato*-like father]. He currently resides in a nice, though weather-beaten, twenty by fifty modular at the Hamilton Inn Mobile Home Park.

Frost, who vowed never to marry again, now cohabitates with a 225 pound woman [she has added sixty-seven of those pounds since moving in three years ago]. Buzz Clocker is big, mean spirited, a lousy housekeeper, loves bowling and happy hours, has a bad complexion, more credit debt than the US treasury, floats on bad knees, and smokes too much.

She provides a double paradox for Frost—a subtle irony in events that have permeated his life—Buzz is both physically unattractive and unappreciative of his efforts.

Once, in trying to rationalize her weight gain, and hoping her swelling body size might miraculously simultaneously increase the goodness in her heart [like the Grinch event!], he crafted a poem which he entitled Jack's Girl is Big. [But he knew he could never show it to her—it was too fantastic, too untrue, probably too delusional.] Jack often used the poetic idiom as a means to test bed ideas—to work out problems. Typical of his poetry—it had power and an element of truth—but would be read by no one. Hopelessly a romantic, Jack

106

was compelled to write and dream big dreams, despite his daily confrontations with a thorny reality. [Sidebar: Ach! Certainly, romantic love provides for complex and difficult interconnections—usually chaotic and non-discernible. But what was he thinking?]

Jack's girl is big...

She's got jowls and big hams for thighs...
Poor thing...
Who knows where she finds those jeans.
Her little blue eyes twinkle like chickadees, and her laugh is a stampede
His girl is big...
Oh, Jack hears the whispers and snickers and nasty remarks
About her size and about him and about them
But Jack will tell you.
He wouldn't trade her for a super model—and here's why...
She loves him—not in the Hollywood kind of way—she's no Bond girl—
But in real terms, real simple terms in the way a man wants to be loved—she loves him...and is nice to him.
She is nice to him and respects him.
When they are sitting together in the Copper Coin, blowing smoke rings from their Camel lights, eating pickled eggs, and cheering at the tele, arm and arm, two big bears on tiny stools,
Well, they are happy, my friend, and their little sudsy pint-clover moment is the galaxy—
Time [and space!] has no meaning for these lovebirds.
Every Friday and Saturday, my friends, you'll see them on the same stools [sometimes three stools!], laughing and loving and putting away fish and chips and drinking and smoking, arm in arm, and loving each other like you can't imagine...
Jack's girl is big, and she always asks him how his day at work went—and asks about his problems, and his sadness, and misgivings.
Jack isn't all that small himself...
And she doesn't complain or try to control him.
Jack's girl is big. And he loves her. And she loves him.
And they are nice to each other without script or agenda...
And what you think doesn't matter to them.
Jack's girl is big. Jack isn't all that small himself.

Frost has no legal connection to this woman, but he is too kind-hearted, too emotionally entangled, to eject such a specimen from his domicile and his life. In short, his loneliness is nearly killing him—and she occupies [on a vast scale] a cavernously large empty spot in his life.

Jack Frost had big dreams earlier in life. He wanted a cabin in the forest. He hoped to obtain a PhD in Spanish literature, perhaps concentrating on Spanish subjective romanticism—most likely concerning the work of Mariano José de Larra [1890-1837—a suicide because of a love affair gone bad!]. But this never came to pass.

Shortly after his second marriage—while he was teaching at Giltner High School—he somehow got this job at Copperfield Community. He had been teaching mostly credit [but non-transfer] Conversational Spanish classes ever since and occasionally took monolingual senior citizens on tours of Juarez or Tijuana or El Golpho de Santa Clara.

Frost continued to apply for other positions at more notable or interesting institutions. He had kept a folder with over 133 rejection notices. He had interviewed at Redhounds, Nebraska State, and Illinois Southern North Central State Polytechnic, but nothing came from these efforts except further rejections. A college football player earlier in life, he had even applied for some assistant athletic director jobs. Never heard a word...

In an effort to improve his prospects, Frost had been enrolled in a University of Topeka at Arlington cohort Ed. Leadership program for a while. The curious rigor, great expense, inadequate students, and endless chatter about restaurants, movies, TV sitcoms, politics, partnering, Cancun, wine tasting parties, Las Vegas, golf, networking, smart phone upgrades, skiing, and job openings drove him away quickly. He didn't want to be an administrator, or social net-worker, team player, or talker.

He had neither the time, money, intellect, nor focus to enroll in a rigorous academic PhD program at this point in his life. Besides, such an academic degree would mean nothing at CCC.

His savings were meager—he lived check to check. He had no idea where the money went. None.

Frost rides an aging Sportster to work most of the time, but some days it is just too cold or icy. Then he rides his bicycle or Razor scooter. Frost has been unable to find the money to fix his truck the last six years [since the engine block cracked], and it lingers solemnly, just off the street, a rusting and mute testament to his financial condition—and the better, happier, suburban times he once enjoyed with wife number two [before she left him for a bug exterminator].

His second wife had cheated on him, ruined him financially, ridiculed him, and left him sinking in emotional quicksand. He could not think of any positive emotional relationship he had ever had with a woman, except his mom, who he was still very close to and visited as often as possible. *"I just wish you could find a nice thin girl and settle down, Jackie. Why are things so hard for you?"* she asked at their last meeting. *"Just enjoy life. My boy, my little Jackie, you think too much. And that poetry your write is so sad. Lighten up a little and have some fun."*

Jack probably wouldn't openly claim that he had experienced a bad childhood, but then, for some strange reason, he was the butt of many unkind remarks from his aunts and uncles and cousins. His extended family members enjoyed minimizing his prospects and his ambitions. *You will never make any money writing poetry or studying Spanish literature, Jackie,* his uncle once told him. *A decir ver dad,* thought Frost now.

Certainly this constant criticism stiffened his resolve to be successful in life [the jury is still out on his achievements, even now].

He had forged a kind of baseline data efficiency approach to existence that allowed him to forge ahead—at the expense of many experiences, many opportunities.

Frost had few friends—he saw S. Chick as an isolated, bizarre work-shirking anachronism. He had once thought often about Julia Flowers—perhaps hoped for something, but he saw her now as someone out of touch, subsidized by a rich husband, living in a fantasy world of dinner parties, pedicures, and happy family life. He occasionally had lunch with Dr. Darling, but Frost was simply not interested in politics. Or intellectual diversity.

He attended meetings of the Hamilton City's Men of Diverse Intellects Club for a few months. The members; Dr. H. Reynolds, Dr. K. Jensen, B. Harres, Stockham Bob, Dr. B. Martin, The Right Reverend D. Forrester, F.

Westerman [Engineer-Fabricator], C. Stryker, Dr. Tomas Gamble, D. Jones, McGill, C. Peterson, PhD, G. Thorpe, M. Newlun, I.M. Tyred, Colonel Knox, Prof. R. Finske [Emeritus, UH], Engineer J. Sego, L. Johnson, Keymaster, Actor R. Hunt, Chef Jhil, D. Jensen Jr., Financier C. Stryker, luthier M. Carroll, Dr. J. Paddison, Prof. Doyle B. [Aeronautical Sciences, CCC], R. Ryan, JD, J. Grady, MD, Prof. Gerald O'Neal [Astronomy, CCC], Dr. S. Halstead, Sgt. Hoyt, T. Baugher, Fire Chief, General T.Huffman [Ret.], and J. Cummer were very bright men, leading figures in town, and had much to say. Frost felt inadequate around them, and simply stopped going.

He had been a fair athlete in his day and had committed himself to a life-time of physical fitness. While his jogging program had slowed, he still had the habit of maintaining a prisoner's workout regimen in the front yard whenever possible [using scattered free weights, jugs of milk, cinder blocks, four by four fence posts—whatever was available]. Sometimes in the summer Jack would lace up his old battered brogans and run through Streeter's Park late at night, breathing in the glorious, damp, richly humid air. At such times he felt alive— and free.

He was lean and strong, but...he smoked and drank too much too, though he had been told countless times he simply had to quit cigarettes.

Recently, his thyroid had begun giving him trouble, his joints were wearing out, and small patches of skin cancer had been cut off his head. He took all of this to be a sign of fatalistic doom—further proof of the bad hand he had been dealt by fate.

Frost had a dreary, tasked commitment to his job. He was always available to help students after class [His daily dilemma?—see students or go face Big Doc Buzz]. He received good reviews and did what was expected of him by the institution. He did not gossip or rant and rave about how great his future retirement would be. [One ex-wife and a shadowy former concubine had already cast lots to soak up the final waters of that diminishing stream.] Beaten up by reality and bad breaks over and over again, he took no giddy pleasure or other emotions in student success vignettes, pep talks [or *"Armageddon is here"* speeches] by administrators, certificates, quality awards, luncheons, conferences, or bake sales.

110

The community college provided a paycheck and benefits—his proletarian efforts went largely unnoticed by students or staff.

The world of happy hours, movie theatres, wine festivals, Disknee Cruises, smart phones, mp3 players, politics, flat screen TV's—well, it all seemed like some sort of script, some sort of puppet show going on that squeezed the spirit and life out of everyone. His quiet reflections—few as they were—while walking through a wooded park or on the banks of a muddy stream—such moments seemed to have priceless value to him—immeasurable moments of poetic ecstasy no one seemed to "get"—or even wished to acknowledge. The scripted circus that went on around him, including his many bouts with a failed domestic life, simply debilitated him.

The twenty-first century buzz of commoditized learning at his college both fascinated and discouraged him. Teaching and learning, he often considered, has been replaced by whimsical conversations about quality, assessment, and careers.

Jack thought, *I go to work and swim in a kind of philosophic compost quagmire, a sinkhole of insincerity, self-service, and corporate pretension.*

He could not fathom, could not grasp, how men like President Dolly and Dean Preston had such big salaries, impressive lake front second homes, large portfolios. They always had new clothes, the latest cars, the trendiest electronic gimmicks. Such people, he thought, seemed to have nothing to offer anyone or anything outside the cloistered, artificial circle of community college life. They performed no observable valuable function, but got bigger raises every year. He wondered if any of them even knew a second language, or read poetry, or reflected on purpose, or generated FTSE, or knew any students, or prayed privately. He wondered.

He knew for certain that if Dolly or Preston vanished or left town unexpectedly, few people would notice their absence.

Frost considered the legions of adjunct (part-time) "professors," working for a pittance, no benefits, no future. They represented probably three-fourths of the college's teaching workforce, but their total salaries combined paled compared to the annual take of a single Dean or VP.

At sixty, Jack had never known a moment of romantic tenderness. There were no gentle eyes to scour his soul, no soft hands to touch his face, no wonder at his poetry or songs. He was a locust—still buzzing, but a shell, a cicada husk stuck on a dried tree. The vampires had destroyed him. *How can it be—all those women, all those children, yet to never know tenderness, to feel support, to be loved and acknowledged? All those years…all the ridicule.*

He marveled that so many males—handsome, homely, and socially gay, both wealthy and attractive—had female companions who were pretty and pleasant, kind and sincere. His unwanted isolation was a cold trill, a nasty wound, a compelling, vengeful voice which had affected his emotional health for decades.

Frost had many issues, many lingering and malingering emotional concerns.

Sometimes at night, he would awaken and see figures in his room. The phantasms were always different. One night he saw a small girl riding a pony without a tail. Another night, a Christmas eve, he saw Chuck Berry playing guitar and singing with Frank Sinatra. He had seen Dick Van Dyke, the Terminator, and a shadowy Argentine dressed all in black except for a white tie [and carrying a wolf-headed cane] a time or two. The figures were never frightening—and they were always gone at daybreak. Once he saw Wilbur the Duck sauntering into his clothes closet; once he saw the barkeep from the Copper Coin and even the adjunct faculty member, Father John, who was singing the Notre Dame Fight song.

Just last night, he had been transfixed by a large, smiling, photo radar robot that flashed his picture then quickly left the room. Frost's reality was slipping…

CeCe "Buzz" Clocker, First shift Barkeep, Copper Coin

Buzz is a big woman—and a great bartender. She remembers customers' names, their favorite beer, the way they like their drinks concocted. She knows about bourbons, vodka, foo-foo umbrella mixes, mint juleps, and all the clubs and taverns from Buckeye, Arizona to Billings, Montana to Boston, Mass. She can drink with the best of them—and was perhaps best known for beginning the always-popular "*birthday kamikaze shots from the toilet plunger*" tradition.

She is coarse and vulgar and fears no man, woman, or beast. Some would say she looks like a horse that was ridden hard and put away sweaty, but there is always a man in her life. Right now she is shacked up with a Spanish instructor from CCC, but before that good ol' Buzz spent about three months down in Tucumcari with a Harley Davidson riding dude named Reginald. She nearly beat ol' Reginald to death in a domestic dispute [*"Who drank all the!@#$%$!&! beer in the fridge?"*] And, after serving a thirty day jail term, came back to Hamilton.

Long before that happy liaison, she lived for a while with the guitar-playing custodian from the college, but he just played country music and it finally made her sick.

Buzz has been a shift bartender here for several years now. Prior to this career, she was a full-time home economics teacher in the Hamilton Unified School District and an adjunct accounting instructor at CCC.

During her ten-year tenure working for HUSD, Buzz constantly butted heads with principals, directors, secretaries, counselors, superintendents [who came and went about as often as college presidents], and teachers. She finally was released from her teaching duties, and she understood why—she was simply smarter than all of 'em.

Buzz had six hours of undergrad accounting credit and a Master's in Special Ed from HSU—this qualified her to be a Professor of Accounting at CCC.

But after working eight years as an adjunct, and often teaching seven courses a semester [at 675 dollars per three hour class], she began to realize she would never get a full-time job. [She told then-Dean of Instruction Hans Goeber to "*take CCC and ![*&][[!it up his ![*&^%&**[!*" and began her full-time calling at the Copper Coin].

Buzz hadn't seen Dr. Hansmuth [von] Goeber down here for a while, since that night he got arrested for drunk driving. [She had heard he was now a President at a community college in Ohio somewhere.]

Despite her falling out with CCC, Professor Clocker had fond memories of Hans from years ago when he would initiate drinking games and sing bawdy and often obtuse songs in German.

"Die Fahne hoch! Die Reihen fest geschlossen!
SA marschiert mit ruhig, festem Schritt.
Kam'raden, die Rotfront und Reaktion erschossen,
Marschier'n im Geist in unser'n Reihen mit."
(Horst Wessel Song, 1929*)*

And "Doc" Buzz is very happy. She loves the smell of old cigarette smoke, popcorn, bacon, and beer. Something about seed company calendars, deer heads on plaques, bowling championship trophies, bobble heads of baseball players, photos of softball teams, autographed bats and hockey sticks, pictures of Marilyn Monroe and Betty Grable—well, these were her people.

Her reputation as a dart player and karaoke performer is secure too. She is an expert at survey analysis, stakeholder satisfaction, quality control and process implementation inside the four walls of the Copper Coin.

Oh, she could be vulgar, and Big Buzz [as the patrons fondly know her] even frightens the bouncers who work there.

If the truth be known, on a good night, "The Buzzer" can make almost as much in tips as she did teaching an entire class for a whole semester at CCC.

Why Buzz got involved with that whacko Spanish teacher was beyond her [except that he subsidized her completely—car, no rent, spending money, insurance, and periodic vacations to Tucumcari].

"Professor" Buzz had initially thought Frost wrote great poetry, but he turned out to be an introspective flop—he might even like men more than women [*He won't touch me anymore, a hunk of burnin' love such as myself,* she thought.]

She has a roll of belly fat the size of a tire—her belly button has not been seen for decades. Her jowls jiggle when she laughs that crazy laugh, and her frequent sneezing fits shake the mirrors and counters.

At fifty, Buzz is really starting to slide. It is hard for even her to imagine she once wore a bikini and competed in the Sturgis swimsuit contest. Cheesy fries, wings, charbroiled burgers, fried mushrooms, bacon wrap peppers—so good and so straight to the thighs. Oh, she still flirts—she has a pretty face, cool metal parts sticking through her nose and cheeks, nice lavender toenails, and she always wears black miniskirts or seventies era hot pants and a bright purple tube top.

Most of the male patrons would say she still looks pretty good [after three or four pitchers…]

She has **"74 or more"** tattooed on her left calf and **"Big Girls need Love Too"** on the right calf. [*"The twin heifers,"* Zontarg calls the tattooed legs.]

Buzz can sit down and argue for hours about NFL contracts, baseball trivia, Sammy Hagar, Tupac, Fords, and Harley Davidson pan heads. She can tell you about Daytona Bike Week, poker runs to Big Bear, her stint as a traveling mud wrestler, and the best desert beer parties she's ever been to.

[More cynical patrons have characterized her as a fourteen year old girl stuck in a Bulgarian weightlifter's old body. They still talk about how [von] Goeber kept a close eye on her—*"Mein Vergeltungswaffe! My Teutonic Princess,"* he would coo to her, when ordering a stein of *""sehr gut kalt beer mit wurst und kraut."*]

The second shift socialist barkeep, McDougal, gave his opinion of Buzz to one of the patrons. *"Well, she's a big bonnie lass but I'd stay clear of her if ye could. She's a mean one, that dar filly. But she knows her liquor. Ach, she is a big oon. Ya, we could have used some of that muscle back in Glasgow on a night or two. Ach, she is a big oon. She reminds me of me faithful, beautiful, always God-fearin' wife, bless her heart, back in Scootland."*

Sometimes Buzz still hangs out with the secretaries from CCC, but those Girls Night Out [GNO] events have declined with the secretaries' maturity. [The fact they all ended up in Las Vegas one night with a bunch of spike-haired bikers didn't help out their marriages, either.]

Buzz doesn't see too many CCC employees at the Copper Coin any more—at least not like she used to. She knows Dean Preston and the counselor Vasquez meet down here occasionally, and the part-time teacher Father John sometimes stops off for an Irish whiskey with Coach Ski. Bob Zontarg still lurks around once in a while, asks for horseradish on his corn beef sandwich [on rye bread], and plays the Kinks' "Lola" once or twice on the jukebox, but he usually comes and goes in a cab.

Sometimes Frost will stop by and give her a ride home or bring her a few dollars for smokes.

Buzz just loves the Copper Coin. She can be herself there. [Better yet, at the Copper Coin Halloween party each fall, she can be whoever she wants to be—a princess, a vixen, a vampire, a starlet. Once she even came as a big sweaty horse, complete with a saddle on her back!]

The Coin maintains big gallon-sized jars of pickled eggs, serves up half-burnt bar pizzas, celebrates twenty-two beers on tap, still stocks a cigarette machine, and nurtures a great rowdy group of fully-engaged stakeholders and process owners.

But sometimes she misses Reginald and his big black boots...and the sound of a Harley Davidson with powder-black street-sweeper pipes...

[Bob Zontarg and his Little Colorado River Band also wrote, but never actually performed, a "Song for Buzz Clocker"—written for several guitars in key of G]:

Her name was Buzz
Because
It was
She's got some rings, and things,
That go jing
She uses you
Too too too
Barbecues
She bums a smoke
Always broke
What a joke!
How can you say that we're wrong?
Playing our seven chord songs
Working class heroes are we
Are you too blind to see?

Instrumental break
Her name was Buzz
Because
it was
She's got some tats, lots of cats
Getting fat
Her name was Buzz
Because
It was
How can you say that we're wrong?
Playing our seven chord songs
Working class heroes are we
Are you too blind to see?
Her name was Buzz
Because
It was

Song…ends with cymbal wash with e minor chord. (Little Colorado River Band circa 1995)

William-Henry Ireland, Director of Public Information CCC

Mr. Ireland came to CCC from a radio station [WAWL] in York, East Nebraska. He spends most of his days drafting copy about student success stories, athletic events, and upcoming board meetings. W-H maintains a snazzy web site that posts information about the college's day-to-day activities, employee awards, student functions, and coming events. [He is paid a full-time salary for mostly part-time work, but every college needs a full-time director of public information.]

W-H has learned to attend many meetings and to serve on many committees. This keeps him abreast of events at the school, keeps him out of the office, and keeps him busy. He plays on the staff intramural basketball team and sponsors the student journalism club. He never misses a golf tournament or a home football game.

A good money manager, his salary is decent—and he drives a nice newer SUV [which he has detailed weekly by the Hamilton City Mobile Auto Detailing Service [HCMADS]—at only forty-nine dollars a visit]—but he is essentially biding his time until he can break into a better job in journalism or TV. William-Henry would like to be a sportscaster. He has an audition tape [which he created using college equipment] "out there" but no responses, yet. His wife, Cathy Ireland-Jones, is secretary to the Registrar.

[He recently made a note to himself to ask her why the exterminator makes three visits to their house each month.]

As Director of Public Information, William has full access, and editorial rights, to consider faculty or staff personal or public achievements, including publications, as suitable for recognition in CCC's monthly newsletter. He had come across a year-old copy of an article, written by Dr. Darling, which was not considered for recognition by the previous Director. Mr. Ireland had some time before his next scheduled meeting and, finding the title a bit intriguing, began to read:

That thing they do: Journalists and the Community College
By Dr. Deuce Darling
Copperfield Biology Faculty

The recent spate of articles in North New Mexico news media—especially the *Hamilton County Democrat*—concerning the potential sale of Copperfield Community College has prompted me to consider the media's perception of community college culture. What is it about the American community college which begs journalistic scrutiny? Certainly there have been high profile cases—a college president being arrested for allegedly selling pot in Iowa, two college presidents forced into "retirement" due to international travel wrongdoings, and the numerous fraud cases in Alabama. One can find more such instances of investigations, allegations, and arrests using any reliable online search engine—the baleful, dark litany is available daily for public view.

But every agency, every corporation, every town in America has its share of alleged wrong doers in high places. Such situations are hardly limited to the community college experience.

Still, there is something about the public's and media's perceptions of the community college that begs further assessment. What can we do to improve our relations with the press? The answer, I think, is a reexamination of our organizational deportment and the resulting relationships we reveal to local constituents.

A December 2005 Chronicle of Post-secondary Ed article described how a community college president decided the local paper had written too many negative stories about the school. His plan of action? "We are stopping all dealings with our local paper."

Public Suspicion

But stopping communication with the local paper or miscommunication with the local paper, or any misarticulating of ideas or purpose can be deadly to a college's enrollment and future. Certainly, the local press provides a primary and hopeful gateway to positive marketing and information.

I think the public is suspicious, to a certain extent, of 21st century community college culture. Perhaps a gradual perceived paradigm shift from stewardship (as daily college cultural emphasis) to the colleges' self-imposed "leadership" has negatively influenced the public at large. Is it possible our newly found corporate images, quality-focused management styles, and self-proclaimed "higher education leader" manifestos have distanced us from our potential students and tax base? Local newspapers, who have traditionally fashioned themselves as public watchdogs, may sense a misplaced aloofness, a kind of pretentiousness, which is never alluring.

First and foremost, I think we should promote an image of being the *local community's* college. Community colleges actually have something in common with their local newspapers—they share the same geographic and political constituency. Consider this—most information, most news, most editorials found in a local small town or city papers have primary significance to residents who reside with the home delivered readership. I would venture a local paper which busies itself with stories the locals do not find interesting will perish. What are the stories promoted at your community college? How does your local paper perceive your organization, your purpose, and your relationship to those who pay your salaries through tax dollars?

The rumored sale of CCC might be a case in point. How should Hamilton County residents react to such a possibility? Are the stewards of a tax supported public institution even empowered to consider such an event? Perhaps an informed press wonders why the most overtly socialistic institutions in American post-secondary education have become so profit focused.

Or, possibly, that historical or traditional part of community college academic culture which has nurtured primary contemporary ideological "marketing" tenets—inspiration and "comeback" vignettes—may have also nourished the public perception the colleges foster hope rather than accomplishment. Such stories may have created a folklore or mythology, finding voice in the print media, which is no longer effective and may even be damaging.

Daily Discourse

One of my colleagues and I enjoy "gently" analyzing our perspectives on the true mission, the true purposes, of the two-year college movement. While she vehemently defends the community college as a higher education entity, I contend our most viable and profitable purpose, would be to embrace our function as institutions with a post-secondary focus. I said, "Kat, if we are higher education institutions, our notions about higher education are different than what the universities believe higher education to be."

She looked at me directly and exclaimed, "Aren't we supposed to be different?"

Her response stunned—and enlightened—me.

We *are* different. Why aren't we able to manage, to assess, to celebrate that *difference* in a positive, mature, community-inspired fashion? Perhaps journalists do "that thing they do" because they may well perceive (better than we wish to admit) much of our working culture appears illusionary—and we often borrow our tenets, our mores, and our folkways from other cultures, because we are absent of a realistic knowledge of ourselves. What do we want?

> We want to be academic in a meaningful way.
> We want to be corporate.
> We want brand recognition.
> We want titles—and lots of them.
> We want to be small business developers.
> We want nationally competitive sports teams.
> We want to be everything and frequently look silly
> trying.

Perhaps we should better understand what we do best—as individual colleges—and nurture that part of our institutions. Let's give the journalists powerful truths to write about—truths our students and their families will embrace and nurture.

Who Are We?

Certainly, we can be noble, loving, and truly helpful. We have improved life for so many. I could fill several pages with the storied successes of my former students. I am so proud of them and the work we have done at Copperfield Community. I wish I could write about these students for the local media.

Perhaps these successes do not quite qualify as "man bites dog" human interest stories.

Or, perhaps our culture has become oddly corporate—this may be what the journalists sense and why they observe our actions with suspicious eyes. Somehow we maintain certain behaviors that are, I'm afraid, ultimately self-defeating. Think about some of your internal organization practices the media reviews and then reports. How do you look to the townsfolk who shop with you in the same grocery stores? Rethink some of your entrenched practices—ground yourself in a post-secondary reality—and I am convinced your media relations will improve and your enrollment will increase. Consider our folkways, our mores, our Zen. Please consider alternatives.

How many times do we conduct national searches then hire the interim anyway? Is attendance at a community college a ticket for a future classified job at the same school? Let's codify our hiring practices to honestly reflect what we intend to do when we seek new employees.

Let's embrace and promote the nonfiction that we can truly help our constituents enter the middle class (through meaningful twenty-first century workforce training). Help your students earn more money, and they will love you.

Reconsider that entire proud talk and media buzz about teaching globally via the internet. There is yet a solid constituency who would prefer classes face to face—even though they might be quite comfortable with the internet. And—don't boast about teaching the Nebraskans or in East New Mexico if you perpetually cancel face-to-face classes because of low enrollment.

When questioned by the media about policies and plans, we often become defensive (even hostile) and exhibit an inability to appropriately respond....in the language of realism and working Americans (those we are probably serving). Speak directly and in clear language—avoid the corporate blustering and buzz speak so common to the boardroom and faculty development literature. Truthfully, such posturing is very unbecoming and lacks sincerity, authenticity, or the demeanor evidenced by wise persons. Surely the banks and chipmakers are looking for people who can speak the clipped tongue of the global corporate giants.

You may have crossed the digital divide and conquered the corporate ethos—but many of your constituency still have analog, down-home interests. Consider ways to meet their needs. (Your goal should be to increase enrollment—not impress folk with fancy posturing, acronyms, start-up programs, and tiring speeches better suited to politicians or Division I football coaches.). Technology, my friends, is represented by a shovel. The shovel helps us, but should not be the focus, the absolute end, of our being, our learning, and our culture.

Community colleges are not corporations, nor are they universities. Embrace a post-secondary mentality—call your faculty instructors (not professors—unless you have a true merit based faculty advancement policy rather than a column and row secondary school-emulating salary schedule) and scale back the salaries (and titles) of administrators. You'll get more work out of both groups—and your constituency will sense your college is grounded in a purposeful reality.

Recruit local athletes—even if it means no more national titles. The townspeople would prefer seeing their own sons and daughters play and lose. What community does your athletes from out-of-state or out-of-nation, represent?

We try to "intellectually" distance ourselves from the secondary schools while sharing much of their complexion (salary schedules, dual enrollment, governing boards, pedagogical associations and emphasis). But we are so much like them. Revisit the concept of grades 13-14. Consider making vocational training your primary focus. Follow the lead of those community colleges that include Technical in their names.

How much money do we spend at overpriced conferences at five star resorts? We are spending the public's "dime"—can we defend such expenditures?

I am convinced data would show, if such a poll were ever conducted, that most Americans believe community colleges are places to improve job training or career advancement.

We have embraced (probably two or three) education leadership programs as the "sole" training ground for our senior administrators. Think about this. We celebrate diversity, but do not practice it. The public must wonder when all of this leadership training will pay off. Become more understanding about leaders by reading biographies, great literature, and philosophy. Tell me truthfully—do you understand the differences between Shakespeare's Richard II and Henry IV? Do you know where Patton went to college before West Point? [Hint—he attended VMI].

Perhaps, if you want to be an academic institution, you should hire staff and faculty with academic backgrounds.

Eventually, nearly all faculty and staff attend BISON. And most administrators have some kind of Quality Award hanging on an office wall. We literally drip with self-aggrandizing quality. I think we should find ways to honestly service the community—outside the college walls—that helps our stakeholders believe, too, that we are quality organizations. Read to school children. Play in a community band. Work at the food bank. Do something each semester and the paybacks, both in press, self-satisfaction, and real quality, will be evident.

"That Thing *We* Do"

I understand a Copperfield Community College administrator once said, "The University can't ignore us. We're the 800 pound gorilla in the room." I can't speak for the University, but I suspect four-year schools are bemused by our speeches, planks, pranks, platforms, and squabbles. [And if they flex their muscles with programs and discounts, they will take many of our students.]

However, I suspect the journalists are *not* ignoring the gorilla. Let's find a way to help them respect our difference...Let's rethink our mission, our purpose, and the community we serve. Let's better inform them of "that thing *we* do" and help them to refocus "that thing they do.

~ * ~

Ireland didn't waste much time. He tossed it in the trash can. "*Too Dangerous!*"

Still waiting for his phone to ring and just minutes away now from that next meeting, killing time and rummaging around in his desk [hoping to find a candy bar in there somewhere, actually!], Ireland found, at the bottom of a drawer, what looked to be a copy of a letter of application. *I have no idea what this is doing here. What in the world? Frost? That rough-looking Spanish teacher who's always flirting with Mrs. Flowers? Hah! Maybe my office used to be the HR office or something. But this letter is to a school in South Dakota! I thought these records were supposed to be private. Why are Dolly's initials scribbled across the top?*

Letter of Application
By Jack Frost, Espanol Professor, CCC

April 21, 2010
Human Resources
ESDSU
Bookings, South Dakota

Greetings,

I wish to apply for the Spanish Instructor position (posting # 000247) as advertised on the ESDSU website.

I am hopeful both my academic credentials (MA in Spanish Education) and my experiences teaching both conversational and transfer Spanish language courses make me a suitable candidate.

I have taught Spanish transfer courses, conversational classes, Spanish literature survey courses, creative Spanish writing, and introductory Spanish linguistics in a variety of modalities, including traditional F2F settings, online (using both WBC and Buckboard course management software), on ITV (teaching both college and secondary school students), and in Hybrid situations—combining F2F, ITV, and online methodologies.

I enjoy writing poetry and maintain several web sites that display my poetry and tortured personal feelings.

My students would tell you I am sincerely interested in their development as Spanish speakers. I enjoy working with students in the language lab or other supplemental instruction settings.

I spend far more time at school than I need to—I would rather work with individuals who need my help than stay home and get depressed further.

I am a member of SPTE and I have been quite active in the North New Mexico Spanish Teachers Association [an SPTE affiliate]. I served on our institution's Spanish Articulation Task Force [SPAT] group for nearly 15 years—

125

the SATF groups from North New Mexico community colleges and universities meet annually to work out transfer and articulation matters for Spanish department courses (between the cc's and universities). I have also worked with the North New Mexico Humanities Council as a Spanish literature and film discussion leader. [I especially enjoy films about dark romantic suicides and ballerinas.]

I spent a great deal of my early life in Nebraska—and received my MA from Nebraska State in 1978. I am quite familiar with the culture and climate of the Great Plains, although I would rather ride motorcycles than horses.

Please consider my application. I would very much like to return to the Midwest, and one of my career dreams (and life dreams) has been to teach at a four-year institution such as ESDSU in Bookings. I am capable, student centered, job-focused, energetic, and confident.

I really need to get away from the macabre community college environment and my current circle of associates. Please help me. Are there any thin but intellectual female faculty members at ESDSU?

I look forward to hearing from you.

Thank you,
Jack Frost
Professor of Espanol
Copperfield Community College
Space 26
Hamilton County Motor Inn
Hamilton City, North New Mexico
8850x

~ * ~

Later, William-H is attending one of Dr. Dolly's extended Cabinet meetings [Extended means everyone in the school is invited. Cabinet, to Dolly, means everyone who is a 12 month non-maintenance or non-clerical employee. *Yet only VP's and Deans hold voting rights.*]

During the last few minutes, Dr. Dolly has been congratulating CCC staff for their hard work, excellent relations with the community, national recognition, and commitment to learning excellence.

"Yass, the good work you are doing here at CCC is a light unto the world. Yass we can be proud of our service to stakeholders, steak-eaters, and students alike. Yass. [KaffKaff]. When I walk the fair streets of our communities, any of our communities, any time of night or day, any season, even when the leaves are falling, hand-in-hand with my lovely wife Molly, I receive so many compliments about our grand institution and about our world class staff—our stakeholders are so pleased with the global state-of-the-market service we provide here at this shining example of the Learn-ed College. Yass."

Mr. Ireland noticed Dr. S. Chick, sitting towards the back, was staring at the Exit Sign. Ireland also noticed Dr. Preston was checking his Blackberry and smiling at Elena Vasquez. Zontarg, the long-haired janitor, was tapping rhythmically on the table and mumbling something to himself about Bon Jovi.

Several students sat quietly, eyes closed, plugged into Ipods. Two faculty members were walking out the door to take cell phone calls. One director was vigorously moving his thumbs as he sent a text off to somewhere.

[The woman sitting next to him erupted in shrieking laughter—perhaps she received his important message.]

Professor Hedlund sat directly in front of the speaking president, eating a container of peach yogurt and snorting periodically. A student track athlete from East Oregon had his head down on the table and was snoring softly.

All of these behaviors, thought Ireland, *were rude but typical. Rude but typical.*

The President had rambled on for an hour or so about budgets, quality initiatives, the Highbrow Learn-ed Commission, and an upcoming consultant visit from Dr. Leonard Sushy.

Then Dolly was making his case, once more, for seeking state approval for his pet project—awarding bachelor's degrees at CCC. Dr. Dolly was quite animated, almost purple-faced as he made his impassioned, fist-pounding plea. [The athlete from East Oregon, awakened by Dolly's shouting, looked around in a daze, probably wondering if he was back in class or the great Northwest.]

Looking Dean Preston Paxton squarely in the eyes, Dolly ventured that *CCC* [a public entity] *might even investigate the possibility of selling itself to an online private university—a transaction that would accelerate CCC's growth into a four-year institution.*

The assembled employees looked uncomfortable and even more confused, but let the President continue, without interruption, his fiery oration.

Is this all he ever talks about? William asked himself. *This is a JuCo, for crying out loud. Does he have the right or authority to put the college—a taxpayer institution—up for sale? Criminy! Where did this guy come from?*

Section Two
Michael and Celeste: The Rise of Philip Dolly
"Time is so old and love so brief
Love is pure gold and time a thief"
(Speak Low—Kurt Weill and Ogden Nash 1943]

Chapter One

Michael P. Staten worked for *The North American Petroleum Energy Corporation [NAPEC]* located in Los Angeles, California. Or, more specifically, he was assigned to its international subsidiary *Petroleum Energy Production Enterprises [PEPÉ]* located in Mesquite, Texas, just outside Dallas. The subsidiary enterprise was doing work internationally, and since 1958, heavy contract work in Argentina. The oil energy company operating as *PEPÉ was* awarded lucrative government investment contracts to supply Argentina with energy production. Equipment and resources PEPÉ supplied made possible the intensified drilling practices necessary to produce sizable expansion of Argentine petroleum output.

Staten had graduated from the University of Michigan at Ann Arbor, with a degree in mechanical engineering just two years before accepting the position with NAPEC. He had benefited from the extensive financial scholarship support provided to him. National higher education funding, resulting from the 1958 National Education Defense Act, helped him finance

129

the last two years of college. He understood his scholarships resulted, in part, from the country's shocked reaction to the 1957 USSR Sputnik satellite launch.

Prior to this, his full-time employment consisted of contract work with agricultural equipment manufacturing company in Illinois, and a one-year internship with a shipbuilding firm near Duluth, Minnesota. After eight months' "hands-on" training at company equipment manufacturing facilities in California and Texas, Staten was assigned to travel to Argentina and assist with the installation of energy equipment manufactured by NAPEC. His October departure date was altered due to travel restrictions imposed by the U.S. just days after the 1962 Cuban Missile crisis.

Having previously not traveled abroad, Mr. Staten received all the essential inoculation shots, a current passport, and a brief description of Argentina's geographic and social aspects [which the company deemed necessary for adaptation for his initial six month assignment]. While preparing for his approaching departure, Staten read over the brief brochure describing his living accommodations in the capital city of Buenos Aries and his shorter stays in the Mendoza province, site of an oil refinery where his mechanical petroleum equipment services were required. He was quite interested in seeing soccer matches, horse racing and, having grown up on a farm and living in the state of Texas for the past year, was really looking forward to tasting Argentina beef. [*Staten loved a good steak.*]

Mr. Staten's DC-4 Pan Am Airlines flight from Dallas International airport departed at 7:30 AM on Sunday morning the twenty-first of April, 1963. Flight plans included a scheduled stop in Washington D.C. and on to the International Ezeiza Airport, "Ministro Pistarini," Buenos Aires—according to what he read in the itinerary. Staten was informed that Argentina was three hours ahead of Washington D.C. [Standard Time].

Once de-planed in Buenos Aires, Mr. Staten became slightly disoriented, directionally, as he attempted to locate his waiting ground transportation. While staring intently at his itinerary, he inadvertently brushed the arm of a man dressed in a dark suit [and wearing a black velvet fedora]. Without uttering a sound, the man's eyes "helpfully" re-positioned Staten to a near exit where a taxi driver held a hand written **PEPÉ** sign. The driver transported Staten directly to his PEPÉ arranged apartment, where he was to receive a full itinerary for his work [which began in earnest the next day].

The majority of Staten's first three weeks in Argentina involved twelve to fourteen hour work days. This provided few opportunities for other activities. Week one entailed receiving scheduled work assignments from corporate PEPÉ representatives; project time frame meetings with uniformed state petroleum entity officials; and a formal tour of the PEPÉ's Buenos Aires corporate operations plant and equipment warehouse. Staten learned production and drilling contracts were directed by the state petroleum entity—Yacimientos Petroliferos Fiscales [YPP].

During his second week of training orientations, Staten had several lunch meetings with Edward Kenny. Ed was a PEPÉ Operations Manager from Ohio who had been on location in Buenos Aires for two years. Through Ed, Staten learned of the strong labor unions in the city and the functions occurring within the operation plant and warehouse. Ed was a friendly and informed fellow, in his early-forties, with a good sense of humor and gregarious laugh. [Sitting at a café, not far from the PEPÉ operations plant...]

"Hey, Mike, one thing you'll need to get used to here is the week day work schedule. We typically begin office and warehouse operations about 8:30 AM. Then at noon, the place shuts down until about 2:00 PM. Most of us do as the locals and enjoy a nice lunch, maybe a short nap. Most all the shops in the city close down during this time anyway. We then work steady until about four, take a short sandwich and coffee break, then resume working till about seven or eight o'clock."

"Well, I'm sure I'll find a way to get accustomed to that, Ed—beats the heck out of the steady nine to six."

"You got that right. You'll also really enjoy the food here, Mike—kind of spicy at first, but man you'll begin to love it. They make really great soups and stews, and the meat is the best I've ever had. The steaks are a favorite of mine, and as you can tell [Ed taps his protruding belly], I'm no slouch at the dinner table!"

Just then the lunch serving waiter came by to get their order. *"Mike, ya gotta try the Guiso, really great stuff."*

"Alright Ed, I'll take your word on that."

"Ok, Pedro, we'll both have the Guiso and plenty of your hot fresh out of the oven bread—with additional butter and dulce de leeche... and a couple of cold beers as well. Gracias! Yass!"

~ * ~

After the delicious and filling Guiso, Ed and Mike took a walk through a commercial part of the city. *"Hey, Ed, there seems to be a lot of construction projects going on in and around the city."*

"Yeah, Mike, much of this construction is part of major government improvements begun about a decade or so ago. This infrastructure development also enabled PEPÉ to secure contract work here, which keeps us employed, Mike!

"The way I understand it, after the war, the political leadership here called for all sorts of social and economic reforms promoting independence. There was a big push to improve the country's infrastructure by intensifying oil drilling to expand petroleum output, being that the majority of their oil is imported. That's what brought PEPÉ here, and good old Yankee know-how! That would be us Mike...Ha! Ha!"

"So how long do you think we'll, I mean PEPÉ, be here, I mean helping with petroleum production and all?"

"Oh, h——, Mike, I hear all the time that foreign contract work is drying up and the Argentines want to be free of us!"

"Yeah, Ed, I picked up on that when meeting with those uniformed state petroleum guys from YPP."

"Ah, don't let those guys spook you, Mike—they work for us just as much as we work for them! They oversee most of the Government bids and agreements with private companies for exploration, drilling, pipeline and plant construction, you know corporate stuff. As I said, the government here has been trying to establish an independent economy, free from foreign influence, for a while now. In order to pull this off, they heavily subsidize manufacturing. How about a cup of coffee, Mike?"

"Sure, Ed, sounds good."

The two stopped at a sidewalk café and pastry shop on a nearby corner. Ed ordered a coffee and a small cookie creation known as *"alfajores."* Mike just had a cup of tea.

"So these guys from the government who oversee foreign oil contacts, the YPP, do they hold other government positions? Why the uniforms?"

"Oh, you'll start getting used to the uniformed folks, Mike. Lots of military and police in uniforms here—good government jobs as I understand. This place has a long history of political disagreements and power struggles among different factions—I mean labor and trade unions, agriculture workers, Marxist, socialists, communists, you name it! Heck, even the Catholic Church gets involved here. It's quite a place, Mike. Hey, didn't corporate NAPEC officials fill you in on the economic, social, and political history of this place before this assignment with PEPÉ?"

Ed continued, *"Here is what I understand, Mike—the political system here operates more socialistically in many ways. I mean, there's been a big push to nationalize a lot of their institutions like health care, education, banking, even some housing. I guess a lot of people here benefit from some of this. I know the military does, and with the strong labor unions, it seems like most middle class folks do alright, too."*

"Their former President, Perón, had a lot to do with what has gone on here after the war. I guess he got really ambitious in his push for economic independence but couldn't get it all done. The hope was that the national economy would not be so dependent on foreign trade. The country essentially subsidized the majority of this growth in hope of long-term benefits. As one could figure, the bill for all that spending would someday come due."

"Anyway, they ran Perón out of office, and the country, when he couldn't mandate or force through some of his big ideas." You should really try one of these alfajores, Mike."

"No thanks, Ed. So the contract PEPÉ has with this Yacimientos Petrolíferos Fiscales—how long do you think we'll assist in operations here?"

"Listen, Mike, I've been here a little over two years, working with the Mendoza project. The output at that plant has been positive, and expansion seems palpable, but international politics and PEPÉ contract work, heck, I don't know...

"Just do your job here, Mike, and fulfill your work-related duties, enjoy the city life when you can, and heck, you'll only be here on six month assignments—and save those pesos!"

Chapter Two

Next morning, around 9:00 AM, Ed met Staten at the PEPÉ operation plant and warehouse. He was introduced to Warehouse Manager "Big Ted" Thompson. Ted stood about six foot four inches tall and looked to weigh about 220 pounds. He wore a blue, front zip jump suit, which covered his khaki colored trousers and a long sleeve checked button down shirt. A pair of steeled toe black ankle high boots was exposed at the base of his jumpsuit as he walked with a confident gait toward Mike and Ed.

"Good morning, gentleman!" Ted proceeded to briefly shake their hands with a firm, large-mitted, callused grip.

"You must be Michael Staten from Texas. That's my home state as well—Abilene—allow me to show you part of the operations here."

Ed and Staten followed Ted through an aisle or two of pallet secured, industrial silver painted machinery used in drilling production. Some large, unopened, metal band strapped crates with the NAPEC logo could also be seen. The elevated ceiling and florescent lighted warehouse was clean and organized. A number of jump suit-uniformed male employees maneuvered yellow propane powered forklifts throughout the facility. All union employees were required to wear a uniform and, although Ted worked for PEPÉ, he chose to sport the union wear as well. The smell of the propane and hum of the forklift motors were heard above the tone of Ted's tempered voice. The warehouse, like any such industrial facility, was a beehive of activity, a carefully articulated and orchestrated productive dance between men and machines.

Staten was to begin work in the warehouse the next day on a couple of projects that would most likely take ten to fourteen days to complete. Staten quickly fostered a friendly and productive relationship with Ted Thompson. The two men collaborated on warehouse assembly projects, and they frequently worked together on PEPÉ procedural paper work in the adjacent office complex.

On Thursday afternoon, during a break, Ted suggested that he and Staten catch a bite for supper at one of Ted's favorite dining spots, not far from the warehouse. Ted also invited a local Argentine forklift operator by the name of Jose' to join them. Staten was pleased to have been included and accepted the invitation. At 7:45 that evening, the three men walked about three blocks to an outdoor café called "Carne Asada de Pablo Pascualo" [Pablo Pascualo's grilled steak].They sat under a shaded overhang where they enjoyed some refreshing local beverages of beer and wine. The men each ordered Pascualo's feature item, a large, perfectly seasoned cut of the tenderest steak which had ever assaulted Staten's taste buds.

"Well, Mike, how you liking Buenos Aires?"

"To tell you the truth, Ted, I haven't had much time to see the place—been fairly busy with PEPÉ work duties."

"You should get to the coastal vacation spots, Mike—the beach resorts at Mar Del Plata are really something to experience. And there is much culture in and around the city; museums, concert halls, movie theaters showing both American and Argentine films, and of course, horse racing. Ah, do you bet the ponies, Mike?"

"I have a couple of times back home."

"Well, we'll have to go Mike, yes…the Hipódromo de San Isidro; we can catch a few races. What do you say?"

"Count me in, Ted."

Easy-going, non-work related banter continued. For the first time in days, Mike began to relax, began to feel comfortable with his surroundings.

"Not been to a football match yet, Mike?"

"No Jose' not yet...but I'm most excited to."

"Well, how about next Saturday, there's a good matchup between San Lorenzo de Almagro and River Plate at El Monumental de Nuñez [River Plate Stadium] at 2:00 PM. I'll take my two boys, what ya say?"

"Well, yeah, that sounds great. How old are your boys?"

"Julio is 11 and Carlos is 8. They both play."

"Well, it could be helpful to see soccer with someone who understands strategy better than I; football in the states is a different game, you know."

"Yeah, you guys wear helmets and kick the ball over goal, rather than in goal."

"Well, if you ever come to the U.S., Jose', I'll take you to a Michigan vs. Ohio State Game—now that's something to see."

Conversation among the three covered a variety of subjects from warehouse operations to local economics and politics. Ted offered some insight on the contrast between universities here and those in the states.

"No tuition here, Mike, and nearly 80,000 students attend the university; most are part-time and take classes after 5 p.m.—due to work obligations. Students are also very politically active."

Ted also noted that Buenos Aires, although best known for its urbane culture and modern cosmopolitan lifestyle, also had its share of slum areas and degrading vices.

"Be careful where you venture beyond the major business district, Mike! Stay clear of what locals refer to as 'villa miseria' [slum town]."

"Yeah, Mike, lots of thieves and drug dealers. Stay clear, amigo."

The following Saturday morning, Jose' picked up Staten in a 1959 Kaiser "Carabela." The four door allowed Staten to sit up front with Jose' with his two boys Julio and Carlos sitting in back.

"Morning, Mike, the boys are pretty excited about the game. I wish it was as easy getting them up and going on a school day."

"I'm looking forward to the game Jose'. Hey, guys! Your Papa tells me you're pretty good soccer players."

Julio looked at his brother while fidgeting with the window handle, giggled, and said, *"Yeah, I scored two goals last game, but we lost. Carlos plays goalie."*

"Well, I'm counting on you two to help me understand soccer strategy at today's game. Do you think you can assist?" The boys laughed and began rustling with each other. Jose' then interceded, "Hey! That's enough, boys; cool it or no 'helado' [ice cream treat] at the game."

"For most games we take the bus to the Belgrano district and walk from the Barrancas de Belgrano [transportation hub], so this is a treat for the boys. But driving has advantages, and there's usually plenty of parking outside the stadium, and we're getting there pretty early. You're going to enjoy this Mike— the game's supposed to be a near sell out."

From the car window on the way to the stadium, Staten noticed what appeared to be an extremely run-down neighborhood. The streets were unpaved and lined with rows of shacks made of scrap tin and wood.

"What is that area there, Jose'?"

"Villa miseria ! The slums I mentioned to you earlier, Mike. Not a great area to visit or get stranded after dark."

"Right in the middle of the city, Jose'?"

"Yeah, certain sections, not so good Mike." *We'll be past them soon enough. There are many in Mendoza too, Mike. Stay clear when you travel there. Many in these "asentamientos" [settlements] are migrants or locals—never able to improve themselves. Sad thing is the children, Mike; they often never escape here."*

Carlos and Julio, stirring in the back seat announced, *"El Monumental de Nuñez Stadium! San Lorenzo de Almagro vs. River Plate."*

Jose' continued. "Quite a sight, wouldn't ya say, Mike? It's considered the national stadium of Argentina."

~ * ~

The arena was quite large, with open seating in a bowl similar to the stadium at Michigan.

Jose' and the boys witnessed an entertaining game won by the home team three to one. What most captured Staten's attention was the animated energy from the play on the field and the rambunctious fans. During the contest, Carlos explained the conditions for a penalty kick, and throughout the game, Julio went on about the exceptional play of a star defensive player. Jose' and Mike enjoyed "choripan" and a soda. The boys had fried "empanadas" and "*milanesas*," and spilled "*helado*" [ice cream] on their shirts. Finally, near the game's end, in the hazy glow of the late afternoon sun, they tired.

While gazing across the vast open stadium, Staten's thoughts drifted. Visions of ancient Roman "bread and circuses" spectacle entertaining the masses to satisfy and potentially divert civil unrest occupied his thoughts.

Before leaving the River Plate stadium parking area, Jose' took a peek underneath the Carabela, then turned to Staten with a grin.

"*Another reason to continue our work in Mendoza*"—and proceeded to open the hood to add a liter of oil he retrieved from the trunk. "*This buggy leaks oil like a sieve, Mike.*" *Ah, I guess I'm still a grasas.*"

"*What's that, Jose'?*"

"'*Greased', Mike, workers with grease on their hands and fingernails.*"

During the drive home, Jose' spoke of the wages, benefits, and advantages of being a union member in the General Conference of Labour [CGT]. He expressed overall support of government influence on social and economic life.

"*Before the Perónists' ambitions, many workers had few rights and were treated badly. My grandparents were often treated as servants. The rich owners would call the industrial workers by racial slurs like 'cabecitasnegras' [little black heads]. "I remember Papa fighting a man for referring to him as 'descamisados' [un-shirted]. We now live much better, Mike. The National Mortgage Bank helped me buy a house and my family has health care at hospital. My wife Carmen is going for Nursing at the tuition free university. Carlos and Julio go to good schools near our house. Really, I can't complain.*"

Staten gathered from conversation with Jose' that former President Perón was more of a "dictator" than President, at least. As Staten understood it, Perón had as many detractors as followers. The Catholic Church also appeared to hold strong political and historical influence with government policies.

Staten began to get a clearer picture of some of the peculiar institutions and conditions in this country, but many things remained unclear to his conservative American sensibility.

Chapter Three

At the beginning of his fourth week on assignment, Staten was relocated out of his apartment in the Capital. He was to assist in the supervision and installment of complicated pump and transfer engineering equipment at the oil refinery facility in Mendoza. Staten traveled the approximately 500 miles from Buenos Aires to Mendoza on a DC-3 aircraft operated by Aerolíneas Argentinas. The airport in Mendoza was not necessarily designed to accommodate such an aircraft, as the plane roughly landed alarmingly shy of the runway's end.

The PEPÉ sponsored housing accommodations also proved a bit sparse, obviously intended as a place to simply work and sleep. Days were busy and, except for Michael's occasional difficulties understanding and communicating with some of the Argentine workers [Staten did not speak Spanish], the installation process was progressing within outlined design frames. While on location there, Staten visited operations at the Valle Grande hydroelectric dam near San Rafael, and enjoyed a number of tastefully prepared delicious Argentine meals accompanied by a sampling of wonderful wines from local vineyards.

~ * ~

The engineering aspect of the project was on task and Staten was scheduled to return to his apartment in Buenos Aires for an extended time before returning to Mendoza. He again was to take a lead role in equipment assembly at the warehouse. Additional industrial hydraulic expansion materials were expected within 14 days from NAPEC's California manufacturing plant through PEPÉ's distribution center in Mesquite, Texas. Upon its arrival, he would supervise and assist assembling oil transfer pumps and mechanized power components on large NAPEC surge process regulators. The fully assembled equipment would then be prepared for shipping, by rail, from Buenos Aires to the refinery in Mendoza. Happily, this meant Staten's days would allow him, for the first time, some real opportunity to explore his surroundings in this dynamic and interesting Capital city. He was also looking forward to working again with Ted Thompson. Michael certainly caught a passion for horse racing, and he was very much looking forward to going to the races.

~ * ~

Saturday of the first week back in the city, Staten and Ted went to the Hipódromo track to take in the ten races scheduled for the afternoon and early evening. With post time nearing, and while scanning his betting cards, Staten casually watched the parade of horses walk by the railing. Each was accompanied by a horse trainer who methodically walked the horse past the gallery of patrons making their race selections.

One particular female trainer immediately caught his attention. She was outfitted in traditional jockey attire: knee high polished boots, pink-colored silk blouse, and tan riding helmet. Next to her strutted a sinewy glistening specimen of a filly named "*Bastante Trotón*" [pretty trotter] who was featured in the fifth race.

As Staten studied the filly's smooth gait, the attractive trainer looked directly in his eyes and stared for more than a comfortable moment then smiled broadly and continued forward. Staten was blushed and taken, captivated, by her classic facial features, petite frame, large olive shaped sparkling moist brown eyes, and copper complexion. Staten circled "*Bastante Trotón*" on his betting card

141

as his eyes traced each stride of the sinewy filly back into the starting staging area.

The fifth race's favorite, "*Bastante Trotón*," ran away from the field, winning by four lengths as expected, but as the favorite, paid only marginal returns. Overall, the race day proved fruitful for both Staten and Ted, for they both came out ahead in a number of ways.

The NAPEC California shipping order came in during the next week as planned, and the assembling warehouse work was going well. In another week, Staten was scheduled to return to Mendoza where his mechanical engineering skills were once again required.

On the last weekend before his Mendoza assignment, Staten was invited by Operation Manager, Edward Kenny, and his wife to attend a play. The production was to be performed by local artists, supported in part, by PEPÉ and a Buenos Aires theatre company. Staten cordially accepted and was to travel with the Kennys to Rosaria for the theatrical performance, about an hour away.

The play was an adaptation of on a novel, *Don Segundo Sombra,* written by an Argentine author named Ricado Güiraldes. Colorful costumes, elaborate set designs, and festive music made the performance quite entertaining. The story was about the life of a boy who becomes a man through the experiences of gaucho life. The spoken dialogue, all in Spanish, captured Staten's attention as he was able to comprehend meaning primarily based on facial expression, tonality, and action.

During one of the final scenes, a *gaucho dance* was performed in rhythms by six flamboyant costumed couples. Suddenly, there, twirling about in an "*Andalusian*" styled, multi layered purple and gold "*trajes de faraleas*" [flamboyant Flamenco dress], was the girl from the Hipódromo race track.

Staten was convinced. Yes, he was certain it was her. Dressed in the traditional countryside skirt, flowing dark brown hair and those olive shaped moist eyes… There was no doubt. It was her!

She certainly didn't recognize him [yet]. Staten was determined to locate her after the performance. He was not quite sure what he was going to say. But he was certain… certain he was going to…speak?

He sat nervously through the final scene, thinking *I'll just excuse myself from the Kennys and say I'm…No, I'll let Ed know I must…oh; um…I'm going to wait near the stage door until she, or the dancers…*

During the curtain call, after the main actors took their bows, Staten applauded then, as the house lights glowed, stood with the Kennys and shuffled to the lobby.

"*How did you enjoy the show, Michael?*" asked Mrs. Kenny.

"*Oh, it was simply wonderful,*" said Staten, then nervously. "*I believe I may know someone in the performance, I mean, I've seen one of the dancers in the city, I mean I think one of the dancers works at the race track.*"

"*What was that Michael—you know one of the actors? Ed! Michael knows one of the actors. Now, how can that be? Have you seen another performance by this company?*"

"*No…I…mean…well, I just think I may have seen one of the dancers before, that's all…excuse me, Mrs. Kenny, I'll be back in a few minutes.*"

Staten could barely collect himself as he walked toward what he believed were the restrooms. A tall man in a fine fitting black suit and hat brushed against him. He then noticed a short hallway where colorfully dressed costumed actors were gathered, chatting and talking in enthusiastic tones only they could understand. A flash of shiny purple material, a twist and turn, and suddenly…there she was!

Staten panicked. Then, after momentary paralysis, he abruptly turned away and clumsily struck the wall smartly with his shoulder. Turning again, he caught a glimpse of her and her of him. She hesitantly glanced downward, and then…locked her eyes upon him. Staten began to move cautiously in her direction. She briefly smiled, while slightly tilting her head, and returned toward her party.

"Umm...Pardón...Hello, Excuse me, Senorita! Hello. I'm...I...think I've seen you before? At...ah...the Hipódromo race track? Yes? No? Si'?"

She giggled ever so slightly, then said softly in an orchestrated Spanish-layered English voice, *"Yes, I believe we have...I mean, yes I think I've seen you before as well...at Hipódromo."*

"You speak English, then?"

"I believe so, yes."

"I'm so sorry. My name is Michael, Michael Staten, and I really enjoyed the play...and

your dance was just...well...great! I...well, the show was wonderful."

"Yes...well...thank you."

"Do you...I mean...what's your...um...."

"I'm Celeste."

"Well it's a pleasure to meet you, Ms. Celeste. I'm with, I mean...do you have time...Is the show over? I mean, do you have any time...see...I'm here with...the Kennys and well, I was wondering... Do you drink coffee?"

"Yes, I do drink coffee, but not usually after an evening show, thank you."

"Oh...ok then...I'm sorry...I've...."

"It's all right, Yes, I...ah...I have to change and...Oh...Are your friends waiting?"

"No... I mean yes, well...maybe, I'll see what they, I mean...what time, how long until

...um..."

"Oh, most likely fifteen to twenty minutes, but I understand if...if that's too..."

"No, great. I mean, I'll find the Kennys and...fifteen minutes? Great...I'll be standing in the lobby...I'll be...I mean...I'll be here...there."

~ * ~

Michael Staten discovered that Celeste Maria Angelica was a member of the *jóvene sactores de teatro* [young actors theatre] company, part-time over the past couple of years but had danced since childhood. She was taught English by Dominican sisters, having attended Catholic schools through elementary and secondary school. Celeste was a student at University of Buenos Aires, and she also worked with her father at the Hipódromo most weekdays and on special race event weekends.

"Papá is at the track by five AM every day, and he needs my help exercising, washing, and pampering the dozen or so horses in his care. Whether sick or well, rain or shine, Papá has to be there—they are his family."

Having been raised on a farm in Nebraska, Michael related with Celeste's commitment to feeding and caring for animals.

"My folks were essentially dairy farmers, but also tended about 200 acres of corn and soy as well. Dad sold most of the Holstein dairy cows when I went away to university. Dad and Mother mostly concentrate on the farming now, and Dad also sells Allis-Chalmers tractors and Gleaner combines near Grand Island, Nebraska, in a town called Aurora." [Interesting enough, Staten has a black and white glossy photo of his father shaking hands with Nikita Khrushchev—who visited the implement dealership during his 1959 American tour.]

Celeste asked few questions but listened attentively. They talked a bit about horse racing.

Celeste seemed quite interested in the American university. The two pleasantly agreed to meet again, most likely when Michael returned from his two week assignment in Mendoza.

Chapter Four

The Tuesday following his return from Mendoza, Celeste was able to join Michael for lunch. Over bowls of *carbonada* [meat stew, potatoes, and corn] in an open outdoor café, they discussed a variety of subjects including the university and cultural interests. Michael was taken by her passion for the arts and emotional references to social issues.

"As a child, I would dress up and dance for my mother and she would applaud…and say 'Keep dancing my child. Dance engages one's spirit and brings joy to both body and soul.'"

"I really enjoy the tango, but it takes much discipline and rehearsal, especially for theatre performance."

Celeste's impassioned speech led Michael to inquire what she was studying at the university.

"At university, we explore many aspects of the humanities, economic theories, political ideologies, art, and music."

"It's nearly impossible to not be aware and concerned of the political climate while living so near the capital. Although it's been only a dozen or so years since women here gained the vote, we have long been conscious and active."

She continued, *"Like many young girls, I was captured by the style, wealth, and glamour of Eva Perón and aspired to be like her. I was moved by her social works and image of personal commitment to inclusive justice. I dreamed of visiting the Children's Republic [a theme park based on tales from the Brothers Grimm] and wearing fancy clothes. But children grow, and so does their naivety."*

Suddenly, her wrinkled brow erased and her darting eyes eased into a glowing smile. *"Oh, Michael, I apologize; it's just that these things hold importance for me. Let's discuss music; I very much enjoy American swing and jazz music—Harry James, Benny Goodman, Count Basie, Charlie Parker, Sonny Rollins."*

Michael smiled broadly. *"I really like Joe Morello's drum solo on Dave Brubeck's 'Take Five'."*

They talked of the genius and unfortunate habits of Art Pepper and Chet Baker and the role of music in film.

Celeste mentioned how much she enjoyed the Gershwin musical *Funny Face*, particularly the dancing scenes. *"Audrey Hepburn is so very beautiful."*

Michael had not seen the film but knew of Fred Astaire. Stan Kenton's *West Side Story* release was an agreed-upon recent favorite.

Having previously taken a course in Renaissance art, Celeste was currently studying seventeenth century Baroque styles, frescos, and Italian piety works.

"I find the artists elicit so much emotion in their works—the colors, physical and realistic moods, portray feelings in me."

Michael was just remotely familiar with Renaissance or Baroque. He had taken a year of modern art at Michigan, studying Impressionism and Post-Impressionism. *"I genuinely appreciate the works of Gauguin, Van Gogh, and Matisse; but my favorites are Renoir and Degas. Maybe Degas' paintings of dancers remind me of you?"*

Celeste smiled and blushed ever so slightly. *"I like some of Picasso. We studied the "Guernica" in history class during secondary school. I also find Salvador Dali intriguing, but sometimes disturbing—although that may be his intention."*

The two shared some *Alfajores de Maizena* [corn starch cookies] and coffee.

The nature of their interaction and conversation was delightful—neither wished to depart. However, Michael needed to return to the warehouse and Celeste had a scheduled university class.

"It would be wonderful if we could meet again. How about next Thursday after my evening class? I can introduce you to some of my university friends."

Michael amicably agreed. Celeste suggested a favorite *confiterías* [café] near the university.

~ * ~

Back at the warehouse for a few days, Michael Staten had to put his engineering skills to an important test. It seemed the sewer system became plugged—he and Big Ted fashioned a primitive spinning rooter-like device and cleaned the pipes. *"I wonder if we should try to patent this thing?"* asked Michael. Said Big Ted, *"I think it was already done about ten years ago. One of the greatest inventions ever! But who knows who holds the patent in Argentina!"*

Argentines and Americans cheered alike when the prototype rooter cleansed the pipes—and commerce could flow again! *The Work Stoppage abated!*

Chapter Five

On Thursday evening, as Michael arrived at the café, he could see Celeste waving from a table on the patio.

"I'm so glad you are here Michael! Were my directions clear?"

"Yes, exact. Very good to see you again, Celeste."

"Please meet my friends Gina Esteban and Eduardo Miranda."

Gina, wearing a multi-patterned blouse, cotton skirt and huarache sandals, greeted Michael. *"Hello, so good to meet you."*

"And you as well, Gina."

Eduardo stood briefly while aggressively shaking Michael's hand. *"Michael the American—yes, Celeste tells us you are a petro engineer."*

The three had been drinking coffee, and Michael ordered one as well.

Eduardo was a thin, nervous, chain smoker wearing a snug fitting long sleeve open collared shirt and straggly goatee. He was quite animated and expressed passionate commitment in his speech. Gina had short dark brown hair with a petite boyish figure. When she spoke, she looked directly in the eyes of the person she was addressing. And when contemplating a point, she would run her slim fingers around the brim of her coffee cup.

"So, Celeste tells me you're quite fond of nineteenth century impressionism?"

"Well, I became a bit familiar with some artists. I mean yes, Gina, I studied just a year of modern art while a student at the university."

Gina commented, *"Yes, I find the cubist movement essential, foundationally, in popularizing still life at the time."*

Michael, fidgeting for something to say…*"Well, yes of, course, many of Cezanne's landscapes contained elements of cubism, which certainly influenced the early twentieth century work of Picasso and Braque."*

Eduardo entered the conversation. *"I find the stark, longing, emotional moods of American realist Edward Hopper powerful. His canvas subjects provide a sense of displaced opportunities, particularly urban loneliness, longing, and failure."*

"Um," Michael responded, *"I'm familiar with some of his work. I remember seeing a rural farmhouse drawing of his…. It looked a lot like Crete, Nebraska. "*

"Michael, are you at all familiar with Caste paintings?"

"No, Eduardo, I've never heard the term. To what does it refer?"

"Well, you're familiar with the Caste system of social hierarchy?"

Michael replied, *"Yes, India comes to mind."*

Eduardo continued, *"Well, caste paintings depict the realities of people living within one caste or another. They are artistic reflections of where people stand, socially. The artists attempt to capture life in a restrictive system that excludes people based on birth, wealth, occupation or other discriminatory repression. The artwork is emotionally very powerful."*

The conversation continued with topics involving social and economic issues. The foursome discussed political ideologies—how governments often set agendas, make promises, and under deliver. Over the course of their conversation, Michael learned of the students' seeming distrust for certain government action. Celeste did not express full agreement with former President Perón's "Perónismo" Justicialist party, referencing many noted social justice accomplishments with suspicion.

Celeste: *In some ways, the Peróns provided workers a set of non-sustainable delusional dreams which could not be fulfilled.*

Michael: *Well, isn't that true of most political leaders' agendas? I mean, our current President made many campaign promises proposing quick economic growth, rehabilitation of depressed areas, improvements in urban housing and development, reforming tax legislation.*

My folks heard promises of revisions to the farm programs which would immediately affect their situation. His administration is also considering major efforts in conserving national resources, expanding aid to education, funding better medical care for the aged...and even sending a man to the moon! Those are pretty ambitious promises.

Gina: *Perón's efforts had made some progress in advancing social justice but with much compromise and sacrifice of individual freedom. He had intolerance for most party opposition, using tactics which deprived media access and alternative voices. His defensive practices led to distrust and dismissal of many good people and fertile ideas. Open expression for many was limited by a kind of disguised repression.*

Eduardo: *Through control of public media, they exploited the ideals and possibilities of social justice to a large number of people and profited most by making labor's cause, their cause.*

Michael could only reflect on their words, recalling his study of Machiavelli's *The Prince*, but thought better than to become deeply involved in their heated discoursive utterances. [Machiavelli wrote in a time of great political upheaval but understood human nature, particularly a leader's common virtues and vices.]

Gina: *The Perónists captured the public's consciousness—which was a good thing. However, their actions often served to limit, rather than expand, freedoms; to suppress rather than foster, and to mandate rather than manifest true social justice. Why, even your American civil rights Socialist, A. Phillip Randolph, understands true social, civil, and economic equality can only be achieved when the humblest share the same rights as the privileged.*

Michael: *Is anyone getting hungry? I could use a little something.*

Celeste suggested they order a few plates of *picadas* [small dishes of cheese, mussels, salami, anchovies, olives and peanuts].

As their order arrived, Eduardo continued, between aggressive drags on his cigarette, some rant about the nationalization of production and labor rights. "*Redistribution of wealth—controlling production, isolationism under the spell of economic independence—self-production of economy goods and services designed to intoxicate the masses—perpetuating a contented 'middle class' existing on government dependency empowered for disempowerment!*"

Staten considered their views—considered the American writers Sinclair Lewis, the naturalist Frank Norris, and John Steinbeck.

He knew there was truth in what they said, but his experiences with class struggle, and the bitter naturalism they so freely discussed had been restricted to literature and art. Gina talked about Che Guevara, and the young Senor Castro in Cuba—her views, like Eduardo's, were tinged with militaristic anger. Michael remained silent for quite a while and listened to the students' discussion.

Celeste was convinced the government was becoming fearful of the new opposition, particularly the likes of university professors, artists, publishers, film makers, musicians, and actors—while Gina and Eduardo spoke of their university study experience and how it affects the way they interpret the world.

Michael sensed their heightened consciousness had a strong potential for actions; change seemed hastened by the forces around them. He thought of his experience at Michigan, considering it more as a place buffered from the day-to-day realities of the world. He certainly understood the correlation between activism and change, but found little time during his studies there for political activism.

Conversation among the students turned to university study. The liberal arts were discussed in terms of the values and virtues prized by Western civilization.

Eduardo embraced "liberating" education as the only suitable approach for a free person. He went on, citing an ancient authority's vision of the "virtuous" citizen as one dedicated to the welfare of the commonwealth, and not of self-interest.

Gina cautioned Eduardo's use of the term virtuous, noting the Latin *vir*, meaning "virility" or "man."

Gina, playfully smirking, *"Eduardo…you may consider reviewing Augustine's Confessions?"*

"Ah, think of me as the rebellious African Augustine…not yet of Platonic virtue!"

Heard at a nearby table was a bearded muse strumming a well-worn acoustic guitar; while vocalizing in a whiney tone.

"Berenjena, planta y fruto…negras…estruja…
Alpargatassí, libros no…excomulgar…"

"What is he singing about?" Michael inquired.

After a long pause, Eduardo began, *"La Nueva Canción. It's Chilean folk music. He's singing about labor and racism, anti-university…'like a garden eggplant, plump and dark…content and ripe for squashing…shoes…not books.' He's commenting on Perón's ex-communication from the church…and social justice issues."*

Gina provided insight on the nature of the social/political intent of the musical voice and the specifics of his verse. *"Perón opposed universities and professors for questioning his methods and goals. Class struggles between students and Perónist workers created much distrust and anger. Perón was excommunicated from the Catholic Church, prior to his ousting and exile. He legalized divorce and prostitution. After Eva's death, he maintained relations with a thirteen year-old child."*

Celeste's eyes burned like dim coals, but she said little for a while.

Staten wondered about her politics, her philosophy, her weltanschauung, but he spent most of the evening listening to Eduardo and Gina debate the meanings of communism, the International Workers of the World, Marxism, and socialism in South America.

He and Celeste gazed at each other and smiled while the other two Comrades maintained an animated conversation.

Satiated with political talk but satisfied with the new friendships and the social good feeling that came out of the evening, Staten bid the group adieu about 11:30 PM. His heart was beating with a new awareness—but the new awareness had nothing to do with Che Guevara or *The Grapes of Wrath*.

Chapter Six

Staten acquired symphony tickets for the *Teatro Colón* through Ed Kenny. The *Teatro Colón* was located along the city's northern outskirts, on Corrientes Avenue, and would be easier to reach by automobile from his south side location. Jose' agreed to lend Staten his Kaiser Carabela. *"Make sure to check the oil; there's a liter in the trunk."*

Celeste was excited to hear the scheduled classical compositions by composer Gilardo Gilardi. Staten also secured dinner reservations at Los Mariposa two hours before the show's 9:00 PM start.

A handsome waiter dressed all in black [except for a white tie and carrying a wolf-headed cane] seated Celeste and Michael. The Los Mariposa restaurant's menu was exquisite, and the ambiance was more than delightful. An open airy high ceiling with ornately capped cornices framed the dining area. The walls were colored with bright lively tones of blue and pink—and accented with a colorful flowered frieze.

The aroma of garlic, olive oil, and fresh stewed vegetables permeated the evening air as plates of meats, pastas, and breads were presented at nearby tables. The butterfly winged *Cena* (dinner) menu was written in a beautifully cursive Spanish calligraphy. Michael, with an impressionable style, ordered the wine, a Mendoza vineyard label he had enjoyed, on occasion, during his recent stay

154

there. Celeste suggested *parrillada* [a mixed grill of steak and other cuts of beef] as the main course.

Delicious hard-crusted warm fresh bread was served with vegetable soup prior to the prized *parrillada*. Michael expressed how much he enjoyed the loaf's rich texture and flavor. He easily became comfortable sopping the bread in soup. Celeste offered a toast which she had heard often as a child. *"May those who eat be bread for others, may those who drink pour out their love... Salute."*

Over supper, Celeste shared some personal family history.

Chapter Seven

The Fisher King

He's the fisher king—What did he bring?
He brought us rain and things from tomorrow
She's the Runza Girl
With the string of pearls
And all her Valentines are still with us
It's the peace of the heart we had for a time
It's the Holy Grail we seek but don't find
Under the street lamps
I hear them both play
He's the tractor man
With the coffee can
He brought us golden bricks back at Christmas
She's the Runza girl
With the string of pearls
And all her Valentines are still with us
It's the peace of the heart we had for a time
It's the Holy Grail we seek but don't find—
Under the street lamps
I hear them both play

(Jack Frost, circa 1994)

Celeste's grandparents, Sebastian Dominick and Maria Theresa Pelligrino, were of Italian decent. Sebastian was a wheat farmer who worked for a family of *estancieros*, or ranchers, near Rosaria. The aristocratic ranchers, the Del Monico family, also had a house in Buenos Aires with business and family connections there.

Maria and Sebastian had three children, two boys and a girl, Bernadette Rachel. The two boys aided Sebastian in the labor of the land, while Bernadette assisted her mother in tending farmhand chores and domestic duties.

Maria made certain Bernadette was baptized Catholic, regularly attended Mass, studied scripture teachings, and embraced spirituality through prayer. Maria also established, in her daughter, an independent and strong willed approach to life. She supported her daughter's dreams and comforted her in failings and disappointments. *"Pray my child, for strength and perseverance and—Never Quit! Never Yield! And Never Give Up!"*

Wheat was a precious grain for the Pellegrinos, and Mother Maria would often describe the spiritual aspects of the grain's life-giving qualities. In a beautiful and soothing Italian voice, she would proclaim the essence of God's choice of bread as a symbol of life.

"Each grain holds a spiritual importance—providing living proof of the Lord's unending love and promise of eternal life. Especially precious is the wheat's germ, for it contains the embryo which provides bread with life giving oils."

She often quoted Genesis 18:6, and Genesis 43:11, adding, *"Wheat has provided the people of the Holy Land staple food for over 4,000 years, and we are blessed to be called as 'Stewards' of its harvest."*

Bernadette would assist her mother as she ground the whole wheat, by hand, into flour. While kneading the dough, Mother Maria would often quote Romans 11:16: *"A whole batch of bread is made holy if the first handful of dough is made holy."* Bread making was one of the most cherished memories Bernadette maintained from her childhood. The preparation of wheat flour and its transformation into an edible loaf of life remained, for her, a fulfilling memory of her Mother and Father.

Celeste's mother, Bernadette, married Miguel Philippe Angelica, an estate rancher who managed grazing land and tended horse stables for the Del Monico family racehorse operations in Buenos Aries. Miguel was of Spanish descent. His family had immigrated to Argentina during the early part of the twentieth century. The two were married in St. Vincent Cathedral, Rosaria. The service was presided over by Miguel's cousin, Fr. John Bolléot, S.J.

Bernadette and Miguel made the transition to the urban center located in greater Buenos Aires after Miguel assumed a more full-time role managing the Del Monico stables near the Hipódromo racetrack.

Bernadette soon discovered that, in Buenos Aires, a substantial gap existed between the burgeoning and cosmopolitan scene and the more remote interior, rural existence of small independent farmers. She sensed the natural rivalry present between middle and lower classes as well as the struggle between agricultural and industrial interests.

The increasing societal distrust between labor and military interests also contributed to a contentious political environment.

Celeste Marie Angelica was born in 1942 during the onset of substantial social and economic reform in Argentina. Her parents, Bernadette and Miguel, had lost a previous child at birth. Complications while carrying Celeste ended Bernadette's ability to have additional children. Celeste became their coveted and beloved *niño de la esperanza* [child of hope].
Bernadette and Miguel raised their daughter, Celeste, with the same love and committed passion as their own parents had raised them. Celeste's memories of her grandmother Maria were limited, Maria having passed away before Celeste reached the age of three. However, Bernadette made certain she embellished the memories of her mother's impassioned traditions to her daughter, Celeste, by often repeating the lessons she so cherished.

~ * ~

The well-appointed meal and pleasant ambiance accentuated Celeste's heartfelt persona. The elegant Colón theatre further enhanced the couple's evening. Warmth and emotion-filled orchestra compositions included sonatas and the esteemed Misa de Gloria. Gilardi's symphonic poem, *Gaucho con botas nuevas,* proved both moving and hypnotic.

~ * ~

Staten was scheduled for work in Mendoza over the next twelve days. While there, he visited the century-old *Escorihuela* winery in the *Godoy Cruz* district. A PEPÉ official and several YPP representatives included Staten in a dinner party at the famed 1884 Restaurant. Conversations focused mainly around the oil-drilling project; however, some references to corporate motives and transformational government did surface. Staten came away with a clearer view that understanding democracy demands a good amount of patience. And, although he did not consider himself political, he sensed that repetition in political discourse was painfully essential for convincing or persuading international understanding.

The dinner with the PEPÉ and YPP officials was quite in contrast to a barbeque he had with some local oil operation workers in Mendoza. The worker's conversations included oil drilling conditions and project schedules. But more often, talk referenced spouses, children, and sports. Besides polo, soccer, and horse racing, Staten learned about a sport called *Pato* (horse ball) where horse riders fight to grab a leather "duck" and place it in a basket net. The aim was to score the largest number of goals by letting the duck go through the opponents´ ring.

The meal menu with the workers was very much different from that offered at the 1884 Restaurant. Something called *asado con cuero* [whole beef roasted complete with hide and hair] was served. Staten chose not to partake; rather, he opted for a bowl of the local *carbonlia* [chili]. Although accustomed to Texas style hot seasoning, Staten's culinary indiscretion resulted in an immediate unquenchable and non-extinguishable thirst, and then considerable subsequent intestinal discomfort. [Sidebar: It was HOT!]

Chapter Eight

One Saturday afternoon in nearby San Telmo, Celeste and Michael spent a good part of the day enjoying the pleasant weather. While strolling along the cobblestone streets, past museums and antique shops in Dorrego Square, Celeste led Michael into a cathedral.

Opening one of the two ornate and substantial weighty doors, they were met by a cool and airy indoor breeze. The marble floor, majestic stain glass, and daunting archways intimidated Michael. Celeste genuflected upon entering the church's main aisle, and Michael did the same. A distinct clicking sound from their footsteps echoed slightly throughout the vast marble chamber. No words were spoken, whispered, or murmured. Michael proceeded cautiously beside Celeste.

He had only been in a Catholic church a couple of times before—once as a child when an uncle had passed away, but that was a small country chapel, nothing quite like this. And for the marriage of Gerald and Debbie, friends from Michigan, but that was at the St. Mary student parish in the University Newman Center.

The Cathedral had two main aisles and what appeared to be a smaller chapel to the right, down a short corridor. Walls in a central hallway were decorated with painted frescoes, depicting some biblical scenes and colored

160

mosaics. Kneeling near the back row pew, Michael observed four darkly-covered elderly women, with clattering rosary beads, devoted in prayer.

Celeste knelt piously, directly adjacent to the immense front alter, beneath a flickering table of dimly lit amber candles. Michael sat quietly in a narrow aisle pew. The smell within the church reminded Michael of old dry varnished furniture, like that found in a neighbor's shed in the heat of summer, or Grandma Staten's upstairs dining room.

About twenty minutes passed before Celeste raised her head, made the sign of the cross, and joined Michael in the pew. It was there in near-silent piety that Celeste, with tear-filled eyes, spoke passionately of her mother.

"Mother Bernadette believed that some efforts to reduce poverty and dignify labor by the Perónists had merit. She regarded Evita's work with the ill, orphans and elderly, and women's suffrage as small incremental steps. Mother's prayer intentions after the Plaza de Mayo incident focused on peace. However, Perón's actions troubled her deeply—she prayed for his reconciliation."

"Shortly following the June sixteenth, 1955 bombing, the St. Michael church was ransacked and fire-bombed by violent Perónist supporters.

"Mother Bernadette died while praying a (novena) in a small basilica there."

"Madre remains an emotionally powerful force in my life. Love and friendship unite our souls. Death cannot tear this union apart. The wounds of grief shall heal."

"I have found comfort in Augustine the philosopher and Saint: 'My love is also my weight'...Mother Bernadette's heart sought and found its eternal place of rest...my hope honors her through prayer."

[As Michael comforted an emotional Celeste, a dark-robed elderly priest appeared just to their left near three vacant confessionals. He spoke not a word as he shuffled silently through a narrow vestibule passage.]

After exiting the cathedral, Celeste and Michael walked slowly hand-in-hand down the crowded cobblestone street.

Their silently-traveled steps manifested a deep epiphanic consciousness within Michael. He became overwhelmed by this whispered truth:

"A Mother is truly the soul of society."

The year of her mother's death, 1955, Celeste was thirteen—the same age as the young girl with whom Perón was said to have relations. Michael understood Celeste's mother's thoughts and concerns for her own daughter—and the social justice causes that would confront her.

After a block or so, Celeste casually noted, *"Most summer weekends these streets are filled with performers, including tango dancers."*

"Have you ever danced here, Celeste?"

"No, Michael, not yet anyway." Her eyes once again offered a smile.

"And many plays and musical festivals are performed in this area, Michael. It's one of the oldest neighborhoods of Buenos Aires."

Crossing the street, Michael noticed what looked to be a "poster art" painting by Henri de Toulouse-Lautrec. It turned out to be advertisement for an upcoming theatrical performance on the main square. Celeste and Michael took to a bench in an adjacent grassy area where children played soccer. A local parish priest was officiating the playful match.

[They noticed, on the opposite end of the field, an older gentleman feeding pigeons. The man departed abruptly upon their arrival, nervously walking away, with what appeared to be a white duck on a leash.]

"My mother often quoted scripture to me," said Celeste. *"I remember her reverence to children: 'Let the little children come to me; do not stop them, for it is such as these that the kingdom of God belongs' (Mk. 10:13-16). We can certainly learn from children…imitate them in their innocence and listen to their simple wisdom. The Irish author, Elizabeth Bowen once said, 'Children are God's spies.' Do you believe that Michael?"*

Staten remained silent.

As the game ended and the children scattered, the priest tethered the soccer ball to a basket on the front of his bicycle and departed.

Uncharacteristically, Michael cleverly stated, *"Well there goes Pedro, the preeminent Papal peddling Priest."*

After a buttery pause, Celeste broke into long and sustained laughter, causing her moist eyes to flood with joy. Finally, after an extended deep breath, she placed her head on Michael's shoulder and kissed his cheek.

["The human mind plans the way, but the Lord directs the steps." Proverbs 16:9]

Chapter Nine

Staten's Pan Am Airlines flight left International Ezeiza Airport on Sunday, October 20, 1963, nearly six months to the day he had arrived. He was scheduled to return to Buenos Aires for another six month assignment after the first of the year. PEPÉ corporate offices in Mesquite, Texas, required Staten receive additional two to three month certification training on new production equipment. This meant he would have the opportunity to spend at least part of the holidays with his folks in Nebraska. He was nervously considering telling his parents about Celeste.

Much of the PEPÉ certification training took place at the corporate office in Mesquite. Most training days involved engineering classroom sessions followed by "hands-on" equipment familiarity.

While engaged in copious note taking and anticipating the extended Thanksgiving Day weekend, Staten was informed of the tragic event that occurred just blocks away. The enormity of that dark Dallas day forever changed both Staten and the world.

~ * ~

During early December, all PEPÉ international business and travel had been suspended indefinitely. And, with the exception of 'essential' correspondence from South and Central American, all PEPÉ operations were terminated. Argentine relations were increasingly dampened by advertent Warren Commission investigation procedures and more discrete "shadow" operatives.

~ * ~

Over the next several months and proceeding year, Michael tried in desperation to reach Celeste. Countless attempts through postal correspondence and long distance telephone messages resulted in dormant, and dominant, silence.

~ * ~

When PEPÉ was restricted from petroleum operations in Central and South America, including major contract work in Argentina, most of its international employee group was reassigned to work in the states. A major reduction in staff placed many former international employees in lower paying positions not always utilizing their professional expertise.

In early 1964, Staten worked with a PEPÉ employed chemical engineer by the name of Benjamin Zuckerman. The needs for chemical engineering research and lab work had been reduced considerably due to international operation closures and demand.

Zuckerman began exploring opportunities in the growing plastics industry. A University of Chicago educated chemist, Zuckerman was both bright and ambitious. Together with another chemist already employed with a plastics firm in Texas, Zuckerman exercised an extreme level of entrepreneur know how and started a company called Z-*Astic*-polymers.

Zuckerman created a recipe list of formulas necessary to making plastics pliable and durable enough to withstand large variations in temperature, as well as adapt to constant temperature alterations. His products also included a soft, moldable, plasticizer C-4 material. Zuckerman soon discovered that fulfilling the variety and number of molds necessary to complete orders required a specific kind of in-house production design component. Knowing Staten's mechanical engineering expertise having worked with him on numerous PEPÉ production models, he asked Staten to join the firm.

Within a short period of time, Staten designed a universal casing mold and hydraulic assembly line equipment capable of accommodating the company's needs. The equipment designed by Staten made possible multiple product runs without having to change the design molds. Three years after beginning the company, Zuckerman and Staten became partners. The company did exceptionally well during the booming plastic needs created in the 1960's and early 1970's.

Staten's infatuation and love of horse racing also flourished during this period, financed in large part by his income earned with *Z-Astic*. He acquired land and ranch facilities in North New Mexico and Nevada which enabled him to board, feed, and train a number of prized racehorses. In 1972, a year before a horse named *Secretariat* stole the hearts of American horse racing, Staten had a horse by the name of D.P. Flyer place at Belmont, at the Preakness, then complete a strong second place finish in the Kentucky Derby.

Dourine Staten

Staten was nearly forty when he decided to marry—more out of convenience than due to a romantic impulse or burning love. A distant friend of his partner's wife introduced him to Dourine Bateman. She was on the "corporate track" as a sales representative, at that time marketing plastic outdoor children's playground equipment. Dourine fulfilled most duties of an executive's wife admirably, and she possessed many of the appropriate accouterments required by her role: ambition, smart business suits, nice hair and nails, an interest in furniture, a taste for fancy restaurants, resorts, dinner parties, first class passage on cruise ships, and a manufactured dedication to charities and fundraisers [and an unthinking and unfeeling support of the husband who subsidized her lifestyle].

The Staten's wedding was a large catered affair, of course, held in an Austin church not far from the university campus. Perry Como sang at the reception, and the Statens took a lovely honeymoon to Sequoia National Park. And then they were a married couple. And the years rolled by.

Chapter Ten
Over Forty Years Later...Rosario, Argentina

Letters were discovered in a vestibule drawer within the sacristy. The narrow veneered vestibule drawer was where altar linens and the priests' vestments were held. Such white daily vestments were typically housed in the third and fourth drawers of the six drawer dresser. Bottom drawers kept special ceremonial chasuble and stoles or second liturgical year garments used for celebrating ecumenical mass or Bishop-attended Benedictions. Deep in the right hand corner of this bottom drawer, three white, somewhat faded envelopes were discovered within the tattered pages of a [1925] copy of José Hernández's "Martin Fierro."

Probably the only reason the book and letters were uncovered at this time was due to Sister Claudia Marie Francisca's insistence on re-folding all Alb vestments in uniformity.

Sister Claudia's initial findings were simply part of her neatness and obsession for organization and cleanliness. She removed the book containing the letters and neatly placed it on the sacristy table landing. Then, after carefully dusting its cover, she arranged it in a similar position among the other green, papal leather-bound volumes of scripture readings often referenced by priests in preparation for daily mass and Sunday sermons. Sister Claudia departed silently, returning to the convent, joining her order to prepare, with the public recitation of the Novena to the Holy Ghost, for the approach of Pentecost.

It was not until Tuesday of the following week when, in preparing for Gospel readings and Sunday's Pentecostal homily, Fr. Francis Tiberio noticed the tip of one letter peering from the seemingly book marked pages of the misplaced copy of "Martin Fierro." Fr. Tiberio removed the first of the three letters, noticing the cursive style displayed a United States mailing address. The other two accompanying letters also displayed similar handwriting and the same U.S.A. address [*624 Plaza Boulevard PEPÉ Corporation, Mesquite, Texas, U.S.A.*].

The letters were addressed to PEPÉ, care of Mr. Michael P. Staten, and the international postage appeared aged on each of the obviously undelivered letters. Fr. Tiberio placed the letters back inside the [1925] copy of the leather bound José Hernández's "Martin Fierro" volume on the counter and completed his Gospel readings and homily preparation.

Nearly an hour had passed before Fr. Tiberio removed himself from the Pentecost Sunday preparation. Besides, he was feeling a bit hungry and knew Isabélla, the rectory's cook, was cooking the noon meal *"milanesa"* [beef dipped in eggs, crumbs, and then fried], one of his favorites. He gathered his preparatory notes, jacket, and the leather bound volume, which contained the letters and shuffled off in anticipation of the noon meal at the rectory.

The smell of *milanesa* permeated the kitchen and the rectory as Fr. Tiberio ambled to his room, placing his notes and the book holding the letters on a small wood desk. He then proceeded to wash up in preparation for lunch. He joined Fr. Gomez Incondella and Monsignor Roberto Pucci at the kitchen dining table.

Weekday lunches were typically served at the kitchen dining table, reserving the more formal rectory dining area for special Sunday and Holy Day gatherings. Dominican prayers were recited as the priests gave heartfelt thanks and appreciation for the food and labor required for preparation and serving this blessed meal.

The three priests were each familiar with the others' habits, and conversations often surrounded parish events and priestly duties. After tasting a few fork fills of the *milanesa*, indicating his satisfaction, Fr. Tiberio mentioned to Monsignor Pucci his discovery of the book and accompanying letters.

Looking over his black-framed glasses, the monsignor paused, indicating a level of confused intrigue, and then requested that Fr. Tiberio bring the book and the letters to the study after lunch.

~ * ~

The letters had been returned as *"undeliverable"*—postmarks dated over a two-year period [January, 1964 through June, 1966]. The following Monday, Monsignor Pucci contacted the Diocese Monsignor Victor Auila who had resided over the parish during the period in question. Monsignor Auila collected the letters and consulted octogenarian Abbot Francis Benedict for counsel. Gazing at length over the handwriting on the letters, the bearded and astute-minded Benedict responded in a whispered, and clearly enlightened, tone.

"For the person whose penmanship marks these notes, charity was not an abstract teaching but the heart and soul of her life. Celeste Angelica remains a beloved niño de la esperanza [child of hope]."

"Celeste came to us shortly after losing her father Miguel. She was an unmarried mother with a two-year old son. Committed to a faith-driven passion, she asked whether the child might reside in the loving care of the parish over a forty-eight hour period. She then handed me a sealed letter requesting that it be opened—if her absence extended beyond the agreed."

"It was June, 1966, one day before a military coup installed Gen. Juan Carlos Onganía president."

~ * ~

In August, 1966, Sister Theresa of the Maryknoll Missionaries arranged adoption measures for the boy with a lay missionary family returning to their home in the U.S.

All the required official adoption procedures were finalized by October. Thaddeus and Elaine Dolly became legal guardians—parents—to the two-year-old boy. The Dollys resided in a small rural community about an hour northwest of St. Paul, Minnesota. Philip grew healthy and strong in a loving upper Midwestern home of fine and deserving parents.

Chapter Eleven

...Conquistador your stallion stands in need of company—and like some angel's haloed brow you reek of purity—I see your armor-plated breast has long since lost its sheen—and in your death mask face there are no signs which can be seen—and though I hoped for something to find I could see no maze to unwind....

"Conquistador" — Brooker/Reid (1967)

Although supposedly "in the works" prior to Dolly's hiring, Michael P. Staten bequeathed five million dollars to the college. The legal transaction transpired within a month of Dolly's hiring. The timing of such a gift enabled the college to build the near gothic and [considered by some] aesthetically pleasing showcase gateway to the Copperfield plant—now under the administration of one Dr. Philip Dolly.

Dolly had benefited almost immediately upon signing his letter of intent for the presidential position at Copperfield. The timing and notoriety of such a large Staten donation made Dolly's arrival appreciably important.

However, well before completion of the building, local dissenters argued publicly about the use of donated funds in constructing such a lavish structure for a "public not-for-profit" educational institution.

[Sidebar: Frankly, the structure looked very much out of place on this otherwise 1960's architecturally structured campus. It did not really fit well with the many clinically constructed concrete buildings, uniform windows, and functional entries.]

The Staten Conference Center entrance doubles as the entry to the administration building, where Dolly has his office. Anyone wishing to visit the president must first enter through this intimidating long hallway and adjacent winding stairwell leading to the reception desk, where his secretary Rebecca sits patiently.

Note of Interest—D.P. Flyer and the Staten Horse Racing Legacy

In conjunction with Copperfield History and Heritage month, Professor Van Dorn assigned her classes an essay topic to explore a historical feature of the college. The assignment required at least two primary resources. A student named Susan Marsh was intrigued by the information plaque located under the bronze horse head near the entrance to the Conference Center. The plaque recognized the donation by Michael P. Staten—primarily resulting from his horse racing interests. The horse head represented his famed Kentucky Derby placing D.P. Flyer.

After some quick traditional and non-traditional research activities, Susan was able to procure electronic photocopies of the following two documents. The first was originally published in the "Official" Derby program. The second was an article included in a 1972 copy of *The Chicago Daily News*.

Ninety-eighth *Running Kentucky Derby—Churchill Downs 1875-1972* ONE MILE and ONE QUARTER
May 6, 1972
D.P. Flyer—Pedigree

Mare—Champion "C. M. Angel"—miler in Argentina
Stallion—Misremembered, "Derby Dolly"—winner of the March 6 1969 Santa Anita H. (G1) at 1 1/4 miles

"C. M. Angel" served as a broodmare. Foaled and bred D.P Flyer in the United States.

In his only start at 1 1/4 miles, two-year old "D.P. Flyer" blazed to a respectable finish in the Pacific Classic (G1) at Del Mar.

Trainer—Terry Caraway

Born in St. Johns, Arizona on June 26, 1943.

Began his career in horse racing at the age of seven by hot walking horses for his father C.J., who trained Thoroughbred and Quarter horses in Ohio, Arizona, and Texas.

Jockey—"Slim Jimmy" Ibenez

Born January 12, 1945 in Havana, Cuba.

First Kentucky Derby mount was supposed to come aboard 1970 favorite *Chi Town Chäch*, but the morning of the race was scratched with an ankle injury.

Won the 1968 Eclipse Award for Outstanding Apprentice Jockey.

At the age of 11, began getting on horses for trainer Dominic Gabriollo in Chicago. The first racing experience for Ibenez came at Fairmount Park Racetrack in Collinsville, Illinois.

Owner

Primary owners are Benjamin Zuckerman and Michael P. Staten.

The Staten family resides in Dallas, Texas, while the Zuckermans make their home in Santa Ana, California.

Chicago Daily News - May 9, 1972
Mickey Wahpeton
"Jimmy Rigged?"

Suspicions have arisen over the legitimacy of *D.P. Flyer's* second place finish at last Saturday's Kentucky Derby. *D.P. Flyer,* ridden by jockey "Slim Jimmy" Ibenez, is rumored to have been "fixed" for placing in the famed race. Potentially "tampered" evidence of drugging the derby favorite, "Speedy Cousin," is currently under analysis. Jockey "Slim Jimmy," a Cuban native, was employed as a horse trainer and jockey for the Chicago based Maywood Park

Tortolini Trotter's Club. He was retained to jockey D.P. Flyer just weeks before the Derby. Ibenez, who reportedly "retired" hours after completing the race, is currently out of the country. Horse owners Michael P. Staten and Benjamin Zuckerman could not be reached for comment.

~ * ~

Upon her husband's death, Dourine Staten was presented with the "legal will" accompanied by a sealed manila folder containing the attorney William G. Bolton's compiled summative reports. Item *b-3a* clarified, and subsequently enforced, the following legally binding benevolent bequest.

"Mr. Philip Dolly, the biological son of Mr. Michael P. Staten, shall receive $3.6 million dollars subject to his 'full mental and physical capacities' to begin hence, five years [60 months] after the death of Mr. Michael P. Staten, and be commenced to recipient, Philip Dolly, and all aforementioned accompanying parties at this date; or on or upon his subsequent retirement of service to Copperfield Community College."

Dourine Staten was then faced with an overwhelming need for funds to pay federal and state inheritance taxes on her deceased husband's estate. The amount due, estimated at $2.5 million, would substantially reduce her current wealth, and most-likely subjugate her to a "middle class" lifestyle—something she deplored and wished to avoid at all costs.

It was also rumored that several months prior to his death, while lavishing in a near-invalid state, Michael P. Staten had used his formidable local political influence to place Hans Goeber in the unfortunately precarious situation which sealed the VP's fate at Copperfield Community—and then Staten leveraged the Governing Board's decision to hire Dolly.

~ * ~

The following three letters became available to Michael P. Staten only months before his death. And until that time, the content of each was known only by Mr. Staten and retained by his attorney William G. Bolton. Only after much probing, and significant legal counsel expense, had Staten's widow

Dourine obtained access to the papers and learned about her husband's brief, yet poignant, South American life... [They are reported below in unedited form.]

3 January, 1964
Mr. Michael P. Staten
c/o PEPÉ Corporation
624 Plaza Boulevard
Mesquite, Texas, U.S.A

Dearest Michael,

I hope and pray all is well with you. Multiple attempts of connection through telephone have been unsuccessful. The Consulate here informs me of potential correspondence conditions restricting U.S.A. contacts. I am hoping written correspondence provides timely appointment.

The nature of my writing is serious and discerning. The gravity of which, I have earnestly contemplated in prayer and consciousness. Our shared intimacy has resulted in my conception. Full gestation brings a projected date of early June. I pray for our acceptance of this most precious and holy gift, and remain faithful in God's wisdom to guide your actions. I apologize for the terseness of my writing which disguises my tranquility of emotions. I wait in anticipation of your reply.

With love and prayer,
Celeste

2 July, 1964
Mr. Michael P. Staten
c/o PEPÉ Corporation
624 Plaza Boulevard
Mesquite, Texas, U.S.A

Dearest Michael,

I write to share our celebration of life, the birth of a glorious baby boy! I have chosen his baptized name Philippe [Philip], in honor of his father's father. I feel, through spiritual grace, your shared love and joy.

The challenges of Motherhood remained overwhelmed by the blessings of this cherished gift. My Papa glows with joyful heart at the sight of his grandchild. Words cannot provide the measure of hope I have for baby Philippe.

Remaining ever faithful, my prayers for your good health continue.

With heartfelt love and concern,
Celeste

22 May, 1966
Mr. Michael P. Staten
c/o PEPÉ Corporation
624 Plaza Boulevard
Mesquite, Texas, U.S.A

Dearest Michael,

I hope and pray you are well and may someday meet your beautiful son. I remain uncertain of the conditions which disallow our correspondence reaching one another. I understand the vehement nationalistic posture of President Arturo Illia has strongly influenced PEPÉ petroleum contracts here.

There remains growing unrest among student and workers within the city and industrial centers. Repression fears among university professors persist, and concerns over a possible coup and threatening military actions are brewing.

There is increased resentment among us and we hold in contempt additional censorship. Despite fears of arrest or imprisonment, my conscious political resolve remains strong.

I assure you the safety of young Philip. I am reminded through daily prayer that holiness is not the absence of problems; but the presence of God.

With peace through action and prayer—
Celeste

~ * ~

Staten's Search for Letters Addendum

After absorbing the gravity of the above Celeste letters' content, Michael Staten employed a "high powered" research fact-finding team to "comb the records" in hope of determining why the missives were "unavailable" for over forty years. The resulting inconclusive "evidence" was revealed to Staten in an 87-page report. Following is a summary of that exhaustive document.

Executive Summary
Re: Correspondence: Letter Availability

The following researched information is provided in two sections 1) what was revealed? And 2) what remains uncertain?

What was revealed?

Pan American Airline passenger records dated Sunday 21 April, 1963 indicated the Washington D.C. to Buenos Aires leg of Staten's flight included Thomas T. Witherspan, a U.S. representative for the Organization of American States (OAS).*

The passenger log also listed Albert Stuart and Taylor Pearce, Foreign Ministry, Susan Estágo, reporter for the Latin America International Bureau, Julia Strouss, Interpretation Stenographer, and Cooley James, Photographer for *The Washington Post*. Available Government documents record U.S. and appropriate affiliates' official business in Argentina as "Alliance for Progress efforts."

[During that time, the USA was committed to stimulate growth and social progress in Latin America in an effort to avert communist interests in subverting "orderly social progress" of nations in modernization transition. The eventual failure of the alliance influenced many Latin American nations to adapt their economies to private enterprise rather than to socialism. These actions have benefited wealthy multinational corporations.]

In early December, 1963, State Department meeting notes ordered Argentina travel restrictions and "Certain Corporate Operatives" in Argentina to immediately cease. Official documents obtained from the U.S. Embassy in Buenos Aires indicated the following. "...On 3 December, 1963, the North American Petroleum Energy Corporation required all *Petroleum Energy Production Enterprises* international business and travel operations to be suspended indefinitely. "Any and all correspondence related with PEPÉ corporate business in Argentina, with the exception of 'essential' determined correspondence from South and Central American, are to immediately cease."

Recently "declassified" journal memos dated 20 February, 1964 provided inconclusive information regarding Whitehouse "insider" discussions over discontinuation of *Petroleum Energy Production Enterprises* operations in Argentina.

Subsequently, "other" sources, offering a more detailed account regarding 'intensified surveillance' and 'sequestered' correspondence, were inaccessible through the National Archives and Records Administration.

[*Approximately 18 minute 10 seconds of taped transcripts were excised by the National Archives and Records Administration as classified information. The missing segment was rumored to have included voices* from *Rusk, Morison, Sorensen, Stevenson, Schlesinger, Shriver, and Goodwin.*]

In late 1965, a *Petroleum Energy Production Enterprises* employee by the name of Edward Kenny was accused of government and "industrial" espionage. The Government accusations could not be proven. Kenny was officially charged with "industrial" espionage, despite pleading ignorance by claiming the "Tyson Effect."

What remains uncertain?

Historical and previously "classified" information stemming from the October 1962 Cuban Missile Crisis and the November 1963 Dallas incident provide threads of connectivity and much uncertain suspicion.

The U.S. aim of isolating Cuba politically and economically was not entirely supported by Latin America in 1960. Argentina remained impartial, believing the issue a private disagreement between U.S. and Cuba, and was opposed to most sanctions. A special U.S. security committee suggested displeasure and disagreement with Cuba's alignment with the Sino-Soviet bloc. In early 1962 Argentina abstained from voting regarding Washington's OAS agenda. Despite being a founding member of the OAS, Cuba was effectively suspended on 21 January, 1962.

Prior to the October crisis, the U.S. gained approval of the OAS for military action under the hemispheric defense provisions of the Inter-American Treaty of Reciprocal Assistance (i.e., the Rio Treaty). Argentina's participation in the quarantine involved the deployment of two Argentine destroyers and the promise of a submarine—and a Marine battalion with lift availability. Informally, three SA-16 aircraft were also offered.

The Dallas incident remains ripe with conspiracy theories, including multiple plot linkages. Theoretical explanations involving Castro, gangsters, FBI, and CIA operatives continue to flourish. Although Argentina had occupied a seemingly politically uncommitted "Cold War" posture, International espionage and Argentine affiliates engaging in subversive activities also abounded. In the early 1960's, Argentine primary export revenues had been wheat and beef. Just prior to November 1963, the U.S. agreed to sell wheat to the Russians to prevent a famine. Hemispheric commerce concerns had CIA-rumored operatives in Argentina monitoring Cuban Soviet activities. And, an undocumented event, supposedly exposed in dated legal filings, linked Ted Sorensen, George Ball, and CIA Director John McCone with writer and political activist Michael Harrington.

Conclusive Summation

Justification for the restive restrictions and full arrested communication involving all aspects of *Petroleum Energy Production Enterprises (PEPÉ)* over a forty-year span remain unresolved. An array of unidentified discrete "shadow" operatives contributed to the research team's inability to formulate complete and accurate disclosure.

Conclusive evidence could not be reached.

Section Three
The Wheel of Fortune Spins: The SUDDEN OVERT DECLINE OF Dr. Philip Dolly
An Absurd Marxist-Capitalist Interpretation

"All the muffins, honey buns, pizza, garbanzo beans, meatballs, meetings, student organizations, leftovers, potlucks, baby showers!
But what is community college purpose if not to fatten the purses of its employees? And why are most of the classified staff former students?"
(William-Henry Ireland, Public Information Director, Copperfield Community College, 2011)

Dean Preston and Henry McDougal Meeting

"*Why yes, Mr. McDougal, I am happy to meet with you concerning the rejection of your application to hold a socialist party rally here at CCC. It's easy to explain—we don't think socialism [or Marxism or communism] or any of such stuff is appropriate on our campus. We don't want our students to get the, uh, wrong idea about CCC.*"

"*Certainly I gathered that, Principal Preston. But I read in your college's mission statement, which I believe describes the heart and soul of your college, that ye celebrate diversity of opinion.*"

"Why yes, so we do. By the way, I am the Dean, not a Principal. Principals work at K-12 schools. Let me read to you our definition of diversity from the CCC policy manual. I think this will help clarify matters to you."

CCC Definition of Diversity

We celebrate diversity and divergence by scrutinizing how people are different. CCC relishes the importance of complete and systematic inclusion of the tired, the lonely, and the poor. CCC ignores differences, usually glorifying wretchedness while questioning male dominance. Diversity includes biometrics related to global issues, mp3 downloads, food abuse, suspicious dual enrollment programs, ethnicity, cell phone colors, anything which will help us get funding, most any conformity factors influencing life, church attendance, veterans status, abilities and disabilities [though as a learn-ed college we don't really think there are any disabilities—only opportunities to excel], challenges, beliefs, mannerisms, syndromes, work habits, gender orientation [though we do believe southerners and Californians probably represent true diversity of thought], personal identity, age, income status, language and communication style, nearness to poverty, red heads, intelligences, and life styles.

"I might add, Mr. McDougal, we encourage thinking outside the box, collaboration, networking, critical thinking, and respect for all genders and walks of life" [*Even for Crazy Scotsmen,* he thought to himself].

McDougal listened attentively and then said, *"So, yah don't think socialism is a legitimate point of discussion on a college campus? Is it not a global issue? A work habit? Thinking? Ach! What do ye mean by diversity? Don't you know socialism and Marxism are legitimate areas of subject matter study and research—and influence academic focus—at universities? It's political science, economics, justice studies, communication, and civics. Doan' you think socialism is worthy of inclusion—as ye discuss it in your diversity definition?"*

"We are not a university, Mr. McDougal, and unlike universities, we are in touch with our community, our stakeholders. They do not want to hear about socialism or communists. The universities fear us. Inclusion is one thing—socialism is another. Community colleges follow best practice theory—socialism is not a best practice."

"But, Mr. Preston, your own President, Mr. Dolly, has said on numerous occasions, that Copperfield Community College is a Higher Education Leader and wants to grant BA

and MA degrees someday. How can you be an academic leader if you are afraid to study and interact with economic theories related to socialism and Marxism?"

"That's Dr. *Preston, Mr. McDougal. And yes, we are a higher education leader, we are just not communists. We know what is best in terms of diversity for our students."*

"Oh, *tell me, Doctor Preston—who was Karl Marx?"* asked McDougal as if he did not know.

"Ah, well, let me think, he was, uh, yass, he was premier of the Soviet Union in the 1950's," said a reddening Dr. Preston.

"And do you know, Mr. Dean Preston, who is Hugo Chavez?"

"Hmm. I believe he is president of Southern El Paso Community College—or at least somewhere over in Texas. Yass."

"Dr. Preston, what do ye think of collective bargaining?" queried the enlightened McDougal.

"Oh, Barb and I don't haggle over prices at garage sales," said the cheery Dean.

"I see. And just what is your doctorate in, Dean Preston?"

A beet-faced Preston replied, *"What do you mean, what is my doctorate in?"*

"Ach, you know, lad—is it a PhD in history, economics, philosophy, or political science?

Ya seem to know a great deal about history," declared the Scotsman in an admiring tone.

"Oh, no. I have an EdD in Educational Leadership."

"What did you study in school lad? What subjects?" asked the now-investigative highlander.

The dean seemed surprised. *"What? Well, we studied, uh, diversity, networking, uh, email etiquette, operating PDA's and smart phones, salary negotiations, student organizations, dancing, program review, quality management, higher education leadership, TQM, collaboration, team development—-you know, an in depth look at management processes and dialogue—oh, and best practice theory."*

"Ach, well, you've convinced me of the foolishness of my plan, Dr. Dean Preston. A knowledgeable man such as yarself has a much better understanding of the dogmatic dangers of socialism than I do. I won't be back to Copperfield. Good day to ye, Mister Preston."

He walked out the office door, smiled at Secretary Nina [*ach, she's a looker!*], and thought, *Good Lord—and they call this a college! I need a pint bad. Ach! At least the Unionists be marching in Madison!*

Nina looked up from the vampire novel she was reading on her Snook when he walked by, smiled absently, and turned the page. She wiped a tear from her eye.

Quite satisfied with the outcome of the meeting, Dean Preston leaned back in his chair, smiled to himself, and thought, *well, that crazy old Scotsman won't be back in here again. I showed the old commie. I wonder if Elena is free for lunch today. Maybe we can catch the **Moondoggs** matinee concert at the Coin...*

Dean Preston heard Nina call to him from her desk. "Oh, *by the way, Dean Preston, my ex-husband had trouble with EdD, too.* You can get help."

Dr. Dolly and the First MRCCN Letter

What the h—-! Dr. Dolly was not happy. His mood had changed from one of ebullience to panic in mere seconds. Here's what happened. One of the CCC faculty, Professor Hedlund, had alerted him to the presence of the following letter to the editor in both the print and online version of the daily local paper, *The Hamilton Democrat*—ostensibly written by some crackpot fringe education reform group signing itself the **Movement to Reform Community College Now**.

It simply appeared from nowhere—but seemed to be directed at everything he stood for—and he was mentioned personally.

He had to put up with this same kind of nonsense back at his former institution. For some reason, too many people saw community colleges as being primarily technical or job training schools. He wondered who these **MRCCN** people were. *What group of stakeholders had he alienated? Maybe they were from the state house in Trinidad. Why were they afraid to sign their names? Could it be the CCC nursing faculty? Administrators from HSU or HU or HMU? Carpenters? Shop Teachers? Why do vocational people always think they better understand learning competencies and assessment?*

[Names, places, events, constituency groups—possible authors—flit through his mind like rabid bats!]

Their kind of thinking, of complaining, of analysis was toxic—and out of touch with the best practices of the community college movement. He was stunned—this letter challenged his very core, his very foundation of beliefs. To have his name mentioned in such a, a, uh, er, uh, trashy letter! He hoped such sentiment would not impede his plans to have CCC granting B.A degrees by the end of the decade! *I want a legacy!*

I'll have Preston or Glen Keynes or Carl Marks over in marketing ferret this out! Maybe William Ireland can help me. What is the board going to say about this? Should I respond? Perhaps we need a committee or task force to address these kooks.

Post-secondary? What is wrong with these people? We are higher education leaders! I've got quality awards to prove it. Who are these people? What gives anybody out in the community the right to challenge community college purpose?

I wonder if some unions are behind the **MRCCN?** *Glen will figure out if these people are local or real. I've never read such misplaced garbage in my life!*

[I hope nobody knows I sent my own kids to Nebraska State!]

"Becky," he shouted to his secretary in the next room, "*What does u-b-i-q-u-i-t-o-u-s mean, anyway?*"

Dolly got on the phone. *"Glen, have you seen this morning's paper?"*

Over in his office, Glen crumpled up the "crisis" placards he displayed on his desk and threw them in the wastebasket. Again.

The letter, as it appeared in that morning's *Hamilton Democrat:*
Dear Editor,

Community colleges consider themselves to be institutions of higher education. But they are more accurately post-secondary education providing entities. Their expansive mission statements mask a simple truth—they should be in the primary business of providing vocational, certificate, and associates in applied science degree [work] training.

What is the community college? Does much of daily community college behavior and practice mimic the secondary school experience? Do community colleges aspire to have equal reputations—and legacies—as four-year colleges and universities? Should community colleges reconsider how they are perceived through the eyes of their K-12 and 15-16 colleagues?

We believe a fundamental dissimilarity exists between the cultures of community colleges and the cultures of four-year colleges and universities. Understanding this variance in culture may help better explain the current "identity crisis" expressed by many observers of today's community colleges.

We are convinced "local residents" believe community colleges are best at providing vocational skills and basic education training—and some studies back up this view. If community colleges are in the business of preparation— preparation for either work force careers or later university experiences, then let us be realistic.

The **MRCCN** believes community colleges are best suited, by learning culture, instructor preparation, administrative skill, and charter, to provide both *old* economy and *new* economy training for residents within their service area. There is no shame in helping people improve their lives. Why then do community colleges pretend [and spin] they are higher education?

That part of community college academic culture which has nurtured their primary ideological tenets—inspiration and "comeback" vignettes—has also maintained the public perception that the colleges foster hope rather than accomplishment. The stigma of weak academics persists. Our neighbors, too, talk about how some students are university material and others will "just go to the community college." [Usually "to find themselves" or "get basic courses out of the way" before they "go on" to a "real" college.]

But vocational programs, especially those monitored and structured by outside agencies, must respect performance-oriented competencies. State level nursing board exams, for example, are exacting and require vigorous preparatory training and study. Massage therapy, CNA's, custodial science, farrier training, radiology—none of these are stand-alone programs.

Academic programs at community colleges should be ancillary to vocational training programs. And we would venture that most of these academic courses could be provided by adjuncts. In fact, increased adjunct salaries—and fewer full-time academic "professor" salaries—might actually procure better academic instruction when more PhD holding adjuncts become involved with teaching.

Money now spent on academic "professors" [Ach!] should be better spent on skilled vocational trainers, equipment, and other infrastructure needs.

We are concerned the current President at Copperfield Community College, Dr. Philip Dolly, continues to over emphasize academic programs at that school. He, like his predecessor and many of his contemporaries, are out of touch with reality. The people want jobs, not philosophy or big speeches. He must not continue to promote academic transfer programming at the expense of immediate job training programs for Hamilton residents. His desire to change CCC into an ersatz liberal arts BA degree granting institution is ludicrous and destructive!

The **MRCCN** believes ubiquitous online course availability, and the universities' new interest in recruiting and nurturing "grade 13-14" students and life-long learners, will continue to further erode university transfer programs at community colleges.

President Obama—and even George W. Bush—have both advocated the community college experience for vocational, compensatory, and work force development training.

Destiny awaits America's community colleges—and destiny awaits Copperfield Community College. Good Golly, Phil Dolly!

Signed—
Movement to Reform Community College Now
[MRCCN]

[Sidebar: The reader can find other examples of the MRCCN's letters to *The Hamilton Democrat* in this book. If you enjoy the status quo, avoid reading them at all costs!]

Dolly's Dream

Dr. Dolly was sleeping fitfully tonight. The meetings, the letter to *The Hamilton Democrat,* the enrollment data—all were troubling him. He had strange dreams. In one

phantasm-bent dream, the College Board members had turned into Centaurs—and whinnied instead of speaking—but he could understand them!

They were neighing, "*Vocational! Vocational! Vocational!*" In another dream, he was a baby, wrapped in swaddling clothes in a manger. He could hear a man speaking. *"Yass, Molly, dis filly will make us a lot of money someday, das for sure! But doan' tell your husband!"*

Baby Phil could smell horses, alfalfa, tack, oats, and other damp aromas of the barn. He was so warm, so comfortable. A large horse walked over and began licking his face.

Dr. Phil Dolly, CCC President, awoke in a cold sweat...

Thunderstorm Rolls across CCC Campus

Dr. Preston was late to the CCC Governing Board meeting—but he was sure the gathering would be delayed anyway because of the intense thunderstorm which had recently rolled through Hamilton City.

The storm had brought heavy rain and some small hail to the thriving city—but apparently damage had been minimal. *Hmm. Darn it. My Lexus is going to get messed up in these puddles,* he thought to himself as he drove onto campus.

He had heard reports that the power blinked off at CCC main for a few minutes, but he noticed all the buildings now had lights—and student pedestrian traffic seemed normal. *Looks like nothing happened from the storm,* he mumbled to himself.

Then he noticed the college's scrolling marquee, which listed details about campus events, student organizations, cheerleading camps—that kind of daily and weekly information—was not working. Or—at least not working correctly. *What the h——,* thought Dr. Preston. *That thing cost CCC $150,000—and it was fried—probably from the storm. No, wait, there it goes. Huh. It is blinking, not scrolling. Just one word—must be damaged badly.*

What was supposed to read "Cop**per**field College n**on**-credit course offerings" displayed something quite different, evidently jinxed by the lightning storm:

Yass, the Marquee was blinking **perón perón perón**...

The Dean was puzzled. *Hah. Crazy. Perón? Perón? Don't we have a pitcher on the baseball team named Perón from Honduras or Costa Rica? Sure we do, but he wouldn't be smart enough to monkey around with the sign! Musta been hit by lightning or something.*

I'll get Zontarg out here to fix it.

Thirteen Ways of Looking at Community Colleges
A Poem by Henry McDougal, Socialist Barkeep, Copper Coin Tavern
Found scribbled on the Copperfield Community College Administration
Building's Men's Restroom Wall
[With special thanks to Wallace Stevens-McDougal's note]

I
Sprawling fifteen city blocks
The county's only post-secondary thing
Was the campus of the college—
II
The college had three challenges
Each lovely
Academic, Technical, and Developmental Education
III
Tired cars overheat in summer parking lots.
A small slice of daily dreams.
IV
Ach, Academic and Vocational
Are one.
Academic and Vocational and Community College
Are one.
V
What do stakeholders desire,
Prestige of higher education
Or utility of vocations
The students graduating
with certificates—or degrees?
VI
Learners who text and tweet
In unrepentant manner

Their shadows fresh and gloating
Emboss the tired teacher
Her class
Reshapes assessments
—And outcomes make no promise.
VII
Oh sleepy men of whimsy
Why do you dream corporate careers?
Can you see how the college
Depends on yearly taxes
And the will of those that pay you?
VIII
We hear the noble speakers
And focus groups and missions
But we know, too
Subjects—and trades—must somehow matter
while we toil and teach our classes.
IX
When the college expanded mission
The budget stretched and tattered
And the staff took pay cuts to maintain
X
At the sight of Grecian athletes
Competing on the track
The mayor shook his head in wonder
And called the local high school.
XI
The instructor flew towards BISON
To receive his trophy
Fearful of the greater teachers
Who made their online way—
In the post-secondary glimmer
Of the Colleges

XII

The budget is moving
The deans must be meeting.

XIII

It was articulation all afternoon [*on the dark and murky moors, ach!*]
And the committees reached agreement
And the courses would transfer
The universities sat and signed the papers
For they need enrollment, too.

Glen Keynes's Epiphany at the Strategic Goals Reconciliation Meeting
"The Edict of Copperfield"

The day had started like most for Glen. He had lifted weights at sun up, drank a cup of rice milk and wheat germ, and checked his calendar for the day's events.

This morning, Glen re-read familiar marked pages in Augustine's *Confessions*, Book 7--a text he found enlightening while studying at Louisiana-North East Texas Religious Seminary many years ago.

He tried to tell his wife goodbye at 6.30 AM, but, plugged into her Ipod, she was busy cleaning the rug and didn't hear him leave.

Something was up, though. He was seeing things differently, today. His immaculately clean house didn't look so good to him.

At 10 AM, he was halfway through a scheduled two hour strategic goals-budget reconciliation meeting. His mind began to drift—or shift—as the meeting continued.

Tables for the meeting were arranged in a large T. Someone had decided white tablecloths would be nice—and seven small fragrant candles glowed in front of each seated administrator.

A large stack of plain doughnuts rose majestically from a brass centerpiece bowl, and a pitcher of grape juice was available for refreshment. Martha Mark, Vice President of Library Services and Pencil Sharpening Advancement, carefully sopped a doughnut in a glass of juice, ate it, and wiped the crumbs from her lips with a clean white napkin.

She gazed at John Luke, registrar, who was seated next to her, then ate another doughnut. *If only this could be the Last Meeting,* she whispered to John Luke.

President Dolly was seated at the "top" of the T—he was flanked on his left by Dean Preston, representing academic concerns. To Dolly's right was Edgar Dowting Thomas, dean of vocational programs.

The Trio had dominated the meeting, arguing about the best use of funds—academic or vocational programs. Dean Thomas would not win, and would, as usual, struggle to find grant monies and external funding to support his excellent skill building vocational programs. Buzzwords flew like mallards in a late October Midwest sky.

Glen knew Dean Preston was wildly supportive of Dolly's view that CCC should offer BA degrees in academic areas. Preston was constantly attending meetings at the State House to promote the concept.

Their behavior is, at best, whimsical, thought Glen.

Glen knew Dean Thomas doubted the efficacy of such ambitions. His occupational programs were sound, enrollments continued to increase, and the community was well- pleased with the solid occupational training provided for various trades and industries. His division had received national awards from Microchop, Moonbuck's, Sunspot Systems, and John Elk Industries.

Voc-Ed's new solar technician program was a huge success, boasting 225 new full-time students and nearly certain job placement for them in the future. His division's motto?

Train for a Job—Go To Work Now.

What is the strange dynamic at work here? Glen asked himself. *Why do Dolly and Preston ignore the truth—Hamilton City wants jobs, not philosophy. Dolly and Preston just won't change direction. They are like actors in a play they have scripted. But what is the script? Why is there such a struggle? Why do we always talk about "both sides of the house"? Is there some kind of class struggle at work here?*

C'mon. The governor of NNM is considering fifty percent budget cuts for community colleges. Put away the egos, you guys! Let's find a way to survive—let's get grounded in reality!

Always tension, always struggle, always some kind of tabled resolution. Nothing robust on the academic "side"—just puffed up professors, pizza, parties, software packages, and proliferating programs.

What is the struggle? Glen was a good Rotary Club attending, Congregational Church member, hardworking American. But his Dartmouth education had taught him more than "mom and apple pie" common sense. He had studied international politics, dabbled in economic theory, and assessed Marxism as well.

Something was bothering him. *What if Dolly and Preston knew the truth— and the truth was that CCC students were not entirely capable of BA degrees—or even quality AA degrees that transferred to Hamilton State. What if the BA degree "carrot" held out to the community was a means to perpetuate enrollment in academic programs? Better enrollment—and returning enrollment—in academic and developmental education would provide an ongoing funding source to support spiraling administrative salaries.*

By packaging and promising success and better futures to a large number of people who were not ready to perform in academic classes, Dolly and Preston could secure their own positions. Was this not a kind of exploitation? Were developmental non-transfer classes really "college?" Did the students represent a kind of proletariat, led to believe in delusional middle class dreams while Dolly and Preston fattened their purses and bought more lake front property? Dolly needed the students, but he needed them to fail and keep coming back. Like a cigar-smoking South American dictator, Dolly provided students with dreams that could not be fulfilled—by making their cause his cause, he would grow richer.

And that latest scheme! Holy Cow! Did Dolly think that he and Preston could somehow personally profit by selling the college?

Yass! More testing, more pre-prerequisites, more developmental education courses supporting "academics," more success vignettes about single moms struggling through college.

[Suddenly, with passion, he remembered seeing, just this morning, one of CCC's female students, several little girls in tow, smoking, weeping, withdrawing from all her courses—she had been muttering something about Dean "Perkins" and Dr. "Chicken." Sad, Very sad.]

Enrollment in developmental math, reading, and writing was soaring. More and more GED's [secondary school equivalencies] were obtained by students each semester.

The support programs for students facing "challenges" in terms of their academic abilities were emerging like forest mushrooms. Everywhere, every day, every hour. Early alert and late start programs, module courses, online and hybrid delivery modalities, international presence, global outreach, college prep curriculum…

Counselors and academic advisors soothed the developmental students, promising better futures, better self-esteem, and—successfully kept them on campus sometimes for decades…

So many acronyms, partnerships, success programs.

What was the purpose of all the student organizations, awards ceremonies, potlucks? To teach skills—or to keep the students [and staff] occupied—or preoccupied?

Somehow, students had lost their right to fail. Students must be kept in school at any cost. Why? Why? Why was the Customer Service metaphor an integral part of community college discourse?

Why was there so much Customer Service training? *Is there a vast conspiracy at work here? Who is really helping who?*

Do all the presidents at community colleges adhere to such a strange "retention at all costs" policy? Is this why they roll out the higher education leader mantra—whenever they can—even in the face of federal pressure to provide occupational training—even when the communities beg for job training?

Think of all the [camo] fatigue-wearing dictators who vowed a love for the people, but grew rich and powerful at their expense.

Glen's mind began racing again. *Is this why they refer to themselves as leaders rather than stewards? Is this why they ignore the data—the information which shows real merit, real quality FTSE comes from vocational programs? Is this why they can't decide on program review rubrics, learning outcomes assessment, and program assessment instruments?*

Perhaps they don't want to know—they don't want to decide—they don't want better retention or more program completers. They want enrollment—continuous enrollment—and now they even count two-year degree completion after six or seven years of study as successful.

192

There is always something on the table, always degree requirement changes, always new staff. And the staff needs to keep their jobs to recognize their own middle class dreams.

He suddenly realized Dean Thomas had legitimate reasons for his doubts. *What was truly successful, or possible, was ignored or minimized at meetings—and struggled to survive.*

Somehow the entire community college movement was metaphoric of a class struggle, a symbiotic relationship between the exploiters and the exploited—the haves [staff] needed the students [have-nots].

Yass! Dolly was orchestrating a finely crafted dance, using the language of the corporations, of the board rooms, holding long and short positions simultaneously, jockeying for ways to increase his power base and bank accounts, making promises that couldn't be kept but served as palliatives for the joyful pot luck-swilling employees. The chaos of management, assessment, and accreditation would guarantee him employment for a time—then another Comrade would come to take his place.

Why had community colleges so fulsomely embraced corporate management practices? Why? Why?

The Global Corporate Menace? Wall Street? The Illuminati? The Bull Moose Party?

Mr. President! Mr. Plumber! Mr. Speaker! Where is the redistribution of wealth at the two-year college? When will the unions march on Trinidad?

He thought of all those Leadership union card holders, lined up single file outside the CCC gates, awaiting their time in history to become the CEO, or CAO, or CFO—waiting to come in, stir up the pot, leave, and get better paying jobs elsewhere, marching off like corporate soldiers, darkening the plains, protected by the Guild, Crimson Chin, or the Invisible Hand, or—well something must be protecting them—some mojo, some witch, some nightmare on elm street, some talisman stronger than Knowledge, Stewardship, or Selfless-ness.

Surely the internet search engine servers were overwhelmed by requests for information from all those millions of online Ed Leadership Degree programs.

Glen was becoming dizzy. He saw halos of light around the heads of the administrative team to the left. He heard rain patter on the roof. He asked to be excused, and pushed through the doorway into a sudden cold down pour, and felt absolved.

Dourine Staten ReDux

The Widow Staten, just heading out the door—grimly realized she might be late to the Hamilton County Woman's Book Discussion Group meeting. Still, she paused to look in the mirror and carefully adjust the Blue Hat perched on her graying head.

I'll get him yet, she thought to herself—then smiled like a grandma at the face in the mirror.

She did not notice a swarthy man, dressed in a black coat and black fedora, carrying a wolf-headed cane, moving away from her hedge, as she walked down the sidewalk towards the MRCCN meeting.

~ * ~

The book discussion this day focused on the writings of a somewhat obscure Argentine writer who had relocated to Copenhagen after the war. His writings, somewhat poetic, provided tender, yet poignant, romantic overtures, particularly when read aloud. A section in today's reading was especially enticing for the widowed Dourine Staten:

"...On a sleeted and snowy Bavarian Rim morning, Whitsun Holiday,

She gazed through pines near Lion Springs

And felt him slipping away, passing painfully, from her heart and mind.

All those years of waiting—and now nothing.... Oh, it isn't cold in Argentina, not at all, yet her spirit slowly froze—

And white flakes nested in her perfect auburn hair.

She pursed her lips and waited for the Woodsman—he was back in the forest, somewhere, coughing and collecting himself—his shadowy presence gave her comfort, but not fulfillment...a puppet with dogs...

Miles and miles away, her lover sat in his decaying Danish chair, immune, while a cold drizzle splattered his face but refused to cleanse his sins.

Surely the storm of passions would move on. Perhaps. Without games, love dissipates..."

With furrowed brow and piercing eyes, Ms. Staten scribbled three short words in the margin of her tattered book. "Ring of fire...ring of fire."

I read the news today oh, boy...
"A Day in the Life" - Lennon/McCartney (1967)

The morning's *Hamilton Democrat* took another swipe at CCC and Dr. Dolly specifically. The news had deeply distracted Dr. Dolly's preparation for the scheduled afternoon cabinet meeting with VP's, Deans, and department heads. The sinister vigilantes identifying themselves only as the MRCCN had published a second letter to the editor.

Dear Editor,

What is going on, Dolly? Are you a college or a high school with ash trays?

Secondary, Post-secondary, or Higher Education?
How do our current colleges appear to the public at large? Although we remain accountable to external, local, and parochial constituents, today's community colleges are not commonly "peer reviewed"—except perhaps by accreditation agencies—.

The K-12 system has parent/teacher conferences, geographically local school boards, and neighborhood schools. Four-year colleges and universities have an inherent, built-in, ongoing review in the form of external rankings, continuous peer-comparisons, and internal and external evaluative measurement. In addition, admission selectivity, graduate school placement, research dollars, athletic teams, and alumni success contribute to the notoriety and successes [or non-successes] of the institution. Their reputation lies with the preservation of academic rigor and inquiry, "secured by the professionalism of the professoriate."

Do community colleges struggle with a kind of misplaced university-envy that manifests itself with position title proliferation, nationally competitive athletic teams, and course offerings abroad? If community colleges believe they set seeds for lifelong learning and inquiry, universities germinate and crossbreed in an attempt to nurture and grow intellectual lives. While universities seem to create, foster, and preserve knowledge, cherish intellect, protect learning, encourage scholarship, and perpetuate inquiry—community colleges seem to protect themselves from...from what? From being found out? Why does this seemingly uncertainty of purpose continue to persist?

Certainly, four-year college and university academic units, as well as athletic departments, international programs, or individual faculty will come under scrutiny by the public at large. But we believe the entire community college enterprise should be securitized now—mostly because of the mysterious and yet artificial culture that has flowered within the colleges—manifested by a kind of corporate swaggering, funding requests for programs that may truly not be in the best fiscal or intellectual interest of stakeholders, and an inability to sustain or support big dreams—an almost constant change and reaction without real planning—a kind of new age reactivity with foundational footing placed insecurely in philosophical compost—a chaotic dialectic without theory base or plan...or hope...

It's Prime Time Community Colleges Embrace Cultural Correctness!

The growing external pressure to create full-time student equivalency [FTSE]—and the internal administrative hunger to achieve "Bullridge" awards—may not accomplish the long term results the community college idealistic forefathers envisioned. Despite the success vignettes, budgets, and buildings, community colleges must be careful not to become credential-granting institutions rather than teaching/learning institutions.

Perhaps the real workforce development-taking place in our community colleges most directly and dramatically involves the career pathways of staff. Innovative programs, conferences, partnerships, and BISON awards are great bullet points for our resumes, but do our daily activities focus on stewardship, productivity, and true personal growth for our students and ourselves?

The universities continue to produce [and this is not necessarily healthy] more PhD's than can find work. Meanwhile at the community colleges, we create positions for the masses who obtain EdD's from seemingly thousands of education leadership degree programs available—at both online and traditional institutions of higher learning.

The degree must be magical. One can be an assistant director of Student Life in early December, making 25K, complete the EdD capstone project by the twenty-third, and become an Associate Senior Vice President of Student Global Diversity in January, and see one's salary triple. Where do all these Ed Leadership people find jobs?

Let's find a way to put real diversity into community college teaching/learning experience. From the boardroom to the lounges, the corporate ethic we have embraced has muzzled the diversity we cheerily profess. Having a compass, a mission, a plan to guide our way is fine. Do we have to be corporate citizens?

Let's be a community of scholars—not a community of dollars.

Let's understand and improve our own culture—even if it means assuming an honest "middle position" following secondary education and preceding university-sponsored higher education. One of those "whispered truths" is the traditional unpopular reference to community colleges as "Grades 13-14." Should we find this distinction insulting? Why?

Perhaps technology has made the notion of comprehensiveness obsolete. There is more to do every day—do we really need to establish a director and a program and a glossy brochure for every blade of grass in the American social structure?

Whispers of Righteous Truth

Community colleges ostensibly celebrate an egalitarian, a democratic ethic. But the celebration, the party, has left tattered confetti on the floor. Mr. President Phil, let's take control of our own destinies by embracing a new ethos—one that does not parallel proprietary institutions or result from a suspect capstone project in some educational leadership program designed to serve K-14 administrators.

Dr. Dolly, develop your intellect, not your career. Let's perform our professional duty—serve the community first, finish and evaluate the pilot projects, minimize efficiency-killing meetings and reorganizations and conversations, and make some deliberate decisions. Let's develop a critical pedagogy of our own and avoid hiring staff and faculty who have simply been credentialed. We are currently dealing with a student demographic who hungers for credentialing; let's consider how damaging such strangely symbiotic relationships might become. We must determine whether we wish to exemplify an intellectual community or a credentialed community.

Let's start "implementing" and stop "ideating." We can begin by implementing real service to our community. We can begin by listening to them with an open heart and an informed intellect. There is no shame in serving the needs of community—whether they are compensatory or transfer needs. We should be the intellectual, academically proficient experts who support and embrace the primary purpose of the community we serve.

Greatness will follow if we truly develop our intellect and do what is in the best interest of our students—on their terms. Let's focus on stewardship, but not in the Rotary Club ring-the-bell at the meeting-of-the month kind of way. Let's stroll down the street of our town, and connect with the people who pay our salary. Take pride in serving the needs of your community—whether they represent old economy or new economy needs.

Let's begin to make decisions with courage and confidence—deliberately and with the best interests of our stakeholders [not our careers] at heart. Let's not pretend to be a higher education institution if we are not delivering the goods.

Dr. Phil, we sense community college management's love affair with corporate structures has extended too much power to external agencies and institutions that do not understand, or accept, the beauty of the community college's transitional purposes.

Let's take back the power—resist corporate citizenry and the namelessness many of our college's mission statements reflect [they all appear so awfully similar]. Let's become a magnet with powerful programs—and not simply adapt fancy stationery that gives the institution some sort of perceived "brand recognition." Students want real day-to-day service—not bizarre logos, or clever slogans, or confusing acronyms.

The uniqueness of the community college position in American education should continue to be critically defined. We would recommend nourishing this uniqueness by choosing a definite focus, vision, and purpose at our institutions, and work together to ensure its quality.

Signed—
Movement to Reform Community College Now

Dr. Darling's Outburst

President Dolly had called an extended-cabinet session to discuss the increasingly touchy accreditation situation related to the Very Important Excellence Tasked New Accountability Measures [VIET NAM] being disseminated to community colleges by the Highbrow Learn-ed Commission. The Highbrow Learned Commission was becoming involved with ranking—or judging—community colleges as a means of improving their instructional and program quality.

Several cabinet level administrators, line of command directors, and invited "key" faculty members were present at this meeting to provide input and analysis of what the new accountability measures and expectations might mean to CCC.

The meeting was catered, of course, and the pleasing aroma of freshly-brewed Moonbuck's filled the tense air in the room.

Dean Preston enjoyed such meetings very much, and nodded in gentle agreement with Dr. Dolly's concerns about the college's assessment plans, strategic goals, and Embedded National Excellence Meta Accountability [ENEMA] project.

After hearing about the ENEMA plan, Dr. Darling could contain himself no longer. The usually calm and reserved Darling stood and addressed the gathered dignitaries, gathering himself up like a late nineteenth century

Balkans prime minister about to address a council of the European Great Powers.

"Dr. Dolly has accurately described many of the issues associated with the possibly malignant issues related to accountability at America's community colleges. Federal and national accountability are most likely coming down from the hill in the near future. One must scrutinize, however, the current toxic nature of community college culture—the American Community college movement has drifted far from its original intent."

"The misplaced commoditization of education is perhaps most powerfully seen at the community college—inflated administrative salaries, meaningless surveys of satisfaction, exploitation of adjuncts, spiraling text book costs, millions of education leadership degree programs which do not prepare graduate students for leading anyone, thousands of programs, pilots, grants, and services that perpetuate a kind of public fraud which promises higher education but is best suited for vocational training. So much leadership puffery…"

Prime Minister Darling continued in his booming voice.

"Some agency, some scientist, some ethnographer, needs to do an honest, unbiased, anthropological based field study [a true ethnography] of community college culture. Real scholars need to assess the actual complexion of the community college event before any valid judgments can be made."

"Do you understand the hidden, probing, cleansing, healing, deep seated, penetrating meaning of your program's acronym? Dr. Preston, do you know what most people think when they hear the word ENEMA?"

Dean Preston's eyes were glazed. *Darling must be referring to some high highbrow chemical formula,* he thought.

Darling left the room. The silence was deafening. Dr. Darling was no longer invited to such meetings.

William-Henry Ireland and "Evita"

Now that was something, said William Ireland to himself as he put down the telephone. He had trouble remembering the caller's name—*Emma? Ernestine? Elena? Erin? Evelyn? Evita?*

Whatever her name was, he had just spent thirty minutes listening to her speaking [or lecturing!] in a questioning monologue. He had written down her questions [sort of posed like statements] to the best of his ability. "Evita" had identified herself only as a resident of Hamilton City and a member of the Movement to Reform Community Colleges Now [MRCCN] group.

He had learned from Evita that President Dolly's secretary, Rebecca B-F, had transferred her phone call to his office because he was the "specialist" on public information.

He knew she was more or less requesting and commenting on public knowledge information—but her discussion seemed strange. He heard her whisper words like "Comrade," "proletariat," "regime," and "revolution." *Very strange,* thought William.

He looked at his notes carefully-why she asked this stuff was beyond him. He told her he would check with the president then research his responses carefully, since he didn't want to get any mis-information "out there." *Why would someone, some plain old citizen, in this community be asking such questions,* he wondered.

Evita's questions... [William's paraphrased but mostly accurate notes]

1. Why are community college administrator salaries so extravagant? And why are they proportionally so much larger than faculty salaries? She advised him she had some data indicating administrative salaries were on the average twenty-five percent higher than faculty salaries back in the 1970's, but were fifty percent higher now.

[*William knew her data was nearly accurate but could not explain it to her. William also knew President Dolly would say salaries had to be kept high because of the demands on administrators and "we need those salaries to attract the best people!"*]

2. Why don't your faculty members pursue doctorates in their academic disciplines? Why do they pursue those EdD Leadership degrees? Why do they spend so much time at meetings and trainings? Why does CCC have a step and column salary schedule like a high school? Are you really grades 13-14?

Hmm, thought William, some *good points here!*

3. Why do you people have national searches for job openings and then hire from within?

[William thought of Hans [von] Goeber!]

4. Why is community college culture so insular and fiercely protected? [William thought he had detected just a hint of a Spanish accent when she said "insular." He also remembered recently reading about administrator defensiveness in some crazy article about media and the community college written by Dr. Darling. *We were told not to read anything that guy wrote. I'll have to dig it out again.]*

5. Why don't you offer more vocational training programs—the people want jobs, not philosophy.

[She must be clairvoyant—Glen Keynes' emerging data supported this. But Dolly refused to listen to anyone!]

6. Why don't our local kids play on your athletic teams? Why do you teach classes in China and Nebraska?

[I'll let the athletic director and the International studies director handle those questions.]

7. Is the rumor true Dolly and his cronies are going to try and sell the college? How can they sell a tax payer-supported institution? Did some big corporation promise him a big fat job if he sells out?

[I'm not touching that one.]

8. Is a Learn-ed college anything like a liberal arts college?

[Beats me!]

He had scratched some other notes about her comments on the proletariat, suppression of the masses, middle class illusions, exploitation, but could barely read his own writing. She had drifted off into some tirade about remedial classes and GED preparation and then hung up abruptly.

He had wanted so badly to ask her about the MRCCN letter which had appeared in *The Hamilton Democrat* newspaper, but he just didn't want to sound defensive. He told her he would send her information addressing her concerns. He wished he could have directed her to the college's online home page to view the mission statement or access online demographic information, but nothing there addressed the questions she raised.

He knew there was no reasonable explanation he could give her for any of her questions.

Come to think of it, most of the people he knew who worked at community colleges were defensive most of the time. He used to think no one on the "outside" understood community colleges—but now he was beginning to question his own marginal grasp of the community college movement.

And he knew he would never speak to Dolly about this—he would send Evita a copy of the board policies or marketing literature or something…

To an extent, her words and queries bothered him. He had always been aware of the *good old boys network*, but her remarks created a more sinister framework for him to consider. Something was taking shape in his mind that he didn't like—something potentially devastating to his career, his middle class ethos, his values, and his perceptual framework.

Was Evita correct? Was the community college "event," the grand eclectic democratic institution, the most American of higher education entities, merely a front for some sort of networked conspiracy? Were these community college presidents committed to maintaining a repressed student fee-paying class [promising higher education but delivering semester after semester of developmental education shrouded in the mysteries of numeracy and literacy] and hiring from within to protect the scheme?

Why were their salaries so high?

Why did Dolly create so many VP positions? Why did so many administrators come from the University of Toledo at Akron? And is the EdD Leadership degree some sort of code for the autocrats and plutocrats—a rite of passage into the fraternity?

Do these presidents consider themselves to be some kind of Nietzsche Supermen— beyond morality, beyond ethics, beyond the law—seemingly noble and yet self-legislating? He took a drink of bottled water. I mustn't start thinking like this. No! The conferences, the quality awards, Bell grant fee structures, data sets, residence halls filled with out-of-nation athletes, the best practice seminars—No No! This world is eccentric, but it cannot be that corrupt.

But why are we always hiring from within? Why do the CEO's move around so much? Why do they avoid both the universities and the secondary schools? Why? Why?

He began to consider the serendipitous nature of community college "planning"—always cloaked by corporate nomenclature and buzz words. What is the community college's actual theoretical framework?

Capitalism-Socialism-Marxism-Unionism—what's the difference? The rich get richer, and the poor seem to just fade away.

What is our school's motto? Something about learning and spending? But who really earns more money at CCC? Who really benefits from the student success stories, the boardroom dramas, the effervescent portrayals of happy students on our web pages, dual enrollment, and the every-other-year sales tax increases "for the kids"?

Why does every employee include a motto or saying underneath their names on emails? Is it some sort of textual code?

[His mind was swirling now—chinchillas spinning on wheels, skyrockets exploding, fireballs blasting through the stratosphere, giant oil slicks in the Gulf, Republicans debating, London burning, volcanoes erupting, five dollar gasoline, ice floes melting, Wall Street occupied, Ohio under siege!]

Surely these people can't be that smart! All the speeches, all the talk, all the success vignettes—smoke screens for a money maker? Hah! Why else could our daily work lives be so whimsical?

We reinvent the wheel every other month, start pilot programs at the drop of a hat but rarely assess their outcomes, never study national research; crank out meaningless proprietary surveys which are shelved and forgotten, worry about branding, mission statements, strategic plans, visions, ha-ha—and then the college changes direction and purpose after the president goes to a conference, reads a book, or hires a consultant.

All of the fusillades of quality control, software training, benchmarking—surely these people aren't clever enough to use all of that window dressing as a means to fatten their own salaries, their own careers, and to support their immense egos! Can't be. Could it be?

I heard Dr. Darling say once that the administrators, the managers, have become the Creators of work at community colleges—he said our actual daily output has only to do with meetings, trainings, and committees—not student learning, not with teaching. I remember him saying clearly and perhaps with clairvoyance, in his booming voice, that "The Managers Have Become the Producers." How odd. How Frightening! But how true!

[Esteban and Rubio, the chinchillas running in his head, picked up the pace...]

All the muffins, honey buns, pizza, garbanzo beans, meatballs, meetings, student organizations, leftovers, potlucks, baby showers!

But what is community college purpose if not to fatten the purses of its employees? **And why are most of the classified staff former students?**

Can't be, thought William, as he saw another email come in about a new online leadership program at Southern East Central Valley Low Galloping Goose Moon Valley University [The Fighting Mallards].

No! No! And then, another email about leftovers in the Dean's office—and another about a bridal shower—and another about roast duck in culinary. No! No!

Evita mentioned class struggle—what was this class struggle she hinted at? Capitalists and socialists? Management and labor? Or the middle class and the lower class— both deluded by the community college illusion of greatness, prosperity, and learned-ness?

William wondered if Henry McDougal was somehow connected to the MRCCN.

He caught himself. *Why was he even pretending to consider the legitimacy of an organization calling itself The Movement to Reform Community Colleges Now?*

He ate a leftover muffin, took a drink of soda, and went back to reading a college football magazine.

Southern East Central Valley Low Galloping Goose Moon Valley University

SECVLGGMVU IT Tech on smart phone:

Dr. Yuan? This is Homer Byte over in IT. We've had over 4600 email requests for information about our on line Ed Leadership doctoral program this week—mostly from the state of North New Mexico.

Yes, yes, "the cash cow."

We're having problems with the server and the system's ability to send out sufficient automated information responses. Do you think we should install a new server?

Dr. Yuan, SECVLGGMVU VP of Proprietary Instructional and Customer Services on landline:

I'll call corporate and get their permission for a new server—and to raise fees thirty percent for our ten month EdD in Ed Leadership program. That cash cow is really mooing!

Third MRCCN Letter to the Editor

Within a week of the second *MRCCN letter, The Hamilton Democrat* published a third installment. The character assassination team had stuck again.

Dear Editor,

Community colleges should be primarily compensatory [developmental education] and AAS degree granting institutions. *Ach*, perhaps community colleges can be considered as terminal middle education [or post-secondary education] institutions. The twenty first century emphasis should be on vocational [workforce development] at American Community Colleges. Please Mr. President Dolly, listen to the masses, lad! Ach!

Transfer education should be re-evaluated.

Community Ed [fee-based and of course, relevant] should be strengthened.

Student   organizations   should   be   expressively   linked to career development/networking

Imagine the new names—

Western Arizona-Phillips Electro Voice Technical College

Hamilton County-Jones Foods Community College

Blue River Valley Polytechnic Community College

Joliet Junior Semiconductor and Radiologic Technology Institute

Let's be respected by the universities.

Let's articulate our AAS degree programs carefully with universities— especially universities with technological emphasis [such as HSU Polytechnic.]

Let's reconsider the current FTSE based funding system.

Let's develop mission statements unique to our programs and purpose. Why do all mission statements for colleges look the same? Why is faculty professional development so closely connected to "organizational learning"?

Let's study and adapt the successful learning outcomes assessment procedures used by those programs [nursing, welding, plumbing etc.] certified and reviewed by external agencies.

Embrace Post-secondary Education! This country needs radiologists, power line technicians, massage therapists, solar panel installers, and heavy equipment operators. America needs more trained staff for our public infrastructure—policemen, firemen, nurses, EMT's, helicopter pilots.

Let's train skilled workers, help them get good jobs, and give them a smattering of appropriate academics [taught by PhD academics who will lend credibility to the academic component] to help students understand life [and their new found riches].

Let's create a niche we [along with John Elk, Microshot, Kraftwork Cheese, Boener Health Care, Big Steel Inc., welding companies, the teacher unions, machine shops] can really own and be proud of!

Poverty and debt are not good! Let's take control of our own destiny—your school can do what other local community colleges fear—become a magnet institution with clearly defined goals, programs, and a staff that is appropriately educated to manage tangible tasks. The companies and corporations and agencies colleges work with [as we train our students] will be helpful in terms of finances, technological support, and leadership. Let's create true partnerships and healthy external linkages—symbiotic relationships that build confidence, morale, and integrity.

Imagine the real time dedicated learning communities that can be developed within the academic component.

Imagine empowered leadership—administrators experienced with technological applications, manufacturing, substance, marketing, project management!

Imagine the simplicity of recruiting students from local high schools—recruiters could describe specific goals, specific careers, and specific programs—and avoid the murky and trite generalizations about learning environments, success vignettes, and the worth of credits! Imagine new relationships with the American military—even better trained soldiers, sailors, airmen, coastguardsmen, and marines!

Think of how different accreditation and accountability and curriculum development might be!

Consider how courses in chemistry and biology and physics and calculus could be repackaged and made popular!

Imagine the theme-based learning [project-based assignments] and service learning

projects that could take place!

Whispers around any community college are that we give everyone a chance at Higher Ed, that our students are learning about going to college, that we provide a supportive culture. True. Community colleges are actually in the business of acculturation; they are exposing cc students to a post-secondary culture of numeracy, literacy [including science, humanities, and social sciences]. Ergo—

The grounding mission for cc's must be vocational and acculturational—not in a theoretical or fantastical sense—but in reality. Helping students with their vocations—and literacies acculturation—is what we already do best in **Middle Ed**—even by our own admission.

Signed—

Movement to Reform Community College Now *[MRCCN]*

Chapter Twelve

A white sport coat and a pink carnation—I'm all dressed up for the dance—A white sport coat and a
pink carnation—I'm all alone in romance.
(Marty Robbins, 1957)

Phil opened his eyes—he was surprised the hardware store below his apartment had opened so early that morning. He could hear voices, hushed and murmuring, and clinking and clattering sounds. *Hmm, he thought in his half-awake state—must be some farmers rummaging through the bins, trying to find the right size screws or bolts or something....* He could smell food, too, oddly enough. Strange, he thought—*smells like hash browns, bacon—rich and heavy. Maybe the hardware guy brought in some coffee and doughnuts for his customers. Good Customer Service, you bet.* An occasional outburst of laughter from down below calmed him...and he drifted off into sleep for just a few more minutes... Then a horse, whinnying in the distance, woke him up for good.

He was quite fortunate to have found this apartment so quickly after getting off the bus here in Mayfield, North West Dakota. Soon after debarking from the snorting White Hound bus, Dr. Phil had picked up a paper to check on housing availability. At that moment, a large man wearing a white sport coat and a pink carnation approached him and asked him if he were looking for a place to live. It seems the fellow had a studio apartment for rent above his hardware store on the town square.

Dolly was astounded at his good fortune—the price was right, and the hardware man was even eager to carry his suitcases for him. His departure from Hamilton City had been swift and certain. He had signed a few papers and left them on his desk at home—essentially he turned over his estate, his bank accounts, to Molly and the kids. He signed a simple letter of resignation ["*I Quit*"—*Philip Dolly*] and left it on Becky's desk.

He had packed a few clothes into a bag and taken a taxi down to the White Hound Bus Station. Dolly swore to himself during the long bus trip that he would never wear a suit again—he would never spend more than 250 a month on rent—he would avoid all contact with community colleges forever. His meteoric rise was over—he came crashing into the wheat fields but felt oddly at ease, at peace, in the bright white light. He mumbled, to himself, *"I have to take a humanities course to get my certificate."*

The letters and pressure from MRCCN had driven him away from Copperfield. This recurring nightmare had pushed Phil Dolly over the edge.

Wheat Germ: A Poem by Philip Dolly
[Found serving as a book mark in one of Phil Dolly's vampire novels by his wife, Molly, approximately one year after his disappearance]

I've got my room at the Co-Op
I'm with the mice and the birds
From my garden of Augers
I can see the Mayfield herds
And in the heat of the summer
When the soil has turned to glass
And I need some cool refreshment
I crank up the mealy gas
When she sat down beside me

Her face was twisted with pain
I had to tell her I was leaving
Gone to a house made out of grain…
And in the thunder and lightning
I ride bold aegis on the storm
I'm on the backs of the horses
To where the Angels were born
And when my folks come to see me
And they climb that shaky spiral
My momma wonders what got me
Was it Trauma was it Viral?
When she sat down beside me
Her face was twisted with pain
I had to tell her I was leaving
Gone to a house made out of Grain…

~ * ~

Strange, Dr. Dolly thought he heard Rebecca, his secretary, speaking to someone outside his room.

"*Rebecca…Rebecca!*"

"*Yes Mr. Dolly—coming…Good morning, Mr. Dolly.*"

"*Well, did you hear that racket last night? Must have been some kind of graduation parties going on—why the wife and I heard that ruckus nearly the entire night. By the way, I'm glad tomorrow is Saturday…it's been a long week with final exams and commencement activities and all. With faculty final exam grades due next Wednesday and the summation meeting for the ASAP team scheduled a week from Tuesday, Oh, and that d——- external stakeholders wrap-up session for the program review team is due before the start of summer school.*"

"*Yes Mr. Dolly, yes…busy times ahead indeed.*"

"*And Rebecca…*"

"*Yes Mr. Dolly*"

"The SAAC closure meeting, faculty contracts, HLC review, and MyPEDS data file completion also deserve attention before the break."

"Yes Mr. Dolly, consider it complete."

"There's a lot to do before Molly and I depart for our lake cabin in Santa Rey for a bit of summer R&R..."

"Oh, Rebecca... The C-SCAPE committee notes and budget proposal agenda items need completion before next Friday, and has the NASPA grant been updated—I don't want those !*[^#*#@! NSF folks breathing heavy down my back again."

"Yes...Yes...Mr. Dolly...why you sure maintain a busy schedule...yes Mr. Dolly...you certainly maintain a busy schedule..."

"Say, Rebecca—are you, Tom, and the kids planning to get away this summer? Make sure you take some time off, Rebecca, you know summer school sessions will be completed soon after the fourth and the start of the fall semester will be here before we know it...THIS fall will be particularly busy..."

"Yes Mr. Dolly...busy, very busy indeed."

Dolly takes a long exasperating sigh, accompanied by a muted groan...then...crossing both arms in front of his chest, he begins shaking his head slowly. *"Do you see the fields of wheat, Rebecca? The fields are waving in the sun, golden, rich and full."*

She thought the rapidly-aging man, the former CEO of CCC, was becoming delirious.

After a long, silent pause, Rebecca said, *"You know Mr. Dolly...you are getting quite thin. Oh Mr. Dolly...sometimes I just wish your appetite was half as good as your imagination. Come along now Mr. Dolly... We have plenty to do this morning...come along."*

"Rebecca!"

"Yes Mr. Dolly?"

"Why do we have an unsustainable policy promoting sustainability? Are we coffee snobs or not?"

"Rebecca!"

"Yes, Mr. Dolly?"

"Rebecca!"

"Yes, Mr. Dolly?"

"Where are the liberal arts?"

"Rebecca!"

"Yes, Mr. Dolly?"

"Ach, do the **Diné** *think I walk* **in Hózhó?"**

"Rebecca! Please! Rebecca!" [Cough-cough!]

"Are we Leaders—or are we Stewards?"

"What do you mean, Dr. Dolly?"

"Rebecca!"

"Yes, Dr. Dolly?"

"You can call me Phil."

Fini'

A strong rough hand was shaking Dr. Phil Dolly. *"Dr. Dolly! Dr. Dolly! Phil! Pub's closed Doc…come on' Doc…time to close tonight.* **I'm tired, too, Dr. Dolly,** *let's go."* Dolly lifted his heavy head from his collapsed folded elbow where it had rested. Attempting to gather in his whereabouts, he gazed strangely at the now-dimmed lights above the bar and the barely visible seed company calendar. A penetrating smell of smoke was still evidenced but now invisible in the darkened tavern. *"Come on, Dr. Dolly. This fellow is Darrel from Western Dakota cab service. He'll take you home, Dr. Dolly."*

Dr. Dolly, with outstretched arms, one on the shoulder of I.M. Tyred to his right, one on the shoulder of Darrel to his left, his scuffed wing tip shoes barely assisting his progress, is carried to the waiting taxi. Darrel said, *"It was tough to find this place. The map didn't show that the Nose Guard pub is located at the corner of Golgotha and Cavalry Streets."*

"Come on, Phil, the 'Nose Guard Pub' is closed."

Sequel

…Their faces gaunt, their eyes were blurred, their shirts all soaked with sweat
He's riding hard to catch that herd, but he ain't caught 'em yet
'Cause they've got to ride forever on that range up in the sky
On horses snorting fire
As they ride on hear their cry

As the riders loped on by him he heard one call his name
If you want to save your soul from Hell a-riding on our range
Then cowboy change your ways today or with us you will ride
Trying to catch the Devil's herd, across these endless skies

YippieyiOhhhhh
YippieyiYaaaaay…

"Ghost Riders in the Sky"—Stan Jones, 1948

[Horses whinny in the loamy North New Mexico light. Large Thunderheads and Giant Dust Clouds loom in the distance. The CCC orchestra was playing a mixed key version of "Also Spake Zarathustra." The new Copperfield Community College President, Dr. Suzette Tacchus, former PR Specialist from Arizona, stood at the podium with her husband, JP "Skipper" Tacchus, just outside the Staten Information Commons Building. She began her remarks.]

[Custodian Zontarg, who had been mowing the lawn, stopped just long enough to shut off his Ipod (*The Zombies!*) and hear the forceful and inspirational speech. Dr. Seemy and her husband had arrived late to the event and sat, nervously, in her just-detailed Lincoln motorcar (which, the big-bellied police chief noticed, clearly occupied a "handicapped-only" parking spot). Coach Ski, seated next to Father John in the audience, was secretively listening to Notre

Dame Football on his pocket transistor radio. S. Chick, finishing a can of smoked oysters, was resting comfortably at home, far from the madding crowd.]

"Yass, my husband "Skipper" and I are happy to be part of the Copperfield Community College family. I have kept my eye on Copperfield for years—your sound tradition of excellent teaching and learning is well-known to me—and to other followers of the community college work force development movement."

[Dust storm begins arriving, splattering crowd with particles—but they sit transfixed by the pulse pounding and fiery oratory of their new president. She seems to be from a different time, a different place, and her influence on them is spellbinding. Elena Vasquez, a red wool European-motif beret propped on her pretty head, listens with passion. Richard Hose and his good friend Wilbur, sitting on the creaky front porch of their home, hear only the approach of distant thunder.]

"We know that CCC has an important and significant place in the hearts and minds of county residents, other stakeholders, and state legislators."

[Light tinkles of corporate laughter from the shirt and tie constituency in crowd—a group of ladies wearing Blue Hats smile and cheer. Newly-minted PhD Kat Van Dorn looks on with bemusement.]

[The aged Scotsman McDougal begins a standing ovation but sits down as Dr. Martha Mark glares at him.]

The new president pauses momentarily, her attention eerily transfixed on a couple walking by, hand-in-hand, just in front of the speaker's podium. He is a scruffy-looking character wearing brogans and a backpack. She is a crisp-looking red head made-up with green eye shadow and shod in ballerina shoes. They are smiling intensely at each other, with an obvious new knowledge that surpasseth community understanding. "The universe, a decir verdad, has changed, my love," he said to his dear companion, in a voice just above whisper level.

Unruffled, the president continues.

"We want to continue the good work here at CCC and transition into becoming a Voc Ed College as defined by [Kaff] [Kaff] the well-known and respected community college theorist, Karl O' Perkins. My hope is that CCC will become the foremost **Vocational Training Leader** *in the Great State of North New Mexico—possibly in the Southwest itself. My goal is to help CCC undergo a metamorphosis [Kaff], a transition, into a top notch*

215

welder, masseuse, mortician, novel writing, surveying, and horticulturist training center during my tenure at CCC." [Kaff Kaff!]

Full Fury of dust storm arrives, sending speaker and listeners scurrying into a nearby barn, where they find shelter from the maddening cyclonic blast outside. Rain begins to fall, washing clean the campus and the words. Damp horses make their way into the barn and compete with deans and directors for space.]

Sitting on a bale of still-green hay, Glen Keynes and William Henry-Ireland huddle together under a blanket.

The puppet show had taken a rain delay breather for now.

Attribution Theory

A legal size envelope with strange post markings was left near the collection basket at St. Rafael Catholic Church in Concho, Arizona. Molly Dolly received the unopened envelope personally delivered by Fr. Paddison. The letter, addressing Ms. Molly Dolly, had international postage.

25 December, 2012
Ms. Dolly,

We have never met, nor shall we. A request by my late husband has prompted this transfer. The sealed contents? I know neither the purpose nor intention.

C. P. Kenny

Molly opened the adhesive-sealed single envelope with caution as a bi-focal peering Fr. Paddison looked on. The cryptic contents—as appearing in unedited form:

As petro's evening found a match
With Pius secured
Fire force had no douse
While storm blew gently the yellow grain blouse

Now red head flirts with Tina
As camo cried Wolf
Now only whispers from white doll house
The pidgin was forced to duck
While storm blew gently the yellow grain blouse
Black planted Jack's flowers
...cloaked with Pan Am Buzz
Oz wears ruby red slippers
For playing in the Scotland's yard
Angels chirp no more
Now only whispers from White doll House
As Cong's rehearse two-step
Benjeez 67 tour
Daily workers march
Mean clean machine
...while salmon the Deuce devoured
Enter the good king
As Zen Visits the 98th Church
...smoke delivered the flyer
Check yellow silk blouse
During plastic man's 80
And the brick RR ride
Now only whispers from white room
As tea set bush fires

Molly Dolly and Fr. Paddison could make no sense of these annotations.
[Sidebar: The Patient Reader will find an explanation for this puzzling, apparently obtuse, material following the Kenny letter just below...]

~ * ~

Also inside the envelope, in a sealed cellophane packet, Molly Dolly discovered the following.

Ms. Dolly,

I'll be brief. Your husband Phil Dolly has, by now, most likely suffered signs of mental delusions. During the mid-1960's and beyond, his father, Michael P. Staten, and others, were part of a covert international organization with espionage links. Philip's biological mother in Argentina was also part of the clandestine operations in South America.

Shortly after Philip's birth, a microchip was planted within his skull. This chip, although primitive by twenty-first century technology, was designed to transmit classified inter-governmental information. Throughout Philip's life, at opportune times, shadow agents, within optical range, would transfer or store data to the chip, now subsequently located within Philip's cranial cavity. Classified operative powers restrict further disclosure. Philip's father and I were key point men with various, now historical, political, economic, and international events.

Although you are reading this after my demise, I fear retribution for future generations remotely affiliated, biologically or otherwise, with any Michael P. Staten progeny. I regret the unfortunate mental state of your husband. The declassified deciphered message relating to the coded historical events Michael P. Staten, myself, and your husband have affected is interpreted within attached document.

May God save our souls,
E. Kenny

The Code Revealed: Operation Wheat Germ

As petro's evening found a match - Peron and Evita cozy with Communist party
With Pius secured - Argentina Catholic Church political capitulation
Fire force had no douse - Celeste's mother Bernadette dies in church fire
While storm blew gently the yellow grain blouse - waves of Cold War political and economic change
Now red head flirts with tina - Soviet Union trades with Argentina

As camo cried Wolf - Castro and Bay of Pigs incident
Now only whispers from White doll House - U. S. uncovers missiles in Cuba
The pidgin was forced to duck - Soviet actions in Cuban missile crisis
While storm blew gently the yellow grain blouse - waves of Cold War political and economic change
Black planted Jack's flowers - Operatives plan Kennedy assassination
...cloaked with Pan Am Buzz - LBJ takes Presidential vow
Oz wears ruby red slippers - Jack Ruby kills Oswald
For playing in the Scotland's yard - Activism in Argentine Socialistic labor revolts
Angels chirp no more - Celeste dies for cause during military coup
Now only whispers from white doll house- Young Philip adopted by Dollys
As Cong's rehearse two-step - LBJ escalates Viet Nam forces
Benjeez 67 tour - Business partner Benjamin Zuckerman visits Jerusalem in 1967
Daily workers march - Chicago Mayor Richard J. Daley forces order during 1968 Convention
Mean clean machine - George Meany (AFL-CIO) organizes labor
...while salmon the Deuce devoured - Alaska oil pipeline continues construction
Enter the good king - Richard Nixon elected
As Zen Visits the 98th Church - Kentucky Derby run
...smoke delivered the flyer - Cuban born jockey rides D.P. Flyer
Check yellow silk blouse - controversy over Derby placing
During plastic man's 80 - *Z-Astic*-polymers continues to expand internationally
And the brick RR ride - Berlin wall falls during Ronald Reagan's term
Now only whispers from white room - Clinton two-term Administration
As tea set bush fires - Preparation for the H. and W. Bush Presidency

Zontarg Has the Last Word—A Poetic Prophecy
The Empty Seat
[Sidebar: This poem was found scribbled and signed on the back outside wall of the Copper Coin Saloon near the fuse box.]

I have a powerful recollection
Of an evening
Any evening
Back when I was twenty-three or so
Some girl I was dating—and another couple
Wandered into a town square tavern
In a small Midwestern town
[I left my guitar out in the car]
We sat down in a booth for burgers and talked about stuff
You know, unreflective material—
And I noticed three older guys,
Probably in their 50's,
Sitting at the bar
Eating pickled eggs and smoking non-filtered cigarettes
Sharing Field and Bream magazine and laughing
Drinking Filler Big Life beer from the golden bottle
And I overheard them talking
About the lives they used to live
And the beatings they took for nothing
And the divorces, failures, and disappointments
Their presence at the bar seemed archetypical to me
A scene played out in French fry smelling bar and grills
Since rural electrification—or perhaps before…
Hardly empathetic,
I vowed I would never be like them—balding and fat, living in a travel trailer down by the river, or renting a room above the dress shop, or struggling to keep a studio clean on the fifth floor of an old brick building that should be condemned.
But now I wonder—perhaps, with even sideways glances, they were laughing at me, knowing full well the beatings remaining ahead, the false dreams, the corporate chaos destined to coax and strangle me,

Clairvoyant, they could see the future of all giddy young me who cavorted in the
Temple of Doom
And now, so many years later, I have a powerful recollection of one empty chair
next to the rough old guy in the striped bibs and seed company cap...
I know I have been anointed [Ach!] to take my place
In the smoky tavern
On the bricked-street square...
On the empty seat
Of failure and redemption...
Sólo los culpables deben estar a la defensive....

[Side bar:Tantum crimen mos sentio ira]

Appendix
Copperfield Community College Acronym Usage [glossary]

A.A. Degree—Two-year degree granted by community colleges—emphasis on academic courses and university transfer ability. Most community colleges think their true purpose is to award such degrees... [A holdover from the old JuCo model, perhaps] Tennyson might refer to this as a wandering fire [or the Holy Grail] which should not be pursued....

Ach!—Scottish vernacular interjection used by socialists and non-socialists alike

A.A.S. Degree—Two-year degree granted by community colleges—emphasis on vocational training courses and a sure ticket to employment, satisfaction, and a bright future

ASS—Academic Support Service. Just one more of a million community college Student Services plans [and acronyms!] designed to help keep under-prepared students in school so they can continue paying fees, occupying seats, and returning to campus year after year....

Adjunct—Part-time instructor—Way overworked, way underpaid. No future anywhere...

B.I.S.O.N.—Big Institute for Staff and Organizational Normalization. A community college organization devoted to profits, networking, barbecues, and making big time money. They honor community college faculty, administrators, and secretaries with 470,000 normalization excellence awards per annum...

DEAL—Distance Education Academic Legislation

DUI—Driving Under Influence

CCC—Copperfield Community College

CCCDC—Copperfield Corpulent Couples Diners Club. Official recognition of a simple fact—Staff and students at community colleges are constantly eating. And gaining weight

CCADM—Creating culture of assessment daily meeting

CSCAN—Committee Serving College Academic Needs

EdD Ed Leadership—the doctorate sought by nearly every community college employee from custodian to interim president. The Holy Grail of the community college career, the leadership doctorate guarantees big salaries, instant promotions, and an insatiable desire for bake sales, potlucks, and conversations about "branding." The great mystery in our society is that we have so many leadership issues since this union card can be obtained almost anywhere. How can we have any problems at all in America since we have so many people with "Leadership" credentials? [Sidebar: Voodoo Academics!]

F-NO—Faculty Negotiating Opportunities

FOOD—Food—the most commonly heard word at community colleges....

FTSE—Full-time student equivalency—a convoluted measurement of student enrollment and state funding for community colleges such as CCC seldom adhered to by state authorities...

Fraud—Fraud

H.E.L.L—Helping English Language Learners

H.S.U.—Hamilton State University—four-year university, also grants master's and doctorates, research II school. Located in Hamilton City, North New Mexico

GED—Secondary school equivalency diploma—a mainstay of community college enrollment

IBC—Industrial Bocker College—campus of CCC [or I've Been Conned]

Learn-ed College—Early twenty-first Century concept embraced by nearly every community college but understood by few. Apparently eliminates thinking from the equation at institutions—every staff member, as well every student, must be learn-ed in a robotic or non-creative sense. We think. Maybe not. Hard to say. Perhaps some sort of philosophic compost. [Sidebar: This is the philosophical compost referenced by Dr. Roz and other Op-Ed writers]

MLB—Major League Baseball
MODCC—Men of Diverse Colors Club

MyPEDS—National database and clearing house for statistically sound and robust educational data rarely accessed by community college staff

National Search—Community college protocol for filling positions. Large amounts of time and energy are spent attracting job opening candidates from all over the nation—but in house or interim candidates are usually hired anyway

NEWDU—North Eastern West Dakota University Research III institution in West Dakota granting BA and MA degrees

NFL—National Football League

N. H. U.—Four-year university, also grants master's and doctorates, Research III school. Located in Falstaff, North New Mexico

RFNC—Responsible Fatherhood Now Club

SAAT—The Student Academic Advancement Team

SCHEME—Strategic Conversation for Highbrow Education Measures Excellence

SCUD—Acronym for Student and Cash Unified Divulger—the faulty software program used for registration and budgets at CCC

SJCMCSECD—Southwest JuCo Mega Conference South East Coyote Division Athletic Conference
SLIP-UP—Summer Language Institute Plan for Undergraduate Participation

TLC—Teaching Learn-ed Center

T-RUN—"Transfer to Real University Now"

Tyson effect—in espionage, important "players" are not aware of their own participation

U.H.—University of Hamilton, four-year university, also grants master's and doctorates, Research II school. Located in Santa Rey North New Mexico

VP—Vice President—The most common administrative position at community colleges. Each community college president usually has between ten to fifteen vice presidents, associate vice presidents, and assistant vice presidents. This category does not include Assistants to the Vice President. The proliferation of this position clearly illustrates the community colleges' desire to cozy up to corporate management practices and pay administrators huge salaries. Strangely enough, the BA degree is often a sufficient credential for obtaining a VP position

Weltanschauung—World View—a term seldom heard or understood at community colleges

Windbag—Windbag

YCC—Young Copperheads Club

YESSSS—Yearly External Stakeholders Strategic Survey Session

YES—Yearning for Expansion into Science

ABOUT THE AUTHORS

Jann M. Contento has a broad range of experiences in higher education including student affairs administration, athletics, and institutional research. He is currently working in a community college setting and has co- authored several articles on leadership and college culture.

Jeffrey Ross, who resides in Gilbert, Arizona with his wife and son, is a writer, rockabilly musician, and former full-time community college teacher. He has had four "Views" pieces published on *InsidehigherEd.com* since 2007, and has authored and co-authored several articles on community college identity, purpose, and culture.